THE SOUND OF FOOTSTEPS

LESLIE FORD

THE SOUND
OF FOOTSTEPS

Old Justice Frazier was the first to
die . . . then a woman was found, sitting
bolt upright in a great chair . . .
staring straight out into space . . .

WILDSIDE PRESS

THE SOUND OF FOOTSTEPS

THE SOUND OF FOOTSTEPS

CHAPTER ONE

IF IT hadn't been for Jerry Blaine's reconditioned coupé's reverting to type coming out of the Laurel race meeting on the 3rd of October, I should never have held in my hands the key to the solution of Justice Frazier's murder and the public scandal that nearly followed. As it was, I didn't know the importance of my quite casual observation to Jerry as we got out of the taxi in Dupont Circle. Jerry gave the driver the wrong address, so that we stopped at the house beyond the Fraziers' and had to walk back. I shiver a little when I realize how very vital those few moments were: my telling Jerry he was a stupid idiot, Jerry's arguing with the driver about thirty-five-cent zones, and our walking back to the Fraziers' just as the man, his back to us, came down the steps, hailed a taxi, and drove away without bothering to look at us. I've wondered ever since what difference it would have made if he had looked around and seen us. Perhaps if he had Justice Frazier would still be here. But maybe not. Now that it's all over I have a curious small feeling of having been a thread in the mysterious loom of Coincidence. But as such, I suppose, I helped make the pattern, flecked with blood and tears as it was, come out a perfect length in the fabric of justice.

Jerry Blaine is one of the army of assistants at the District Supreme Court, had just finished an unsavory divorce case, and was fairly fed up with life in general and in the District of Columbia in particular. He rang me up just as I was going out to lunch, and I agreed to go to the races with him if he wouldn't bet more than two dollars on any horse and would be sure to get me back in time for Priscilla Stone's slumming party. He promised both and did neither. He lost $10.90 on Lone Star, and the car stalled just as he was making the left turn for Washington as you come out of the track. There was nothing for us to do but be shoved over to one side of the road and wait patiently until everybody else had gone home and we could get a mechanic. What with one thing and another, we got back about nine o'clock and still had to eat and dress. I declined to take another chance on Jerry's car, and my own was in the garage getting a fender straightened; so Jerry called for me in a taxi about 10:30.

That intelligent people should make any effort to get to one of Priscilla Stone's parties must seem odd to anyone who reads her column in the Washington *Chronicle*. There's no doubt about it, she publishes the silliest drivel that appears in print. The English society gossip writers are her only possible peers. There's also no doubt that she makes an excellent living doing it. She's even rather proud of her position in the newspaper world, and takes all our gibes with a certain smug good nature. You can almost imagine her smiling and complacently patting her check book before she loans one of the political reporters enough to pay his landlady or his bootlegger.

The thing about Priscilla's parties is the guest of honor. She never gives a party without a reason, and the reason is usually, if not always, the most important, or interesting, or scandalous person in the Capital at the moment. Which one of these classifications fits the guest of honor makes no difference. Priscilla has a fine lack of discrimination that makes her positively Elizabethan. If Al Capone were in town on Monday she'd have him at a party even if the night before she'd had a supper after vespers for Dean Inge. So if you were lucky enough to hear her flighty, cooing voice over the phone, you accepted at once and broke your dinner engagement with the Turkish chargé d'affaires as soon as she hung up. But never for a moment did you admit that Priscilla was anything but a perfect fool with an unconscious genius for people.

She phoned me on Saturday that Senator Mellish had expressed a wish to see a real speakeasy and would I go and did I think Jerry Blaine would come along. I said I thought Jerry would be delighted to go in spite of Senator Mellish, and that I'd be delighted, but *why* Senator Mellish? I can still hear her simple, rather vague but honeyed tones:

"Really, dear, he's a *wonder*ful man. He's not *nearly* as dreadful as the papers say. He really believes all the things he's fighting for."

"That's all the worse," I said. "And if true, then why go to a speakeasy?"

"Because he has to know the inside of the thing he's fighting. Don't you think so? He can't clean up Washington unless he really knows what it's like, can he?"

"Well, why bother at all?"

"I don't know, but that's what he wants to do. And it's really brave of him, too. Why, do you know, Diane, he told me he'd actually had threats made against his *life?* Trying to make him stop, you know. I think it's *dreadful,* don't you?"

I agreed to go, of course. As a matter of fact I thought it would be amusing to see Senator Mellish, the hell-for-leather, fire-eating, gospel-singing patriot and militant evangelical of the upper house. I'd read his blatant diatribes on the moral unsoundness of the present generation without actually believing he existed in the flesh. I was especially interested, as I'd just heard that he and Justice Frazier had had a violent disagreement before the Turner Committee on Law Enforcement. Anyway, I promised Priscilla that Jerry and I would meet her at 10:00 at the Fraziers' on Dupont Circle and we'd go from there.

We were to start from the Fraziers', I imagined,

for several reasons. Jocelyn was going, for one, and Thalia Xanthopoulos, who was staying with Jocelyn, for another; and I imagine Priscilla thought Senator Mellish would be immensely impressed at beginning his educational pilgrimage into the nether world from so exalted a point. I'm sure he wouldn't have got to the Fraziers' any other way. Justice Frazier has a very definite notion of political dignity and social prestige. It's hard to get into the house on Dupont Circle no matter what your position in the Capital—and on your position in the Capital depends a lot whether you can get in. If you're a half-witted firebrand from that great State Blank, no matter how important you are to the Democratic majority in the Senate you have no chance of being admitted unless somebody waves a potent rabbit's foot. Senator Mellish manages things very well, but Priscilla Stone manages them better.

I'd give almost anything, now that I know him, to have seen the Senator at the Fraziers' that night. As it was, they'd left before Jerry and I rode up to the house next door. So I missed him. While Jerry was having it out with the taxi driver, I was standing facing the Fraziers' house. The light under the portico is fairly bright, and I saw the door open. I thought for a moment it was Priscilla's party coming out, although I knew instantly then that it wasn't, because there weren't any cars in front. A man came out and the door closed. He stopped a moment, and I saw the flare of a match as he lighted a cigarette. There was something familiar about him, I thought; but when I saw him walk briskly down the steps that indefinite idea vanished, and I saw at once that I didn't know him.

I moved on towards the house. Jerry joined me as the man came down the steps and turned quickly to the left.

"Who's that?" Jerry asked.

"I suppose it's a friend of the family," I said patiently. "And by the way," I went on, as the man hailed a taxi that was coming towards us around the Circle and disappeared into it without a glance in our direction, "why did you let that taxi go? These people are gone, and we'll have to get another one as soon as we find out where they are."

Jerry rang the bell. "I'll take care of that," he said calmly.

There's something about the great green door of the Frazier mansion in the Circle that impresses me every time I ring the bell and stand waiting for Horace to answer it. I've been going to the Fraziers', in one capacity or another, since I was two. My mother and Mrs. Frazier were close friends, and Justice Frazier and my father were at the University of Virginia together, in the same law firm, and later on the District Supreme Court bench together, before my father's death. So I've always gone there. I remember the excitement of Jocelyn's arrival, and the great disgust my ten years felt for her one week. Her mother died when she was four, and I've had a curious position in the house ever since. My husband died during the war and my own life has been very active, but never too much so to exclude Jocelyn and her problems as hostess in one of the most exclusive houses in Washington.

When I was a child the green door was so big that I could scarcely reach the knob, as I first remember it. My nurse always knocked the great brass knocker they used then. Then I remember coming home from school one vacation and going there, and realizing that I was grown up, because I could reach the knocker myself. Somehow there was a great mystery about the door. I always held my breath rather, waiting to see if Horace or something—never very clear just what—would open it. Of course it always was Horace. I can't remember a time he didn't, until this very night; but I always had the feeling that some day somebody else would open it, and that something momentous and dreadful would happen then.

I was right, in a sense. We stood there, Jerry and I, a long time—so it seems now—waiting for the door to open. I was crystallizing in my own mind all the things this door had meant, and thinking a little condescendingly of my childish habit of making things into symbols, and linking them all up with my own life. Then the door opened, and I stopped all that business of introspection, because Justice Frazier himself stood in the great dim open doorway. His face was the saddest face

I've ever seen. I knew, with a suddenness that was almost a blow, that he'd come to the door expecting to see somebody else.

"Come in," he said, after a perceptible hesitation. "The rest of them have gone on. They left the address; come in."

We stepped into the hall and stood there rather self-consciously. It seemed almost as if we had burst into a house of death wearing cap and bells. Even Jerry was subdued. Justice Frazier closed the door with what seemed ponderous deliberation and led the way down the dim old Victorian hall towards the library.

I had never noticed before that he moved more slowly and less vigorously than I had remembered. His head, with its fine white mane, and his broad shoulders, once straight as an arrow, were a little stooped. It seemed that years must have elapsed since I stood out on the porch last. I suddenly felt that everything was different; Justice Frazier was an old man now, and I was older, too. I looked around as if I were seeing the house that I knew so well for the first time after being away many years. Even the enormous crystal candelabra hanging in the center of the hall had shrunk. I should have thought, somehow, that they were much bigger. A great feeling of pity surged through me, and I was glad when Justice Frazier stopped just as we got to the library and turned around.

"By the way, Blaine," he said very earnestly to

Jerry, "I would like to speak to Diane a moment. Would you mind?"

"Not at all, sir," Jerry said hastily. "I'll just wait in the drawing room."

Justice Frazier inclined his head and stood aside for me to go in. I heard Jerry skid on one of the small rugs in his hurry to get across the hall, and then close the door behind himself a little ostentatiously. It was embarrassing, because Jerry is a rising lawyer and regards Justice Frazier about as a good Moslem regards Allah.

"Sit down, my dear," Justice Frazier said, with something of the smile I knew. "I don't want to be —what is it you say?—stuffy; but I want to speak to you a moment."

I sat down in the leather chair at the side of the great mahogany table where he worked, and he sat in his chair in front of it. The library has always been a holy of holies even to those of us who feel perfectly free in the rest of the house. Book-lined, mellow calf mingling with bright modern cloth and somber morocco, the walls were lovely. The deep old-gold curtains were drawn, and a coal fire burned in the grate; it had suddenly turned very cold in Washington. I had a sinking feeling, sitting there. I waited. He didn't speak for a little while. I noticed a pile of letters at the side of the table nearest me. I couldn't help reading the name on the top one: Major the Hon. J. P. V. Heath, The Mayflower Hotel, City. I guessed that Justice Frazier had been writing all of these letters, and

I guessed also that the subject of them was what
he was going to talk to me about. Then it occurred
to me, incongruously, that he was going to advise
me to quit going around with Jerry. The ridicu-
lous notion cropped up in my head that he was going to say:

"A young widow—because you're comparatively
young, my dear; thirty isn't old—must be careful. Blaine's a nice boy, but . . ." And so on.

Instead he said, "I want to speak to you about
Jocelyn, Diane. I'm involved in a curious matter
that seems, just now, to have the possibilities of
. . . tragedy."

"Are you ill, Justice Frazier?" I asked quickly,
leaning forward and putting my hand on his arm.
He looked ill, and I was frightened.

He smiled and shook his head.

"No, my dear child. I'm not ill—what is it
Antonio says?—unless it is in mind. No, nor mind
either. I can't tell you very plainly. I wish I could.
But I will tell you that I'm starting a course of
action in connection with certain public matters
that is a fight to the finish. I think I know the
finish; but that isn't what I want with you. Diane,
I want a promise from you. That you'll take care
of Jocelyn if anything happens to me."

I started to protest, and he shook his head.

"Of course it's possible this is just the foolish
notion of an old man, but I want your promise. I
want you to watch out for her until she marries or
does something for herself. Keep her from going

to the wretched places she's going to to-night. Or if she must go, go with her. Keep her, if you can, from a lot of these people. Especially young Xanthopoulos. She's got sense, but she has to have someone help her to keep on her feet. If I can depend on you, well, I'll feel better."

He stopped suddenly, smiled, put his hands over mine, and looked searchingly at me.

"And now you want to go. We'll talk about another matter later. Good-night, my dear. Radstock tells me you're going to be at Monckton to-morrow?"

I couldn't say anything. I've adored Justice Frazier all my life, and somehow I was greatly moved. We shook hands almost solemnly, and I smiled as well as I could—there was no need of my promising anything, because he knew I'd do anything I could—and hurried out, and had to come back for the address of the speakeasy.

A speakeasy isn't very much fun when there's tragedy hanging heavily in the air.

CHAPTER TWO

WE GOT a taxi and went to Joe's. It's the usual sort of thing, just off Pennsylvania Avenue. The sycamore tree in front makes it easy to locate, and Priscilla has made it about as obvious as the Capitol dome. It started out as a good beer saloon, frequented mostly by newspapermen and the police, until a young reporter took Priscilla there. She took it up in her column, and with the help of the sycamore tree and a certain popular policeman whose beat it was on made its location so definite that people almost had to take notice of it. I remember Jerry said that if he hadn't known Priscilla he'd have thought she was trying to have the place raided. Then suddenly she stopped writing about it. Jerry said that Joe, the proprietor, got Caleb Williams of the *Times* to call her off; he also says she gets a big discount on her parties. I remember one note of hers that Jerry said set the whole place in acute annoyance. "Last night," it went, "we were at J——'s lovely place at the sign of the old sycamore tree, just off P—— Avenue;" or something like that. "Patrolman O'G———" was there. He'd just dropped in on his round, so it seems, and it was funny seeing him drinking b—— with his cap on the back of his head. By the way, J—— has the best beer in town, so Count von B—— tells me, and he ought to know. Incidentally, Count von B—— . . ." And so on.

After a few weeks of this Joe was almost beside himself, with limousines driving up and ordinary people strolling in. Patrolman O'Grady got moved out to Wesley Heights to patrol the landed bourgeoisie, who never invited him in to their parties. Caleb Williams went out to interview him as one of his "Life's Little Ironies," and said the poor fellow was a broken man, and talked of taking his family to Baltimore to live, where a man could have a glass of beer in peace. More than that, Count von B—— is now attached to the embassy in Pekin, thanks, it's reported, to the dry diplomacy of Senator Mellish.

When Jerry and I got there Priscilla and her party were upstairs, and all a little tight, even Mellish, I thought. I didn't know then that he was always just such a pompous ass. They were sitting at a big round table in the corner of the dingy, garish room, and Frank the pot boy was keeping them supplied with grenadine lemonade. Or so Priscilla said. There certainly wasn't very much gin in mine.

Senator Mellish was seated next to Priscilla against the wall. His pictures don't do him justice. He has a tremendous crest of coal black hair, rather wavy. When he makes an utterance he tosses his forelock back and his sharp black eyes snap and shoot sparks all over the place. He has a nose like a giant hawk's and his mouth is much more like a shark's than a dead codfish's, as Caleb suggests. There's nothing dead about Senator Mellish. He was dressed in an ordinary dinner jacket, but had added a slightly flowing tie so that he looked a little theatrical. He had a bad audience, of course. All of us are pretty much used to political Savonarolas come out of the West and he flashed to a slightly bored house. Priscilla did her best, which is pretty good if your ego is insatiable. Mellish's is.

Jocelyn was in high spirits, too high, I thought, devoting herself exclusively to Pericles Xanthopoulos, with a grudging word thrown to Norman Vaughan now and then.

She's a lovely thing, blonde, fair-skinned, with clear, very steady grey eyes. No one could doubt the sort of moral stuff Jocelyn Frazier is made of after looking at her. She's slight and lithe and has a dignity that is much more than her twenty years. She's splendid. It was obvious that both Xanthopoulos and Vaughan thought so too.

Thalia Xanthopoulos—it's pronounced "Tálya" —sat between her brother and Vaughan. She's half Greek. Her mother was one of the Adlers of Philadelphia who married an impoverished Greek prince. He already had one son, Pericles, who was about six at the time of the marriage. The prince died shortly after Thalia's birth and her mother brought both children to Washington to live. Thalia is in appearance a perfect Greek, straight black hair, fine regular classical features and live dark eyes and warm ivory skin. Otherwise she's American. She's about Jocelyn's age and as keen as a whip. Her mother spends most of her time abroad, and Thalia and her brother live with an aunt of the Philadelphia school of 1890. As a result Pericles lives at his club and Thalia spends most of her time with Jocelyn.

Pericles Xanthopoulos has a nominal job under some branch of the present government, but no one seems to know what it is. Whatever it is, it doesn't take much time, although it demands a lot of rushing about to New York, Havana, Paris and what not. We thought Priscilla was running him to earth for a while, but nothing came of it. For a couple of months he couldn't leave his rooms without her noting it.

Prince Pericles Xanthopoulos left for New York this morning. I hope he's back for Mrs. H——'s tea. It will be pretty dull without him. . . .

Pericles X————— (he'll be a real prince when the monarchy is restored) was in Georgetown yesterday. It's splendid to find a Greek so much interested in our Colonial architecture. If I were he a broken pediment would remind me of the Parthenon and I'd weep.

Caleb remarked that whatever dragged Pericles to Georgetown might have been pre-war but he'd bet it wasn't any earlier.

Pericles looks Greek and is Greek. He's a perfectly charming person. Why Justice Frazier should feel alarmed about Jocelyn's marrying him I don't know. It's probably because, cultivated man of the world that he is, he still feels a certain national prejudice against a foreigner. He's a Virginian of the old school, and I suppose it's natural enough that he should feel rather strongly about it. He's never objected to Thalia, but of course he'd known her mother and her mother's family. I imagine it was easy enough to be tolerant of the Adlers' *mésalliances*. They made so many of them. No Frazier ever did.

Norman Vaughan was talking to Thalia, but he hardly took his eyes off Jocelyn. Even Senator Mellish noticed it. I saw him look sharply from one to the other of them. I was surprised that he didn't make an obvious witticism. He looked as if it were on the tip of his tongue. Jocelyn's cool beauty is somewhat disarming, and the expression in her eyes when she wasn't smiling at something was curiously abstracted. Her father's words kept coming back to me. I wondered if she had guessed that something was wrong. Because I was convinced that there was something very wrong indeed, and I couldn't quite see how Jocelyn, as close to her father as she has always been, could fail to sense it even if he didn't speak of it.

The conversation was very stupid. Mellish talked fluently, his rich Chautauqua voice rising and falling, people turning to look at him, Jerry groaning something about hiring a hall, and Priscilla coaxing and cajoling her lion deeper and deeper into the jungle, so to speak, of his own ego-tism. That woman is priceless. The only thing she couldn't do was get him tight. I know she was trying to, if only to give Caleb Williams a little copy to sell to the *American Mercury*. But he wasn't getting tight, and anyway Caleb wasn't pay-ing any attention to us.

He was at a small table across the room, his back to us. He was leaning forward, both elbows on the table, talking violently—as usual—to a large man who was listening with a half-amused, slightly whimsical expression on his face. Caleb was exactly his own self; when I next looked over at him he had said his say and was slumped down in his chair, one hand in his pocket and the other partly covering a yawn.

I didn't then know the large man with him. I do now. It's difficult to recall what I thought of him, just seeing him there with Caleb that night.

Caleb's connected with half of Washington— all of it, in fact, that's of any importance. He was destined for the law and went to the Harvard Law School after Amherst. He went into an uncle's law office then and was frightfully unhappy. He went to Oxford for a year and came home and got a job on the *Times*. His father was disgusted and his mother amused. She was delighted to have Caleb do anything at all, but for him to do it and like it was too good to be true. As a matter of fact under his air of devastating boredom and flip-pant disrespect for life in general he conceals a tremendous earnestness. He'd cut anybody's throat who said so, however.

Priscilla had dipped into her bag of tricks to find something to bring him over to our table. She didn't want him, particularly, but I could see she had scented game in his friend. He certainly had an authentic air of "distinction," and he was obviously an Englishman. From the quality of Priscilla's smile, when she looked their way, and from the determined front of Caleb's back, it was evident that they understood each other perfectly. Priscilla wanted Caleb's friend, and offered Senator Mellish, tight if possible, as payment in kind. Caleb had appraised the offer, and refused to barter. But Priscilla is cleverer in some things than Caleb ever will be. I could see her soft, persistent little brain working. Then she leaned across the table.

"Jocelyn, why don't you ask Caleb to join us? He's over there at that table, and I want him to meet Senator Mellish."

She asked it as sweetly as if she'd just that second seen Caleb.

I don't think anybody at the table could have missed the faint flush that brushed Jocelyn's cheeks, or the little shrug that accented her shoulders against the peach velvet lining of the ermine cloak over the back of her chair. Just then the noisy party at the table between us left, and Jocelyn raised her voice slightly and said, "Caleb, why don't you come over here?"

Caleb responded at once. Nobody but myself noticed Thalia just then. Perhaps she's not as American as I'd imagined.

Caleb and his friend pushed back their chairs and came over, anyway. Caleb presented his friend, and you could see Priscilla handing over the Senator with a gesture. Then without the loss of a moment she enveloped, figuratively speaking, her acquisition.

"I've been trying to meet you, Major Heath," she began. "Grace Cunliffe-Watson told me you were as shy as a rabbit. Do sit down."

Major Heath bowed and did sit down. He's an enormous man, and I suppose he must have been in the tropics for years, because he has that intense sunburn that makes a man almost black. His hair looked light in contrast, though it's really a fairly dark brown. It begins a little back, too, giving him an imposing forehead. His eyes, I noticed, were a curious steely grey that twinkled pleasantly at some sort of hidden joke and were cold as icicles when you looked back again. His jaw was firmly set, and yet his mouth was very kindly, except that it had the same trick of changing into something unpleasantly like a steel trap under your very eyes.

It was interesting to see him and Mellish meet; Major Heath English to the core, urbane, yet solid and capable. He was as big as Mellish, if not bigger, but Mellish seemed to have so much more exterior, a sort of pretentious inflation. He looked more like a facade than anything actually three-dimensional. Perhaps that's not accurate—I suppose a bag of air has three dimensions, even when it's pricked. Not that Senator Mellish ever was pricked at all. He was quite noble in his willingness, on this occasion, to admit to a foreigner that the English parliamentary system had many admirable points. If it could ever be felt that the English might possibly have become a decadent people, it would be found that gin was responsible. He had read in a book that public houses displayed signs "Drunk for a Penny," "Dead Drunk for Twopence," and what could any nation hope for when that obtained?

Major Heath smiled deprecatingly.

"Of course that was in the eighteenth century, Senator Mellish," he said pleasantly. "I'm sure we're not as lucky now. I assure you it costs a great deal more than that. I haven't the Home Office figures, but you could get them. Of course that was gin, too, and we don't—I fancy—as a people drink as much gin as you do, nowadays. I mean Americans, of course. In fact I think we had practically quit gin until you introduced the cocktail so universally."

"My dear sir," Senator Mellish countered. "There is actually very little drinking in this country. It is confined to a very few people, and those only in the cities."

"I'm very glad to hear it," Major Heath returned, with a smile. "Because I've really never drunk as much in my life as I have this last month.

The terrors of a prohibition country are very real, in my mind."

"Not as real as the terrors of alcohol, sir," Senator Mellish answered with a flashing eye.

"Oh, but that's just what he means," Priscilla cried gaily. "You see . . ."

She explained. Caleb groaned, "My God, let's go home!"

Priscilla was not letting people off so easily.

"Are you going out to Monckton Hall tomorrow, Caleb?"

"I am not. I've got to go to Baltimore to cover a Better Babies meeting. Anyway I wasn't invited. Old Radstock's off me; I tried to help him downstairs at the Cosmos Club and he got sore. I'd forgot he was so damn sensitive about his foot."

"You're an idiot anyway," Jocelyn put in feelingly. "You're always helping the wrong people. It's a wonder he didn't take his stick to you."

"Have you met Mr. Radstock, Major Heath?" Priscilla asked, anxiously trying to anneal her various groups. "You know him, don't you, Senator Mellish?"

Major Heath said no and Senator Mellish yes. Priscilla bestowed the same smile on each and went on.

"He's a charming man. Quite an English country gentleman—wouldn't you say, Diane?"

Priscilla never expected you to answer her questions, but as your silence implied assent you seldom felt you were let out of any effort. Of course I've never thought of Jacob Radstock as anything but a Virginia country gentleman, and I know him better than most people do. He is sensitive about his lameness, but then Caleb has an irresistible faculty of doing—as well as saying—the exactly wrong thing. I know sometimes, though, he does it on purpose. He once quoted someone to me to the effect that a gentleman was a person who was never unconsciously rude.

Priscilla was explaining the Radstocks to Major Heath.

"You'll be asked out before long. Mr. Radstock has a genius for interesting people. Everyone who comes to Washington—of that sort—goes out there. And it's one of the show places of America in its own right."

"Besides that," Senator Mellish put in, "Radstock, in spite of his antecedents, does splendid service in being an example of right thinking."

It's hard to give a right impression of Senator Mellish, but he did talk just like a badly written book.

Caleb looked curiously at him.

"Don't tell me he's gone dry?" he demanded dramatically. "Thank God I'm not going. I need more than right thinking when I'm through with the Bigger and Better and More Babies."

After a little more of this Priscilla managed to ensnare Major Heath in a tête-à-tête and I was left with the Senator. He was rather difficult to talk to. The Farm Board, the tariff, elicited a pontifical nod, but he was expansive on the rumored changes in the police organization of the District. I said something vapid about how Napoleon would have handled prohibition enforcement.

"That's what we need to-day, madam," he declared vigorously. "A Napoleon—someone with vision. Vision! A Napoleon with vision."

He went on from that to an astonishingly florid tale of his recent experiences in the underworld. It sounded almost as if he had a shrewd idea that he himself was the Napoleon with vision. Perhaps the implication was entirely in my own mind. He told me one really interesting story of how Harry Mello the gangster had taken him to some dive where society people, politicians, diplomats, and so on were gambling cheek to jowl with notorious members of the underworld. That situation seems to obsess him. As Caleb remarked, he didn't seem to mind what people did if they confined themselves to their own rift in the social strata.

Priscilla caught Harry Mello's name and mentally bounced over to us.

"You don't mean, Senator, you went with Harry Mello? I'd be terrified he wouldn't bring me back."

"Ah, but here I am!"

The Senator appeared not to hear Caleb's perfectly audible remark that that was the trouble with gangsters—no discrimination.

"I was able and glad to do a little favor for

Mello," he went on, "in a purely private capacity, and I may say he's repaid me in a thousand invaluable ways."

I was sorry he'd said that. I saw Priscilla and Caleb exchange professional glances. Politicians ought never to admit being repaid, especially by people like Harry Mello.

The conversation shifted back to small groups. I wasn't much interested in Mellish's Napoleon complex, and I must admit he wasn't particularly interested in me. I couldn't help being aware that his gaze shifted fairly often to Thalia Xanthopoulos, who was quietly talking to Caleb. He was decidedly interested in her. What the quality of his interest was I couldn't tell for the life of me, except that it wasn't the ordinary sort of thing.

We finally broke up about half-past one. It wasn't a very gay party. Everyone seemed a little low, and Joe's grenadine highballs only made us lower. I couldn't get the business of Justice Frazier out of my mind, although it was rather in the background. So much so, that it wasn't until we were out on the street that I connected the Major Heath who was standing next to me with the name on the envelope on Justice Frazier's desk. It struck me quite suddenly, and I said, a little like Priscilla, I'm afraid, "You're going to get a letter tomorrow, Major Heath."

He must have thought I was a half-wit, but he only grinned.

"How do you know? Are you the Madame Rosa I've been hearing about?"

If I had had an ounce of sense that would have stopped me.

"No," I said. "I saw it on Just——"

I saw the steely warning in his eyes just as he interrupted me with another grin.

"Don't raise my hopes too much. She'll probably change her mind and not send it. I might miss my lunch waiting."

Then I understood that I was on dangerous ground. But why? I looked around. Thalia and Senator Mellish were just behind me; but I saw that Major Heath was looking at Jocelyn and Pericles Xanthopoulos, who stood talking by the sycamore tree. Just then Jerry came up with a taxi.

I was very glad to get away from the lot of them. So he knew about it, too!

★   ★   ★

[From the Washington *Chronicle*]

What Everybody's Doing

By Priscilla Stone

Major the Hon. J. P. V. Heath, D. S. O., seemed immensely intrigued last night when I saw him ostensibly investigating one of our most interesting social phenomena ("Joe's"). He's going to be in the Capital another month, he tells me. I think he's one of the most distinguished-looking Englishmen we've seen for a long time. He isn't shy, either, like so many of his countrymen, except that he won't tell why he's here. I suspect some lovely diplomatic mission. Anyway, he's not *lecturing*. That's always a comfort.

★   ★   ★

John Radstock is at home this week-end, and everybody's going to Monckton Hall. Ducking's good and Norman Vaughan will be there, so we'll be sure to have grand food. He won the Gun Club trophy last year, by the way. I'm sure I wouldn't get up at two in the morning to go ducking, but then I'd never get anything if I did. The interest of a week-end at Monckton isn't dependent on getting up at two, though—Mr. Radstock always sees to that.

Senator and Mrs. Mellish are going to be there, and Justice Frazier and Jocelyn. Of course Prince Pericles Xanthopoulos and his sister Thalia are coming—if that suggests anything to anybody.

With three of the most eligible bachelors in town at Monckton Hall I wonder what Lady V——t will do Sunday evening. Her at-home will be even duller than usual.

Speaking of dull diplomats, have you heard that Diane Volney is "re-doing" Monckton Hall? She tells me she got a lot of Louis Quinze cherry-red damask panels from the walls of a château drawing room in Burgundy for the Chippendale room.—I don't mean that either Diane or Monckton has anything to do with dull diplomats. That's just it. Diane refused flatly to do the interior of his new house on ———— Street for a certain very wealthy embassy secretary. I fancy she couldn't picture his wife pouring tea, or cocktails either, in one of her gorgeous rooms.

She'll be at Monckton Hall for the whole winter. That's my idea of heaven. I wish they invited columnists places for longer than one week-end!!

CHAPTER THREE

THE next morning at half-past eight Geneva, my highly colored *bonne-à-tout-faire,* drew the curtains and put my breakfast tray on my lap. The paper on it was neatly folded with Priscilla Stone's column, "What Everybody's Doing," uppermost. It was an annoying habit that four years of more or less obvious displeasure on my part had failed to affect in the least. Every morning Geneva examined the papers carefully for my name or the names of any of my friends she knew, and she undoubtedly knows them all much better—at least more intimately—than I do, because she knows their servants and looks at them from a much less decorative angle. If our names appear in any capacity, from birth to death or engagement to divorce and back again, she folds that item so that it is the first thing I must read. I can hardly persuade her to bring me the New York *Times* at all. I refrained from comment until Mrs. Houston-Pelham advertised for her lost Mexican Hairless the same day Tea Pot Dome blew up and spattered more interesting friends.

I understand Geneva better now and I know that the only thing that keeps her tied to my electric

range and assuring me a perfectly ordered apartment is the pleasing publicity that Priscilla and
her ilk give me and my friends. I've always regarded the so-called loyalty of the colored race as
a figment of a romantic, slightly befuddled im-
agination—Northern largely, because Southern-
ers are practical and not too insistent about sins of
omission of the sort. I've never known but one
whose so-called loyalty stood a very great test. But
there I'm getting ahead of my story.

I'm sure of one thing, that if Geneva couldn't
say "Mah madam is goin' to Monckton Hall this
week-end," or "Mistah Justice Frazier was talkin'
to mah madam on the telephone this mornin'," and
all the rest of it, my small household wouldn't be
nearly so carefully run.

Oddly enough, Geneva isn't the only sort who's
impressed by "What Everybody's Doing." Priscilla has a very large following, and takes it all
with impressive seriousness. She reads her own
"fan" mail and answers it herself; how she has
hours enough in a day I don't know. As an advertising vehicle she hasn't an equal in the Capital. A
casual word in her column about a new dress
shoppe or a different permanent wave has far more
pull than a spread of Queen Marie or all the wives
of all the meat packers in Chicago. And she's
honest about it. A large manufacturer of expen-
sive cosmetics sent her enough cold cream, tissue
builder, face powder, and wrinkle remover to
stock a beauty parlor, trusting that she'd mention

his wares favorably some windy morning. No indeed! She looked at me once with her great gazelle eyes and said, "But I don't think they do any good. I think Ivory soap and water is the best, don't you, Diane?"

I admitted a fondness for more sophisticated treatment, and she said, "Well, you'd better take all this truck, because I couldn't honestly tell my public that I use it when I don't—could I?"

I agreed with her perfectly. She couldn't.

And as for the embassy secretary and his wife, whose house I refused to do, I was intensely annoyed. It's quite true that I did refuse to decorate their new house, in spite of the free hand and unlimited means they offered me. Equally true that it was entirely because of the woman that I turned it down. She's perfectly frightful. But I never mentioned the affair to anyone, least of all to Priscilla Stone. One might as well try to mix a cocktail in a sieve. Anything Priscilla finds out appears the next morning, under her own name or somebody else's; she's constitutionally and professionally a vendor of news. I could imagine my fat pale friend, the wife of the embassy secretary, sitting in her mauve and amber boudoir reading that column, fat useless tears dribbling down her fat useless cheeks, mortified, hurt, and probably a little frightened that everybody would recognize her at once, all because some ass told Priscilla Stone an amusing anecdote about a not very amusing person. Priscilla, whose pen is dipped at times in a pot of naïve venom, couldn't ever know the terrible distress she caused.

But she *is* excellent advertising. In the course of time I'll probably get twenty jobs that I don't want, and maybe one I do, because of her column that morning. It's all such a free-gratis-for-nothing sort of thing; you can't buy it, but she'll gladly give it to you—as long as in her own opinion she "keeps faith with her public."

She's an amazing woman and a perfect fool.

I finished my breakfast, bathed, dressed, and helped Geneva pack my bag for Monckton Hall. I was much more distressed than I liked to admit about this business of Mrs.—I'll call her Smith, because she still lives in Washington although she's divorced the embassy secretary. She isn't a bad sort; pots of money from her father—he made a sort of glue that people eat for dessert—completely uneducated, no background, no taste, but pitifully eager and very sensitive. I remembered with a pang that that very day Mrs. Malcolmson, who was well over the threshold that Mrs. "Smith" was giving her soul to cross, was giving a luncheon for her. And she obviously couldn't go. She'd be the butt of so much that was unspoken; or worse, of the appallingly hypocritical sympathy that women goad one another with. I felt frightfully sorry for her and for Priscilla too. Of all the things one can say about Priscilla Stone, that isn't one of them. She's not intentionally malicious; she wouldn't hurt a fly. At the same time she has what

is almost a genius for her job. Anyone else—even
someone who personally knew and actively disliked Mrs. "Smith"—might have hunted for days
for the one thing that would ruin her, and never
hit on such a simple remark as Priscilla's morning
item. It was the one chink in the armor of self-
esteem that was vulnerable. That was Priscilla's
genius. And that makes this fine vacuous naïveté
so bewildering. She's perfectly unaware that
everyone is afraid of her. She's like a child with
a stick of dynamite. Caleb says they handle her
with fur mittens at the *Chronicle* for fear she'll
wake up some day and find out her power.

I thought for a moment I'd call up Mrs.
"Smith" and tell her I would do her house for
her if she liked, but I didn't. I'm afraid at heart
I'm not a very kind person. I was sorry later that
I hadn't.

Meanwhile I had, as Geneva says, "a job of
work" to do. I promised Mr. Radstock I'd be
down at Monckton Hall the week before, but one
of my youngsters had broken his arm and I had
to go up to Andover to assure him of my sympathy
and forbid him to turn out for football. Mr. Radstock asked me especially to come for the week-
end and help him (as I have done many times)
with his guests. But now I was hurrying down because I wanted to talk to him before the rest of
them came.

It was a little after eleven when I turned off the
Washington and Jefferson Highway into the

private road that winds three beautiful wooded miles to the open plantation. The road crosses an open field to the two white gateposts that mark the beginning of the driveway that leads to the porch. It's on these posts that the two white carved pineapples stand that were a talisman for us when we were children. My father used to drive out to Monckton Hall in his carriage—he firmly regarded the motor car as an invention of the devil —and we would lean perilously out to see who could touch the tip of the pineapple on his side. Whoever could had his very next wish come true. It always came true, because we always wished for Aunty Maria's sugar pie or turkey stuffed with chestnuts. I still have an irresistible impulse to lean out when I drive through and touch the tip of the old white wood carved fruit. I'm afraid my wishes are not so simple now.

John and his father were sitting on the porch when I drove up. John came down with flattering enthusiasm, in which I thought I noticed the slightest undertone of something like uneasiness.

"Hello, Diane! Great to see you! How're the kids?"

"Fine, thanks!" We shook hands and I ran up the steps to Mr. Radstock, whom I'm afraid I've always found much more interesting than John. John's all right but rather dull.

"You're looking fit. How are you?"

"I'm glad you've come, Diane," he said with one of his half formal, half intimate smiles that always left me not quite sure what he meant. "Nice to have you here."

"It's good to be here, Mr. Radstock," I answered very sincerely. "I can't really believe you're going to let me re-do Monckton Hall. It's the sort of thing that doesn't really happen, you know."

He smiled and took my arm in his free one.

"Let's go in. John'll take your car out. I want to see you before the others come. Leave your bag there. Sebastian will get it."

The old colored man appeared at the door just then.

"Howdy, Miss Diane! It's mighty nice to see you, Miss—how you-all bin?"

"Fine, Sebastian. You're looking splendid. How's that boy of yours?" I replied, shaking the old man's hand.

"He's mighty fine, Miss Diane. He's playin' in a orchestry in Chicago. It's called Coon Cotton's orchestry an' he plays in a hotel. You hears him ovah the radio, Miss."

"That's great, Sebastian. You'll tell me about him."

"Yas indeed, Miss, 'deed Ah will."

The old man picked up my bags and followed Mr. Radstock and me into the house. John drove my car off to the garage that is tucked away behind a copse a quarter-mile or so from the house.

"Will you smoke a cigarette before you go up, Diane?" Mr. Radstock asked. "Let's go in here."

He led the way to the library to the right of the hall. He lit my cigarette and sat down without saying anything else for a moment. I had the curious feeling that he had something to tell me, too. I said, without much point, "Aren't you ever sorry you don't smoke?"

"I do smoke."

"A mild cigar after dinner. You can hardly call that smoking."

"That's exactly the trouble with your generation, Diane," he returned quietly. He was very serious. "You haven't the faintest idea of moderation—not in anything. You start smoking with your first cup of coffee in the morning, or earlier, and you throw your last butt on the floor after you've turned out your light at night—oh, not you particularly, but most of the young people I have at my house. You haven't the remotest conception that a single glass of good port after dinner is far better than all the gin cocktails in the world."

"Oh, dear!" I interrupted him in mock horror. "You sound exactly like Senator Mellish. Are you going soap-boxing for the return of Puritanism? I suppose that explains why he's here this weekend."

He smiled and offered me another cigarette.

"Not in the least. Moderation is all I want. A return of good taste. The Greeks were quite right, Diane; moderation in all things. From what I hear of Mellish—I haven't met him—he is grossly immoderate."

"But still in the right direction, Mr. Radstock—he'll consider your one glass of port and your one cigar as gross intemperance. He'll read you a lecture on them this evening. He'll probably leave the table with the ladies to keep from being a party to them. Unless he's still being clinical."

"Clinical?"

"Exactly. Last night Priscilla took him to a speakeasy to see life raw and red in the very act of pulsating. Dullest evening I've ever spent. But it won't teach him anything. I don't suppose he has any conception of what it means to be bored. He kept casting a fishy eye about the place—you could just see him making it into his next speech. Dens of iniquity, silken swathed society damsels cheek by jowl with foreign filth.—When you hear it, that will be Jocelyn and Pericles Xanthopoulos."

"Dear, dear!" Mr. Radstock chuckled and frowned in elaborate consternation. "You've been writing his speeches? Somebody told me it was Priscilla."

"Priscilla hasn't sense enough. Caleb Williams may be doing it—they sound like some of his heavy satire. But I think he has too much respect for the Integrity of the Fourth Estate, as he calls it. Caleb, I mean."

A slight frown passed across Mr. Radstock's ordinarily tranquil face. I gathered that Caleb was right in regarding himself as out of favor at Monckton Hall. I again thought it strange, as I had often done, that Mr. Radstock should be so sensitive about his lameness, and I remembered an old childhood scene when I had once found a cardinal with a broken leg and had hid it under a flower pot so I wouldn't have to explain about it to my father and Mr. Radstock who were coming towards me down the path. Lameness was never mentioned.

"He probably writes them himself, Diane, I'm afraid," he remarked coolly. "Anyway, I regard excess in anything as very bad—piety as well as wickedness. It's usually a cloak in that case. However, I'm interested in Mellish as a distinctly American phenomenon."

"He won't fit in with your other Americana very well."

I glanced about the room. It was filled with fine early American furniture and knickknacks of one sort and another. The books in the two high mahogany cases were all early Colonial imprints. There was a portrait of John Marshall over the mantel.

He smiled at that.

"I shan't keep him. There's no use in avoiding the caricatures, however. Do you know, when I go to the House I think what a pity it is we haven't a Gillray to-day. They ought to be perpetuated, these Mellishes. They need somebody to confer immortality on them as Gillray has done for Fox, the Regent, and Queen Charlotte."

"Surely we have a new crop every year?"

"I'm more hopeful than that. I think they're an

aspect of our gilded age, and that they'll disappear along with grog shops, dray horses, bull-roarers, and all useless sorts of things. But that's not getting us anywhere, and all the people will be along shortly."

"Who is coming?" I asked.

"Just a chosen few. I planned it to be much more extensive, but I'm getting old, Diane. The prospect of half the Hunt Club down here was so alarming that I cut them all out. I intended, as a matter of fact, to ask the Fraziers and Mellish down. Mellish because I wanted to see him up close, and the Fraziers for all the obvious reasons. Jocelyn and John chiefly."

"Really?" I asked, pricking up my ears.

"I don't know how really," he replied. "He'll tell you all about it, I imagine. That, in fact, is one of the things I want to talk to you about."

"To me?" I said, incredulously.

"To you. I want to know, Diane, who this crowd is that Jocelyn is going about with."

"What crowd do you mean?" I asked. I was very much surprised. Justice Frazier's words came back to me: "Keep Jocelyn from going to the wretched places she's going to to-night. Or if she must go, go with her." I couldn't think what had occurred so suddenly to the two of them at the same time.

"I mean the crowd last night, for instance. Where were you—some speakeasy or other?"

"Why, Mr. Radstock," I exclaimed, "surely you

know who they all are. You've invited them down here for a week-end; it's the same old crowd. You must know what they're all about. Anyway, you certainly know Norman Vaughan and the two Xanthopouli. I was there. Priscilla you've known since she was a child. Mellish was there. They seem a very ordinary lot to me. Certainly harmless enough, drinking pink lemonade in a nice family speakeasy."

Mr. Radstock was silent. That something was on his mind was perfectly apparent. Ordinarily, or at least at any other time, I should have assumed that a Virginia gentleman of the old school was objecting to the girl his son hoped to marry going to places that his mother wouldn't have gone to. But my conversation with Justice Frazier the night before gave it an entirely different background, and I was considerably puzzled.

"The only other people there were myself and Jerry Blaine. We went to see Priscilla's lion do his tricks. We might as well have stayed at home and tuned in on the radio," I went on. "Especially when Priscilla lost interest."

"Priscilla lost interest?" asked Mr. Radstock. In fact it was the last thing one could expect of Priscilla.

"I mean in Senator Mellish," I replied. "She sighted fairer fields. Caleb had an Englishman with him, a Major Heath. After that Senator Mellish couldn't jump through a single hoop."

Mr. Radstock thought a moment.

"Major Heath? I've heard the name."

"You may have heard of him from Justice Frazier."

I was quite proud of myself with that. I knew perfectly that there was some collusion between the two old friends. They were both worried about Jocelyn's crowd, and neither knew that the other had spoken to me. Mr. Radstock looked at me, a faint smile in his eyes. We understood each other perfectly.

"Did Blanchard tell you about Major Heath?" he asked.

I laughed.

"No, he didn't." Perhaps I was a little sheepish. "He was talking about the crowd Jocelyn was with last night—just as you are. He's worried about her, as you probably know a lot better than I do. He asked me to look out for her if anything happened to him. I was very much distressed. He'd been writing a lot of letters, and I happened to see Major Heath's name on the top one. Then I met him with Caleb. He seems to be rather cropping up everywhere."

Mr. Radstock didn't say anything for a few minutes. His face in repose has always fascinated me. I sat staring at him now a little longer than was polite, I'm afraid. He has a determined face, but his hazel eyes are very calm, as if years of physical inactivity and living among books and old gardens had purged most of the stormier emotions out of him. Unlike so many crippled people there was nothing inert or futile, however, about him. Perhaps it was because I knew his history so well that I saw so much in his face. It always impressed me as being very wise, as if he'd had all possible experience and had come through it and could look at life objectively.

He looked up—he'd been gazing at the rug or somewhere beyond it—and caught me half gaping at him, I suppose. He smiled suddenly, a very friendly smile.

"Do you know, Diane, I really don't know anything about these people at all. If you asked me about Thalia Xanthopoulos, all I could tell you is that I once drank champagne out of her mother's slipper. You probably know enough about the late Eighties to know that that was a very devilish thing to do. I know that everybody in Philadelphia, especially old Mrs. Adler, breathed a little easier in their stays when she married—the first time. They didn't approve of the Greek prince. That's all I know of Thalia. It's more than I know of her brother."

"That only leaves Priscilla and Norman Vaughan."

"I know Vaughan belongs to every club in the Capital, that he's a fine shot and a charming man. I don't know whether he ever had a mother."

"You've got to take some things on faith, Mr. Radstock," I said.

"And that leaves Priscilla," he went on, with a half-smile, ticking them off, so it seemed, one by one. "I do know Priscilla. I may say she's the only woman in the world about whom I've ever felt confident in making such a statement."

I laughed. Poor Priscilla! No woman in the world ever strived so hard to be mystifying with so little success. How many times when the discussion had got on the eternal subject of how to hold a husband, or a friend, has not Priscilla said, "I think it's mystery that does it, don't you, Diane?" And on the mantel in her very swell apartment she has a large onyx sphinx.

Mr. Radstock got up and went to the window.

"I hear them coming, Diane," he said, with a trace of weariness in his voice that startled me into a sudden memory of the scene in front of Joe's place as we were leaving it the night before. I had the curious feeling for the second time since I had arrived that I was transferring the significance of one set of events to an entirely new setting, and getting precisely the same reaction from totally different things. Mr. Radstock came back to the table where I was standing.

"I'm getting old, I think, Diane," he said a little mockingly. "I find myself hearing those cars out there and thinking how pleasant it will be when it's all over and they all go home again. Hospitable attitude, isn't it?"

It wasn't Cassandra alone whom the gods cursed so that her prophecies should never be believed. Or maybe it's only that the tellers of fairy tales are wiser than they know. I don't think I ever heard a casual remark that became more bitterly true a little while later.

We went out to welcome the laughing mob that trouped into the hall.

"My *dear,* you wouldn't believe it! Somebody stole a lot of Justice Frazier's letters last night, and he and Jocelyn can't get out until after lunch. . . ."

And so on. As Caleb once remarked about Priscilla, it's too damn bad she's not a radio so you could turn her off.

CHAPTER FOUR

I'LL NEVER forget lunch at Monckton Hall that
noon. Maybe I was hypersensitive. Maybe none of
the things that happened later were in the air, and
it was after all just what it seemed to be, a perfectly charming luncheon in the genial Virginia
manner of its host. To me, however, the very
smoothness of it was terrifying. Everyone had an
air of complete *rapport*. We might have been on
a desert island with a million years ahead of us,
it was so completely apart and unhurried. I've
never before seen any of those people so polished,
so courteous, and so entirely at ease with themselves and the world. Underneath it ran the mellow current of Senator Mellish's liquid voice, and
above and behind and through it Priscilla's chatter darted and spattered and bounced away again.

Only two of us didn't play the game—if game it
was; I still don't know. Mrs. Mellish, at Mr. Radstock's right, said almost nothing. I sat at the other
end of the table with a fixed smile, listening to the
Senator on my right and John Radstock on my
left. But I think no one noticed either Mrs. Mellish or me. The smooth rhythm flowed around us
and covered us up, and all we did was smile and

44

nod, keeping time with it as if it were sort of a ritualistic dance.

All this gradually beat in on me until I became so acutely aware of it that I wanted to scream, to break it up some way. But on it went, punctuated with Sebastian's white-cotton-gloved hands appearing, just as rhythmically, now to left, now to right, removing plates, bringing others: nothing ever stopping. I kept watching Sebastian's hands. I hardly noticed him; just those absurd white hands, silently and deftly doing their job. No one else seemed conscious of them. I don't think I've been so before, and I've seen them hundreds of times. But nobody seemed conscious of anything else! They talked on, quietly, with curious dignity, smiling, now and then laughing. I felt myself receding into the background watching them, and every one of them seemed to have someone else just behind him, something stark and primitive— ready to spring. I looked at Mrs. Mellish to see what she was thinking of, to see if she had this other self behind her chair like the rest of them.

Sebastian was putting her avocado salad before her. She looked down; the sight of his white hands must have startled her, for she jumped, then recovered herself. I saw her glance sharply at her husband to see if he had noticed it. He hadn't. He was telling Priscilla about a canyon in Wyoming he'd given to the Boy Scouts.

It must be difficult to be married to a great man who apparently doesn't like you to jump when you're startled. I felt rather sorry for her. She looked as though if she had a soul she'd hardly dare call it her own.

Mrs. Mellish was a frail little thing, not fragile though, for her hands bore evidence of hard work —years at a washtub or sewing coarse seams. Her eyes were pale blue, and one fear after another seemed to chase through them. She had reddish hair that must have been quite lovely when she was young. It was ridiculously marcelled now so that her head looked like a strawberry pastry. When she spoke, which she seldom did, her voice startled you. It was thin, sharp, and insistent. I got the impression that in its native habitat, away from the critical eye of a superior husband, that voice would never stop.

She was silent enough at lunch. It seems curious now, but the picture I have of that week-end is a talkie. When I think, I can hear the whole background of Priscilla's chatter, like a river full of ducks; and at the same time, paradoxical as it is, I can hear Mrs. Mellish's perfect silence.

She was particularly odd in contrast with Pericles Xanthopoulos, who sat on her left. They were opposite poles in worldliness, certainly, although he did his best to think of homely things to amuse her. Our eyes met once when I heard him telling her how his nurse used to make a black honey bread and how delighted he would be to get her the recipe. And I heard one bit about goat's milk and cheese just as I heard Thalia remark to Norman Vaughan that she and Pericles expected to spend the winter with Grand Duke Leopold in the Midi.

At only one point in this interminably facile lunch did a personal note enter.

Sebastian brought in some excellent sauterne. He filled everyone's glass except Mr. Radstock's. Senator Mellish had drunk half of his before he noticed that his host was not drinking.

"I'm surprised, Mr. Radstock," he said, with large suavity, "that you do not take wine."

"Probably not as much as Mr. Radstock is surprised that you do," Thalia, at Mr. Radstock's left, remarked promptly.

There was a quick light in Mr. Radstock's eyes, but he replied gravely:

"Oh, not at all. I happen to be a devotee of port, Senator. I seldom touch anything else. But guests have as much liberty as we can manage for them in the matter. I've been very much interested, now, in the country's reaction—and I use the word advisedly—to Mr. Hoover. What do you . . ."

That was neutral ground, as they are both Democrats; Senator Mellish of course was powerless to resist, and we were saved from an explanation of the Senator's views on When-in-Rome-do-as-the-Romans-do. It was a favorite defense. He seemed to spend most of his life in Rome.

So it went on. We might have been a lot of people meeting one another for the first time under very pleasant circumstances. Just that once was there the remotest indication that any of us were familiar with the prejudices, problems, or even occupations of the others. We were in sort of a social vacuum, and I was—or seemed to be—the only person there who was uneasy. Except Mrs. Mellish, of course, and that, I thought, was simply bad breeding—she had no poise. Mr. Radstock most of all seemed to have forgot that he had suspicions—of what sort Heaven only knew—of everybody there. He was charming to Thalia, who has always been a little awed by him.

"It's Mother," she once said to me. "All her old friends are severe with me because she married Father instead of some Philadelphia stock broker. If they'd only look at a calendar they'd see it wasn't my fault. I wasn't born for a whole year."

"Does it occur to you that you're quite as shocking as your mother was?" I inquired by way of reproof.

"I couldn't be," she retorted. "No one nowadays can possibly be as shocking as they could in the Nineties. A sip of champagne was more deadly than a complete pass-out is now. Anyway, I don't want to be; then I'd likely react to my ghastly youth and become a frightful prude like Mother is now. That's really shocking."

She and Mr. Radstock were getting on beautifully just then. Norman Vaughan was leaning over the table, telling them about some adventure of his in India when he ran into somebody's sacred cow and crippled it at some frightful cost, and discovered later that the cow was kept at difficult corners for just that purpose until somebody actually killed her. He's been everywhere and done so many things that he seldom has to repeat his stories—an excellent thing—and Thalia and Mr. Radstock were listening to him with enjoyment. Thalia's a really beautiful girl. I was glad, because it would make it much pleasanter for Jocelyn if Mr. Radstock liked her most intimate friend.

We had coffee in the back drawing room. Priscilla bore Mrs. Mellish off to a sofa in the corner and began a course of cross-questioning that must have bewildered the poor woman. Mr. Radstock and Senator Mellish were examining some early cartoons of the Boston Tea Party. Then I noticed John in the hall frantically signaling me to the summer house. Thalia and her brother were busily deciphering an inscription in Greek under a portrait of William Pitt and talking in low tones about something quite different. I couldn't help but be aware of the urgency in Thalia's low voice.

Norman Vaughan was talking to me and he heard it too.

"What does it say, Thalia?" he interrupted lightly.

"I'm sure I don't know. Pericles pretends to, but he doesn't fool anybody. He was sent down from Oxford because he couldn't read Homer."

Xanthopoulos laughed good-naturedly.

"I probably know more ancient Greek than you do Old English, at that," he retorted. I slipped out just as the Senator came forward with something about Homer's grandeur.

John was waiting impatiently.

"We can't go down there," he said in a low voice. "That damn Greek is staring out of the window. Let's go to the old office."

The "office" was the wing on the right side of the house. It contained Mr. Radstock's large library and the little room he used as a study on the ground floor, and his bedroom and bath on the second floor. It had been the office of the estate originally, and the name clung long after the Radstocks had quit being large landholders and the wing had been converted successively into nursery, schoolroom, guest house, and finally library and living quarters for Mr. Radstock.

I'd been in the office a very few times, and then only for a few moments. The wing was connected with the main part of the house by a covered "hyphen" that opened off the library where Mr. Radstock and I had talked before lunch. Originally there was no entrance from the house, and Mr. Radstock had made one at the left of the fireplace. There were shell cupboards on either side of the fireplace, and it was one of them that swung out, opening into a small stairway that led to the flagged pavement of the hyphen. It was in a sense

a hidden door, although no secret was ever made
of it. What I mean is that to anyone looking at it
casually, it is obviously nothing but a shell cupboard, but no attempt has ever been made to pre-
tend it isn't also something else. It was one of the
things that threw people off so much, when Senator Mellish later discovered it all for himself, by
the logical process of reasoning that someone had
left the room who hadn't been seen to leave. Everyone who knows the house, however, knows it is a
door that was made to keep Mr. Radstock from
having to limp outside and around to get to his
study.

John and I sat down on the old leather sofa in
front of the fire that burned pleasantly in the
grate.

"Look here, Diane," he demanded abruptly,
"what's all this stuff about Jocelyn?"

"What do you mean, John?" I said.

"You know. The way she's running about with
this crowd that that priceless fool Priscilla has
in tow—speakeasies, race tracks, fortune tellers,
and the rest of it."

He glared into the fire and kicked the fender.

"I'm sure I don't know what you have on your
mind," I replied calmly. "But I think I'd get it
off. I'd ask Jocelyn when she comes."

"And that's another thing," he said doggedly.
"Why didn't she come for lunch?"

"I don't know any more than that Priscilla told
us somebody's taken some important letters from

Justice Frazier. I suppose he naturally wanted to do something about it, and I suppose Jocelyn probably stayed to drive him out."

My explanation was hardly very convincing, if he was really worried, but it seemed to relieve his tension a little. I offered him a cigarette from my case.

"Oh, sorry!" he apologized, fishing about in his pockets for a match. "No, thanks, I'll smoke a Camel. You see, Diane, I'm not just making a damn fool of myself about this. I came down last night and met—well, somebody you don't know. He was slinging the local dirt all around, and he said somebody had his hooks in Jocelyn."

"What on earth do you mean?" I demanded.

"Just what I said. What's-his-name didn't know much about it, but he says Jocelyn's always seen in strange places lately and something queer's up. I couldn't very well choke any more out of him in the smoking room and I had to let it go. I thought you'd know about it."

John Radstock is a strange person for so ordinary a young stockbroker-like fellow. I was surprised even then at him, sitting there, his jaw set, his hands gripped so tightly that the knucklebones showed white through the drawn skin.

"Why don't you speak to Jocelyn, when she comes?" I asked quietly, rather more worried now that this business gave a new significance to her father's conversation and to Mr. Radstock's.

He didn't look away from the fire. "I can't very well."

"You're just the one who can," I said, very untruthfully.

"Wrong," he replied shortly. "She thinks I'm an old horse with one nose in my law books and the other in the grave. She'd tell me, and properly, to mind my own business."

"Not if you go at it properly." I knew, however, that whichever way he did go at it would be the wrong way.

"Don't be funny, Diane," he said, pleadingly. I was surprised at his earnestness—he's ordinarily so beastly matter-of-fact. "I'm dead serious; I mean it. I think that kid's got involved in something that's too much for her, and she hasn't anybody to look out for her. I don't like the people she goes around with. Her father's got his head in the clouds, and he couldn't help her anyway, even if he thought about it. Oh, I've heard other things, too, and I tell you, Diane, there's something wrong!"

I was silent a moment at that. Then I said, "Have you told your father about it?"

"Of course not. Dad's like Justice Frazier. Sweet young girls didn't get in messes in their day. And you know how much stock Dad takes in anything I say."

"I see."

If the Radstocks didn't choose to confide in each

other, it was hardly my business to confide for them. And I know, of course, that they aren't awfully good friends. I don't mean that they're not on good terms, but simply that there's nothing warm about their relationship. It's perfectly casual. John lives in New York and his father at Monckton Hall. I've never blamed Mr. Radstock. John's nice but not very exciting.

For a moment I thought of telling John what his father and Justice Frazier had said to me, but I decided not to. It was just as well, as it turned out, that I didn't.

"Do you think Jocelyn is in—danger?" I asked, trying to light another cigarette nonchalantly.

My companion was still buried in despair. "I don't know. Maybe it's just her immortal soul I'm worrying about. But there's something rotten somewhere."

He spoke with an attempt at flippancy, but he meant what he said.

It hadn't occurred to me before that John admitted women to have immortal souls. On that matter I thought I could reassure him a little.

"After all, John," I said practically, "the people right here in this house to-day form a solid wedge in her crowd of friends, except the Mellishes, and Priscilla perhaps. Thalia, her brother, and Norman Vaughan are good friends of hers. They see her oftener, probably, than the hundreds of others she goes around with from time to time."

"I know they do," he returned a little bitterly.

"And I don't think much of them, either. I told Father that and he said he had his very good reasons for inviting them down. That for you, my son. I asked him why he didn't have Jerry Blaine, so I'd have somebody to talk to. He said he thought it would be good for me to talk to Senator Fathead."

He gave the fire a poke that scattered it completely. As he did so we heard the purr of a motor outside.

"There she is now," he said sharply, raising his head.

I kept mine still, for I had heard something else, above the noise of the car, and closer. It was the sound of a door closing quietly, very near us. I touched John's arm and motioned to him to be still. We heard nothing. John got up, and with a strange glance at me looked out of the library door into the hyphen stairway. I followed him. The passageway was empty.

"What was it?" he said.

"I heard somebody in the passage," I said. "Or I thought I did. You know the little click an old latch makes? I thought I heard someone open or close the door."

He looked strangely at me again. I knew what he was thinking: what difference did it make? At that moment I could have given no answer.

Nevertheless he went to the window that looked out over the back garden toward the river.

"Well," he said, with a shrug, "there's nobody

but friends in sight, if you call 'em that. Take
your choice. Xanthopoulos is going down towards
the river. Mrs. Mellish and your friend Priscilla
are strolling about—she's certainly working over-
time on those birds. She think he's going to be
the next President? There's Mellish by himself.
Damn it, he's strolling about, too. Wouldn't you
think he'd stop existing when he's alone?"

This running comment on the garden scene, as
viewed from the library window, came to me, sitting as calmly as I could in front of the fire again.

"There's Jocelyn and Thalia. What're they doing? Probably going out to have a look at the
stables. Isn't it interesting; fine, chilly October
day, and everybody wandering about in the garden. Well, that's the lot—shall we go back to the
house? I've got to phone Caleb; I promised to give
him some dope for a story to-night. This'll be a
good time. . . . But I'll tell you what, Diane,"
he added. "This bunch gives me a pain in the
neck."

We went back to the library without speaking.
It was empty when we got there. In the hall we
met Sebastian bringing the coffee tray out of the
drawing room. Everyone else had disappeared.

I left John in the hall and went upstairs. I wrote
three letters. When I came down at half-past four,
everyone was back in the house. Priscilla was chattering away at a great rate—no greater, really,
than usual—on the drawing-room sofa. Jocelyn
was in a big chair by the fire, her eyes half closed,

listening. Mrs. Mellish was knitting a green sock on the sofa across the room from the fireplace. Thalia was watching her, a half-smile on her usually immobile face. John and Vaughan and Pericles were scattered about, half listening to Priscilla, all watching Jocelyn more or less openly. It didn't seem a particularly engaging group.

I suggested to John that he mix us a drink.

"I'm sorry! I didn't think of it. Come on, Thalia!"

"Righto!" She rose like a lithe little cat from a saucer of milk and with sudden life danced after him towards the pantry.

I said something to Pericles about a print in the small library and we sauntered in to look at it.

Senator Mellish was comfortably, if somewhat ostentatiously, ensconced in a deep upholstered chair, reading a rather elaborately ponderous volume. I glanced over his shoulder; it was Renan's Life of Christ.

Everyone was at hand but Mr. Radstock and Justice Frazier. How very clever of them to have business to talk over in Mr. Radstock's study, I thought with a smile. I was quite wrong. Five minutes later, just as John and Thalia appeared with a tray of tinkling highballs, the colored gardener came to the door of the drawing room and signaled awkwardly to John to come out into the hall. I had one look at his ashy face and rolling eyes.

A moment later John came back and beckoned

to me. I suppose everyone knew, had known the moment before, that something was wrong. Everything I had felt in them at the luncheon table seemed suddenly to break out.

"What in God's name is the matter?" Thalia's passionate, frightened cry seemed to tear across the tinkling, jangling atmosphere. There was an instant of silence. Then Jocelyn got up, white and shaken.

"It's Father!" She seemed to whisper it. "What's happened to my father? John! Oh, Diane! Oh, Dad, Dad!"

She ran from the room and past the colored man, standing awkwardly in the doorway, out into the garden, John and I closely after her.

It was her father. Justice Frazier's great body lay inert on the flagged pavement behind the box hedge. He was dead.

CHAPTER FIVE

POOR little Jocelyn! She looked so pitifully small and fragile, kneeling there on the gray stones beside the silent huddled figure of her father, her yellow head bent, her slim shoulders quivering under the tight-fitting blue jersey frock. Suddenly she raised her head with a wild, beseeching look in her eyes.

"Keep them away, John!" she cried. "Keep them away! Don't let them come and see him like this! Oh, Daddy, Daddy!"

With a heart-breaking sob she dropped forward on the heavy mass that death had made of the splendid figure of Justice Blanchard Frazier.

"Oh, Daddy, don't you hear me?" she cried softly, urgently. "It's Jocelyn, Daddy—don't you hear me?"

I turned away. John stepped out into the garden path. The commotion of hurrying steps and excited voices stopped short. No one spoke—not even Priscilla. John motioned them silently back to the house, and I had the sudden feeling that it was his set white face that silenced them—not any respect for the dead. Incongruous as it seems, it kept going through my head that Priscilla was passing up the scoop of a lifetime, if indeed she was passing it up.

I turned back to the tragic little figure on the pavement still lost in overwhelming grief.

"Come, Jocelyn," I said, bending down and drawing her gently to her feet. "You must come away, dear. It's going to be bitterly hard, and you've got to face it—as he'd have done," I ended tritely. There was so little to say! I've never felt so keenly the intensity of anyone's loneliness. She stood there utterly alone, so close to what had been her dearest friend, but separated by an in-finity of nothingness. She didn't speak, and I couldn't make her move.

"You must go, Jocelyn," John begged her gently. "Don't you see? You must go with Diane. I'll stay here, but you can't. Please!"

She seemed aware of us then for the first time. She closed her eyes. I thought she was going to faint, but she didn't. Instead she said, in a dead calm voice, "He knew it was coming—but not like this."

"My gallant little daughter," Justice Frazier had called her once when she broke an arm and didn't whimper. Gallant little Jocelyn! Alone and game to the core!

We started to the house, she and I, leaving John back there in the fast gathering dusk with the body of Justice Frazier. I thought just then, and I've thought of it many times since that day, that back there behind the great box hedge, huddled, pitched forward in his stride, shot like a Chicago gangster, lay the one man I knew who should have died like the Good Old Man in Blake's engraving.

Near the house, coming as quickly as he could, we met Mr. Radstock.

"Jocelyn, Diane, what's this!" he cried. His kindly face said so much more that Jocelyn's thin little armor crumpled. He smoothed the sleek wavy head buried in his shoulder.

"There, there, little girl, there, there." He spoke very softly, and disengaged her after a moment. "Go with Diane. I'll go down there."

I picked up his cane that had fallen and handed it to him, and took Jocelyn on to the house. We went quickly upstairs. I barely noticed the strained faces through the drawing-room door as we passed. I thought Jocelyn hadn't at all, when suddenly her eyes filled with tears and she laughed a low bitter laugh, so remote from that terrible "It's Jocelyn, Daddy," of a few moments ago that I looked at her in alarm.

"Don't you see, Diane?" she half sobbed, half laughed bitterly. "Don't you see? It's a party in a parlour, all silent and all damned."

Surely Wordsworth was never quoted so terribly before in Monckton Hall.

Upstairs I gave her some codine that I happened to have in my bag, and sat with her, listening to the sudden outbursts of memories of the past that kept coming to her mind. After a bit she went to sleep and I left her.

The police were there when I went downstairs. I found that Sheriff Carter from the Fairfax County Court House was in charge. He had several other men with him, including a surgeon— Dr. Perry, I think his name was. It was the first time I'd seen the police functioning and I was chiefly impressed with the way they tried to "pass the buck." None of them seemed to want to commit himself. They roamed mechanically about the house, looking in closets and cupboards. "Hunting for the death gun," a wizened little fellow informed me in a whisper. They might have been excellent prohibition enforcers, but they didn't seem, in some way, very able to cope with that curious sophisticated lot in the back drawing room.

Sheriff Carter did his best. He parked an enormous evil-smelling cigar (pronounced "see-gar") on the front steps, and picked his way with some lack of ease through the aristocratic maze of Monckton Hall. Obviously and quite frankly he regretted the fact that the prosecuting attorney was in Washington, and that the burden of this particular business should fall on his stalwart if not subtle shoulders. I've seen a lot of Sheriff Carter since, and I have the greatest admiration for him as a man and as an officer of the law. But as he said to me after Mr. Whipple, the prosecuting attorney, came on the scene, "It's just as well your sort of people don't commit most of the crimes—they'd have to have one of you for sheriff and he wouldn't be worth a continental." He was quite right. I'd hate to have his job.

As a matter of fact, when he got down to business he was efficient. He did all his routine work, out there behind the hedge, quietly and with very little disturbance. They brought the body inside, John and his father coming with them, and took it upstairs. I came in the drawing room just as they started up. Somebody had thoughtfully closed the door, but we heard the steps quite clearly, carrying a heavy burden. We were all spellbound, as if we were morbidly counting the heavy labored tread—thud, thud, thud—and the lighter tread of the two who were following.

And then a very strange thing happened, or what I thought at the time was so. Quite suddenly there was a quick movement in the room. All of us had been so intent, involuntarily, on that measured, dreadful progress, that we had forgot one another. But we all turned when Priscilla stepped, or almost ran, with astonishing quickness to the hall door, her face alive with extraordinary intensity, her head slightly raised, listening intently. Quickly and noiselessly she opened the door and listened again. We were all watching her agape, completely dumfounded. Thalia broke the dramatic tenseness of the situation by saying, in her hardest and most nonchalant voice, "It's the Delsarte Method. Hark, I hear footsteps approaching on horseback; oh, say! what may they be?"

Priscilla calmly turned her childlike features towards us and closed the door.

"Wrong, Thalia," she said sweetly. "I thought I heard Jocelyn's door open upstairs, and I didn't want her to see them taking—him—up."

There was a moment's silence. Then Thalia said humbly, "I'm sorry. I didn't mean to be horrid."

"That's all right, my dear." Mrs. Mellish spoke up as briskly as she would have done in her own Ladies' Aid Society back home. "We're all pretty upset, I guess."

She beamed with a sort of sharp good will.

And we were. I hadn't realized before just how much we were, until I looked around the room when she said that.

The chief of the lot was her own husband, the Honorable Reuben Mellish. Somebody might have pricked him with one of his wife's knitting needles. For the time being his façade had completely collapsed. He was sitting next to his wife on the sofa by the fire, staring into it, nervously biting his rather pendulous lower lip, his hands folding and unfolding restlessly.

Priscilla, her nose for news back into play, was watching him like a cat.

His wife, oddly enough, was taking it all very well. She sat primly by her husband's side, knitting. It occurred to me that she was thinking how she would put it when she wrote home about it, and trying to find just the right platitude about it. At least I was half through thinking that when I

became aware that she was not looking at the click-
ing needles at all. Her eyes, shaded by her long
pale lashes, were fixed steadily on Priscilla. I think
she knew Priscilla had been baiting her husband.
At any rate, she went on knitting placidly and
watching Priscilla like a lynx.

Then she said, with almost a smug satisfaction,
"His death will be a great loss to the community."

Looking back now I realize that I was the only
person at Monckton Hall just then who had the
background against which each new event showed
up so clearly—with the possible exception of one
person. Without that background everything must
have appeared normally not normal. I mean that
coming into the drawing room where the seven
of us were, no one, unless he knew what I knew,
would have seen anything unusual in Pericles's
excessive perturbation, much less in Norman
Vaughan's even more excessive nonchalance. After
all a serious incident had occurred, resulting in
the death of one of the most eminent jurists in the
country. Whether it was murder was yet to be
proved, although we'd accepted it as such without
question. It was impossible to connect suicide with
the name of Frazier. But whether the murder—
if murder it was—was deliberate or accidental,
remained to be seen. I don't think the notion of a
deliberate, premeditated killing had entered anyone's mind so far. And so an entirely unprejudiced
observer coming into the room just then would
hardly have noticed Priscilla and Mrs. Mellish,

one watching the Senator—doubtless greatly moved by the sudden death of so eminent a man— and the other watching the watcher.

Even less would there have been anything noteworthy about the two Xanthopouli and Norman Vaughan. Undoubtedly Pericles was a highly strung Southern type. That would account for the swarthy handsome features twitching almost convulsively now and then, and the hand that shook as he lighted one cigarette from the stub of another. He stood, or rather half stood, half reclined, against the window seat near the hall door, watching it nervously, wiping his forehead now and then with a large colored handkerchief. He was in odd contrast to his sister, who sat beside him in a highback chair, cool and calm as some dark lily, against the dull blue brocatelle of the upholstery. Not a muscle moved or a foot or finger shifted to indicate that she was ever aware that her best friend's father had just made his last journey up the stairs of Monckton Hall.

I read somewhere once that a famous detective always watched people's feet for signs of telltale nervousness. If he did, he never caught a Thalia or a Norman Vaughan. He would have missed the pallor that ever so faintly waxened the delicate olive of Thalia's perfect classical face.

And Norman Vaughan was as cool as Thalia. He flicked the ash from his cigarette into a cloisonné ashtray on the table a couple of feet away with disturbing accuracy. I had the feeling that he was testing his own steadiness. I wish I could explain Norman. It isn't fair to say he was merely —as a certain lady on Massachusetts Avenue says of him and many other things—"perfectly *comme il faut.*" But it is true that he does everything he attempts perfectly. The best shot at half a dozen gun clubs, plays better golf than anyone at half a dozen country clubs, does amateur theatricals so cleverly that you're afraid to refuse a crippled beggar on the streets for fear Norman will tell the next dinner party that you're frightfully stingy. But above all I think it's his perfectly fitting, perfectly harmonizing clothes that annoy me most. If only sometimes his faultless collar wasn't quite so faultless, and his cravat, socks and shirts—and undershirts for all I know—didn't so infallibly match. Caleb Williams told me once, with something between awe and revulsion, that Norman always brushed his hair carefully before he went to bed. But as I say that isn't fair, and if Norman is a reincarnation of Apollo and Narcissus—sort of two gods in one person—it's hardly his fault. He's wealthy and one of the most popular eligible men in Washington. Where he gets his money or why anyone should want to marry him, I don't know. Probably one of the reasons for my feeling this about him is that in the twelve years since the war, when he first appeared in Washington society, he's never shown any particular interest in me. I throw that out to circumvent my friends, and his, who read this. I'm perfectly willing to grant that being a perennially popular bachelor in Washington isn't as simple as it sounds. Norman Vaughan is one of the few I know who end a season without having insulted a single hostess unintentionally, and with no crows' feet around his eyes.

As I said, an unprejudiced observer coming in would have seen none of this. No doubt I was hyperæsthetic. Both Justice Frazier and Mr. Radstock had spoken of Pericles, and Caleb had said enough in one form or another about Senator Mellish so that anything that happened when they were about was bound to be colored in my mind by what I was pleased to think of as my special background.

No one had said anything since Mrs. Mellish's remark about the loss to the community. It wasn't a dead silence that had ensued, however; it was curiously vital. I think if Major Heath's Madame Rosa—who by the way is a popular clairvoyant among political ladies in the Capital—had been there she would have heard a frightful din of thought waves crashing against one another—my own not least.

Just then John opened the door and came in, looking very sober but in some way much relieved. He closed it carefully and went over to the sofa, where Priscilla was, and sat down. We waited interminably until he spoke, which he did finally, quite abruptly.

"They say that Justice Frazier was shot at some

distance. They don't know, of course, how far away it was, or what sort of a gun was used, until they take the body to the mortuary and extract the bullet."

"Do those people have all the charge of this business?" Thalia asked, quite sharply, to my surprise.

"Certainly. We're in Fairfax County, and they're the police."

"Oh, can't you get somebody from Washington?"

I thought John looked curiously at her.

"We're not in the District jurisdiction," he said. "Give them a chance. Carter said the district attorney would be here to-night and take charge. Meanwhile you'll all have to be as patient as you can. It's not going to be pleasant, especially when the papers get wind of it."

"Oh, dear!" Mrs. Mellish said simply. "Can't you stop them, Miss Stone?"

Thalia's sardonic laugh startled us. "Ha, ha," she said mirthlessly. "Her paper's probably had an extra out for two hours. Hullo, there's the door bell now; that'll be the rest of the bunch."

She opened the door, and we sat as an audience to a curious scene in the hall.

Mr. Radstock was there with the sheriff and two other men, who had Jem, one of the Radstock colored retainers, by the arms. He was shaking like a leaf.

"I'm not trying to hinder you, Carter," Mr. Radstock was saying; "I'm merely trying to protect one of my boys. You haven't got a shred of evidence to arrest this fellow on."

"He has a gun, sir, and a shot has been fired from it," Sheriff Carter said. "And he can't give much of an account of himself."

"Quite so. But you'll find a good many guns around here, and you can't expect a scared nigger to be very coherent."

Sheriff Carter looked doubtful.

"And you know, Carter, I stand responsible for the boy. I'm not going to have him dragged away to jail unless you have some real evidence against him."

The sheriff looked as if he were not entirely convinced, and at the same time as if he had not really been very sure that Jem had anything to do with it in the first place. So that scene ended; and meantime I had seen Sebastian come slowly from the dining room on his way to the front door to answer the bell we all had heard. He came back just as the sheriff and his men escorted the Negro boy out by the garden door.

"There's two gennelmen, suh. Mr. Caleb an' Majuh Heath. They says they got to see you, suh."

"Aha!" said Thalia. "Little sister right again. Miss Priscilla Stone paging cub reporter!"

We all looked aghast at Priscilla. So she couldn't forego it after all!

Her wide hazel eyes opened a trifle wider.

"You *happen* to be wrong, my dear," she said, a sort of gentle reproof in her voice. "It *wasn't* I at all!"

"Somebody, wasn't it?" Thalia asked sardonically. "Caleb hasn't sense enough to see a payroll robbery on Connecticut Avenue, much less nose out a murder in the country."

It was Mrs. Mellish who spoke up. "But perhaps his friend Major Heath has," she said brightly. We all looked from one to the other of them.

CHAPTER SIX

IT TOOK more than that to silence Thalia. She looked for a second as if she had much more to say about that; then she shrugged her shoulders.

"Not, of course," she said calmly, rising and closing the door, "that we're being beastly interested in somebody else's business."

Mrs. Mellish did not retreat an inch. There was even a little tone of unpleasantness in her thin voice as she said, "It seems to me that in a case of this kind it *becomes* everybody's business."

She certainly had come out like a Japanese wood flower in a finger bowl. Trouble, at least other people's trouble, was her meat. But Senator Mellish was not one to lose his form for long; and he was visibly rounding back into his usual shape. They seemed to me like a perfect domestic teetertotter, and his end was coming up.

"I think that will do, my dear," he sounded ominously. But not before Thalia had well launched herself on an impudent retort.

"Exactly Priscilla's attitude. Are you sure, Mrs. Mellish, you aren't a special correspondent yourself? Maybe it was *you* called them in."

Mrs. Mellish ruffled up like an indignant sparrow. "I'm sure Mr. Williams is a very nice boy," she said warmly. "He took me on a shopping tour when I first came to the Capital, and I found him politeness itself."

The Senator coughed, as Jove reproving a small wayward thunderbolt. He rose impressively, again a large and pompous figure. I think we all felt that whatever happened, we would have him to cope with; and more than that, I think that's exactly what he wanted us to feel. From that moment, except when they were separated, Mrs. Mellish ceased, as far as we could see, to have any identity except that of attendant dove—if such could be said to come out of the lower Middle West.

"Come, my dear," he said. "I think we might go upstairs. I'm sure the presence of so many strangers in a house of sorrow must be disturbing."

It sounded like a line from Webley's *One Thousand Appropriate Remarks for all Occasions,* but I suppose he really thinks in such terms. Anyway, he cast a significant glance at the rest of us and conducted his wife through the library door opposite the garden windows. That, as a matter of fact, was a thoughtful act that should have told me more about the man. The rest of us would have gone directly out the hall door and up the steps, saying "So sorry!" when we ran into Mr. Radstock coping with the law or his present callers. Of course they still had to go through the hall, but by entering at the far door they gave decent warning of their coming. Nor did it occur to me then that it showed, besides such an unexpected thoughtfulness, a definite knowledge of the plan of the house. I shouldn't have supposed then that he had learned his way about so well.

"That's more tact than you've got, Norman," Thalia remarked. "More than that, I think it's a jolly good idea. What do you say, Priscilla?"

We all muttered something and prepared to follow.

John muttered something also and mentally propelled us to the door. "Do you mind waiting a bit, Diane?" he said in a low voice, stopping me. "Oh, by the way! Father said dinner will be at eight o'clock. I'll have Sebastian bring a cocktail to your rooms. It'll look better, and we all need a drink."

I heard the irrepressible Thalia from the other room: "Aye, lads, we're getting back to normalcy. First sensible thing I've heard to-day."

John shut the door and came back to me.

"Diane!" he said urgently. "There's something terribly wrong here."

"Obviously," I said. "Justice Frazier has been shot."

"That's the point," he returned earnestly. "And you know as well as I do that no colored boy around here did it."

"I don't think so," I said slowly. "Though I can't believe anybody else here did it. At any rate, they didn't arrest Jem. And if they do you can defend him; that'll be a fine story for Priscilla."

One of the things about all this, of course, is that John is a lawyer. For six years he's sat at a desk in

the firm of Darrow, Davis & Untermeyer in Wall
Street. I know he's had a dozen invitations from
Washington, but he's refused them and stayed in
New York. In one way it's a good thing, because
no doubt his father's reputation as a consultant
would be something of a handicap here, and the
people he's with have a vast practice. Besides, as
I've said, his father has never shown any great
desire to have him here.

"In the first place," he retorted with some heat,
"I'm not a criminal lawyer. You people don't know
the simplest difference between one court and another. Anyway, that's not the point."

"What is?" I asked.

"Well, look here." He leaned towards me, his
not particularly good-looking but intelligent face
very serious. "I think this is some sort of a political
racket; and I think this crowd Jocelyn's been running with are mixed up in it."

"What do you mean?" I said. "Justice Frazier
has been out of politics for ages."

"There's where you're dead wrong, Diane," he
said. "I got positive information just yesterday
that he'd been offered a place in the Cabinet."

That was news, and I thought about it a minute.
"How can Jocelyn's friends be mixed up in that?"
I said then.

He shook his head.

"Dunno! But I think Father thinks the same—
though he's not saying so."

"Did your father know about the Cabinet position?" I asked after a little. This certainly was all very peculiar, interpreted in light of my "background" again.

"Not sure. I told him. He just smiled and remarked that in his day they didn't entrust young lawyers with political secrets. So I gathered that perhaps he'd known it for weeks."

A Cabinet position; and now he's dead—so my thoughts ran, in an excellent non-sequitur.

"Was that really Caleb?" I asked.

"I guess so. Wonder if that damn Priscilla dragged him down here. And who's his friend? Know him?"

"I've met him. All I know is that he's an Englishman, and that he's been over here two months doing something or other. Even Priscilla doesn't seem to know just what. So you can't expect me to."

Sebastian came in just when John was saying something impolite about Priscilla, or maybe it was Caleb or both.

"Mistuh Jacob wants you-all to come to his steddy, Mistuh John," he said. His voice shook just a little. Negroes always take death of any sort pleasantly hard, but this must have really been a great shock to the old man. He was born at Monckton Hall, and its friends have always been his friends.

"Who's there, Sebastian?" John asked.

"It's Mistuh Caleb and the gennelman what was with him, suh. Ah guess he's a foreign gennelman, least Ah cain't unduhstan' what he says, suh. You better go now, suh; an' Miss Diane, Ah reckon you better go lie down."

Sebastian could never remember that we were grown up. He had always warned us and stood between us and the consequences of too laggard obedience to our betters.

"All right—going!" John said, with a smile. "And Sebastian, mix a highball all around and take it up to people's rooms before dinner."

"Yes, suh. Ah—you don' mean to the Senator, does you?"

"No. Skip him."

"I guess you don' mean to the Madam neither, then."

"No, no, no." John went out with some signs of impatience, and Sebastian shook his head. "Mistuh John, he's powerful careless about the amendities, Miss Diane; he shore is. Now you run along, an' Ah'll straighten up in here 'fore they all comes down."

I nodded and got a book and started out into the hall when the old darky stopped me.

"How's the little missie standin' it?" he asked, tears in his eyes.

There were tears in mine, too. They're so kind, those old colored people; you never realize it until you come up against a fundamental of some sort.

"She's asleep now," I said. "I'll have a look at her when I go up."

"Yas'm. Ah moved Miss Jocelyn's things in Miss

Priscilla's room so's she'd be next to you. An' Ah moved Miss Priscilla's things in the blue room with Miss Tolly. Was that all right?"

"That was all right, Sebastian."

I went upstairs wondering if that was his idea or Mr. Radstock's.

Jocelyn was asleep. She lay like a tired child in the delicately carved fourposter with its old chintz curtains. A low moan now and then showed that sleep was only a lull, and an imperfect one, in this tragic interlude.

I tipped over to lock the door into the hall, but it had already been done. I was glad that somebody else was thinking of Jocelyn.

In my own room I tried to figure it out. John thought that Justice Frazier was the victim of a conspiracy. I wondered if Major Heath would think so. We aren't a murderous people, and whatever we may think of some of the men who make up political Washington we don't ordinarily go out and shoot them in cold blood. After all Blanchard Frazier was the finest type of American statesman. It was inconceivable that Major Heath could think he would be involved in anything remotely connected with racketeering. But there was the cold fact of his murder, and the fact that he feared something or somebody quite definitely. Major Heath's presence downstairs—quite apart from how he'd got there—was a grim confirmation of John's theory.

I thought then that his association with Caleb

didn't seem so much a happenstance as it had done before, for I knew that Major Heath was a private inquiry agent, over on some job for his Home Secretary, and that his mission was finished and he was getting ready to go back. How Justice Frazier had ever got in touch with him, and for what purpose, I didn't know.

I was thinking all this over, and I had the feeling that I was about to have a noteworthy idea, when there was a quiet tap-tap at my door and Thalia came in, arrayed in an elaborate lounging robe of silver and blue velvet.

"I've had the devil's own time keeping Priscilla from roaming the jungle for meat for to-morrow's column," she said calmly, collapsing on the chaise-longue. "Got a cigarette? I'm out."

"Where's Priscilla now?" I asked, handing her a package and a paper of matches.

"Taking a bath. At least she drew a tub. I think she was waiting, all dressed, to leave when she heard me go out. So I locked the door."

She pulled a large old-fashioned key out of her pocket and put it on the table.

"Thalia!" I cried. "What on earth's the matter with you? You can't go around locking people in."

"Can't I?" she inquired blandly, blowing a ring of smoke into the lamp by her side and watching it curl up through the top of the shade. "Why not?"

"Because," I said. "It isn't done, in the first place. In the second, you'd better be careful of the way you treat Priscilla Stone. She's fond of you so far, I think, but if you keep up this insolence of yours, you're going to be sorry the next time you give a party."

"Sorry about that drivel she writes?" she said, with a curl of the lip. "Anyway, I'm not going to give any more parties. So I don't care anyway."

"Very well," I said. "But you'd better run back and unlock that door and get dressed."

Thalia's small, exquisite head came up abruptly with determination.

"That woman does not get out of the bath," she said coolly, "until I go downstairs with her."

Then she leaned forward and her manner changed quickly.

"Don't you see, Diane, that if she gets loose she'll talk to all the servants, and to Jocelyn, and all that, and what a swell story it'll make?"

All of her debonair insouciance was gone. Her voice was passionately intense, and her dark eyes were flashing through the tears she couldn't control.

"You people make me sick!" she cried then. "There's Justice Frazier dead, Jocelyn with no one in the world who really gives a damn about her, and downstairs they putter about with a country sheriff and a Negro gardener—and that woman watching everybody like a cat, ready to spread them all over the front page of a million papers so she'll get fifteen dollars a week more, and nobody tries to stop her! I'll stop her if I have to drown her in the tub instead of locking her in! Do you hear me, Diane? I won't have it!"

This, I gathered, was the Xanthopoulos coming out. I'm sure no Adler of Philadelphia was ever so much concerned about anything.

I tried to be soothing.

"I'll talk to Priscilla," I said. "I don't think you're being fair. After all, she's Jocelyn's friend, and her mother and Jocelyn's father were friends, and I think she'll see the difference between this and a regular story."

"Hell!" Thalia said rudely. "If all you people would get over the notion that just because our fathers and mothers knew one another we're all swell people ourselves, you'd be able to see farther than the nose on your face. The only person I have any confidence in is Norman Vaughan. And that's for the one and only reason that my mother didn't know his father—if he had one, and he looks to me as if he didn't."

"Thalia!" I said firmly. "Give me that key, and go and lie down for a while!"

She looked at me for a moment. Then she said penitently, "Oh, I'm sorry, Diane! Maybe I'm stupid, but this seems to me all a sort of ghastly plot of some kind, and I *hate* Priscilla Stone. I have ever since I was at school in England and some kind friend sent me those rotten things she wrote about Mother and her Russian prince."

"She didn't know you then, Thalia," I said gently, if not very convincingly to myself, at least.

"After all, it *is* her job. And she doesn't say nearly as dreadful things as she might, sometimes."

Thalia flushed slightly.

"I know Mother does ghastly things," she said. "It isn't that—it's not what she says nearly as much as what she doesn't say."

"But that's only because you know the inside of what she's writing about. Think how few of us there are who do know, compared with the thousands who read her truck that don't know at all."

"That's true," Thalia conceded doubtfully. "But of course, Diane, *we* are the ones that count."

I supposed that was a legitimate attitude for the daughter of a Greek prince and a Philadelphia Adler to adopt, so I didn't make the reply I thought of—or maybe I didn't think of it till later. As it happened she was right. It was I who misunderstood and who made the implication she didn't mean. If I'd let her explain then and there what she meant, I might have saved more than I knew was at stake. But as it was I said nothing, and after a little she went on impulsively, "May I go in and see Jocelyn—just look at her? I'll be quiet."

"Do," I said; "and do be quiet. She needs all the rest she can get."

She rose and flattened her half-burned cigarette in the tray and went noiselessly into the room where Jocelyn was sleeping.

She had barely disappeared when there was another tap at the door, and John stuck his head in.

"Receiving?" he asked. "Or dressing?"

"Neither, so come in. What now?"

"It seems, my dear Diane——" he began. "But first, has Sebastian brought those drinks around yet?"

"Not yet," I said. "Go on."

"This man Heath, then, is a friend of Justice Frazier's, and he wants to know who shot him."

I waited for him to go on.

"It seems that Justice Frazier was worried about something. What it was, either the Englishman won't say and doesn't know, or won't say and does know. At any rate Justice Frazier called on him a couple of days ago to talk about it. They have a couple of common friends, and I believe had already met socially. Well, there you have it. This man Heath wants to investigate—it seems further, I should have said, that that's his profession, or his hobby, or something—and I've got the uncomfortable feeling, Diane, from looking at the fellow, that he's going to do it."

Thalia emerged from Jocelyn's bedroom just as I said, "All right; let him do it, then. Why shouldn't he?"

"Because," she said in her cool voice, "it's going to be damned uncomfortable for some of the Radstock guests."

She and John stared silently at each other for a moment, with obvious antagonism. Then she smiled a fleeting ironic little smile.

"If nobody minds I'll go dress for dinner," she announced sweetly, and glided, a lithe, shimmering, velvety figure, out of the room.

We watched where she'd been a moment. Then John turned to me.

"What was she doing in there?"

"She went in to have a look at Jocelyn. She'd have been right out if you hadn't come."

"Did you let her in?"

I nodded.

"You're a fine watchdog, aren't you? Father had you moved here, and locked the hall door, so nobody could get in. You hold open court."

"Why not, John? You can't think Thalia's mixed up in this!"

"I don't think anything about Thalia," he answered rudely. "But I'll tell you this, Thalia's got a brother; and since I've been talking to Heath I'm willing to suspect anybody from Father down. For God's sake be careful of her, Diane! You're the only one who can!"

I sat staring almost stupidly at him. I was recalling my last fifteen minutes with Thalia.

John shook himself vigorously with what was half a shudder, and forced a smile.

"Well, I'll go dress. No, I won't; here's Sebastian. May I have a drink here with you before I go?"

I nodded, and he opened the door and took two of the tall frosted glasses with the fresh mint growing out of them and brought them back. We sat there silently until we'd finished them.

"Well," he said then, "now I *will* go. By the way—would you mind locking your door when you come down?"

"Not at all." I replied.

CHAPTER SEVEN

EVERYONE was in the back drawing room when I
went down after carefully locking my door. Maybe Thalia was right in suspecting everybody of
something or other, and maybe too John was right
even about Thalia.

Mr. Radstock held out his hand and drew me
to the little group by the fireplace.

"You told me you'd met Major Heath, Diane,"
he said gravely.

"Yes, I have; how do you do?"

We shook hands. I thought I felt something in
the friendly grip of his great fist that recognized
a special bond between us. At least I thought so
until my eyes met his perfectly cold gray ones, and
then I was a little miffed. I suppose I expected him
to assume at once that we were allies, without stopping to think that he had no reason at all to think
we were. It's always a little shock to find that
other people don't take you at your own estimate.

"Hullo, Caleb!" I said, recovering at once and
deciding that I could be as cold and formal as
Major Heath, if that was what he wanted.

So colossal was my conceit, however, that even
then I accepted this aloofness of his as a sort of
cue.

"I thought you were doing Better Babies, or something, to-day," I said, and was aware at once that I'd said just the wrong thing.

Major Heath evidently expected something of the sort, or he was very quick indeed. He remarked naturally, "I'm always surprised, you know, at the interest your country has in child welfare. I was very much interested in going through the Johns Hopkins Hospital not long ago with a doctor friend. I remember we met a charming young woman there carrying a tiny black creature through the corridor, all wrapped up in a blanket. She said it had been in the hospital since birth —paralyzed, or something."

"I believe your hospital system is supposed to be much better than ours, sir," remarked Mr. Radstock gracefully.

"That's awfully good of you. I think they're very different. You manage more concentrated effort, which we lose by our nursing-home system."

I don't know how long this absurd conversation, which didn't interest anybody in the least, would have gone on if Sebastian had not appeared just then to announce dinner.

That began the second demented meal we had had that day. The undertones this time were slightly different. We had gone through one cycle, it seemed, and were now on another. Or else something catastrophic had started us all over again.

Major Heath sat next to me at my left, Senator Mellish was still at my right. The rest of them were pretty much as before, except that John had managed to get Caleb Williams next to Mrs. Mellish. Priscilla was next to Caleb, looking very well in a black lace dinner frock of the Victorian era with bows, ruffles, and ribbons scattered about it. It's certainly her period, just as the slim sleek eggshell satin that Thalia wore was hers. I haven't the remotest notion what Mrs. Mellish had on, except that it was a floral affair, totally nondescript, that probably cost a frightful amount. It spoke something for Major Heath and Caleb that although they weren't dressed nobody was the least conscious of it, and I thought I caught a mildly grateful smile from Mr. Radstock that they—particularly Major Heath—were there, and kept the conversation going at a lively, intelligent rate.

Priscilla, curiously, was a flop. I've never seen her not the life of the party before; but she wasn't saying one word. She had her fixed bright smile that Thalia said fairly screamed: "I'm listening, you wonderful man!" and John was trying to say something worthy of it. But I saw her eyes, and I don't think she heard one word of what he was saying. She was intent, with deadly earnestness, on something else.

Mrs. Mellish and Caleb were recalling Mrs. Mellish's first Washington days, when Caleb was with the Associated Press and had been assigned shopping duty—for spite, he thought.

"I don't suppose you remember the seeress you took me to, do you, Mr. Williams?"

Here Caleb made an error.

"You mean the fortune teller on O Street?" he said. "Yeah, sure. What's her name? Madame Rosa. She's a great old girl."

His amusement, mostly polite anyway, came to an even shorter end than normally. Mrs. Mellish was indignant.

"You're speaking of a very splendid woman, Mr. Williams," she said, almost shortly. "I know a great many people who go to see her constantly. And they find her a great comfort and a great inspiration."

Caleb gave the impression that he was trying to think quickly and not succeeding.

"And I was under the impression," Mrs. Mellish continued, a slightly querulous note creeping into her voice, "that you were broader-minded than that. I'm very disappointed."

It was again Major Heath who came to the rescue. He stopped some tale of robbery in the East India Docks that he was telling and said smoothly, "By the way, Williams, aren't you thinking of the other Rosa who was discredited by the Psychical Research Society? Not the lady Mrs. Mellish means. You were telling me something about her the other day."

Caleb drew a deep breath.

"Oh, yes, yes," he said. "That's right, Mrs. Mellish. My mistake! I'm thinking of a woman—*I* know, she was called Madame Rosalie. She wore a red wig and called herself an Indian Seminole seeress. They unmasked her. It was terrible. She turned out to be a man and came from Newark. I remember now. We newspaper people had a thundering lot of trouble with her. She was always calling up and giving tips about race horses, and —mortgages, and that sort of thing. *You're* thinking about Madame *Rosa.*"

"Yes," said Mrs. Mellish eagerly. I had never realized before that such people really have a strong influence. On any other subject Caleb's absurd story wouldn't have fooled her for a second.

"Oh, well!" said Caleb; "that's different. *She's* a clairvoyant."

"Yes," said Mrs. Mellish, simply. "You remember—well, she . . ."

Major Heath returned without so much as a "Let's see, where was I?" to the point at which the Chinaman disappeared in the mews, and went on with his tale. So both Caleb and I had had our first lesson, and I had the disconcerting notion that for a time, anyway, we would be under an intelligent censorship, which if it couldn't stop our saying things could at least repair the damage as it was done. I also gave up the error that men can't talk, eat, and listen to everything that goes on all at the same time. At that, I think Thalia was the only one at the table—except, of course, Mr. Radstock, who has a very shrewd wit—who got it. Even Priscilla missed it. She perked up with her wide-open gray eyes—she's really awfully good-looking—just a second too late.

Things had resumed their natural flow when the white gloves of Sebastian appeared rhythmically placing dessert plates with finger bowls on them in front of us. Caleb could further cover up his tracks by asking Mrs. Mellish if the doilies were crocheted or knitted, as he moved his Sandwich glass bowl to one side. That entirely restored her serenity. If the young man didn't know knitting from crocheting, he couldn't in any case be expected to know a seeress from a charlatan.

As we went into the drawing room, leaving the men to their port—a cherished custom at Monckton Hall even in these days—Thalia whispered to me that we ought to hire Major Heath to look after Caleb all the time.

We found that Mrs. Mellish was properly launched on the subject of Madame Rosa. "Do you know her, Miss Stone?" she asked.

"Just slightly," Priscilla answered sweetly. "I have a number of friends who are—clients of hers."

"And do they like her?"

"Oh, very much," Priscilla purred. Thalia with elaborate yawns roamed around, opening boxes and books, looking, she said, for a cigarette.

"Everyone consults her," Mrs. Mellish went on with evidently genuine admiration. "They say she predicts every important event exactly as it happens."

She looked around for confirmation of that universal opinion, and would have gone on, I think, because she obviously had something on her mind, if it hadn't been for Thalia. Priscilla was sympathetic, and I was interested, having known of Madame Rosa from half my friends who were clients of hers and swore by her. But Thalia, who had very good reason for knowing her better than any of us, was obviously disinterested, if not openly hostile.

"Have you consulted her, Mrs. Mellish?"

That was in Priscilla's most honeyed vacuous tone.

Mrs. Mellish hesitated plainly, looked at the door and at the now very disconcerting figure of Thalia draped, or rather sprawling, in the most unladylike fashion in the high-back chair near the door, humming discordantly and keeping time with a waving cigarette.

Then Mrs. Mellish nervously interrupted herself in whatever answer she was about to make. "Would you please hand Miss Xanthopoulos that ashtray, Mrs. Volney?"

"Too late," Thalia drawled calmly. "Too late. Anyway, ashes are good for the rugs. I ought to know. I guess my father peddled them around the Dôme and the Rotonde."

Mrs. Mellish looked at her in horror. Not that she knew where or what the Dôme and the Rotonde were.

"That's absurd, Thalia," I remarked, putting

an ash tray on her lap. "Those people are Armenians."

"All the same in this country. Most people think we must keep a restaurant somewhere and shine shoes between meals. I'm tired of that, so I'm boosting the rug business."

She went on humming her song and now purposely throwing ashes about.

Priscilla coughed. "About Madame Rosa——" she began gently, with a mildly savage glance at Thalia.

"Wish the Radstocks had a radio," that young lady remarked.

"There is one, in the other room, dear," Priscilla said. "Why don't you go play it?"

"Because I'm dying to hear about Madame Rosa. Go on, Mrs. Mellish. Do!"

Mrs. Mellish glanced again at the door. "I don't really know anything especial about her," she said with hesitation.

"Did you consult her, my dear?" Priscilla smiled.

"Only once or twice, and then in the gravest crises."

"Of course. Those are times one needs help."

"Oh, yes! I think it would be wrong to inquire into the future, unless it was really of vital importance. That's what Madame Rosa said once, when I went there just to test her with some trivial matter. She looked at me. I felt so small. And she said, 'Madame, you know in your heart where your ring is. You really want to know about your husband's career.' She was right. I really did."

"Did what?" asked Thalia, throwing her cigarette at the hearth, missing it, and scrambling under the sofa after it. "Know where the ring was or want to know about his career?"

"Well, both."

I expected to hear a muffled, "Then why don't you say so?" come from under the sofa; but just then the men began coming in and she was occupied with getting back on her feet. Our apparently trivial little scene was over. I hadn't realized at first that it was a perfectly conscious battle between Thalia and Priscilla; nor did I know then how deeply this Madame Rosa was involved in the drama we were playing. Only when I heard of her again, some days later, did I realize what a hold a person of her sort could get over an impressionable woman.

Mr. Radstock came to the fireplace and stood before it, leaning slightly on his stick. He raised his hand for attention, and everybody, expecting, I imagine, some word or explanation on the recent tragedy, was silent.

"Close the door, please, Vaughan," he said. We waited with the gravest expectancy until he continued, which was only when Norman Vaughan had closed the door and resumed his seat.

"Nothing need be said of the appalling event that took place here this afternoon. Blanchard

Frazier meant a good deal more to Monckton Hall than any of you can ever know."

He was still for a moment, then went on in a firmer voice:

"Major Heath here has reason to believe that Justice Frazier expected something of the kind to happen, and was prepared for it—in the true sense of the word. I know myself that he has been troubled of late, and I think he wanted to-day to talk to me about his private affairs. You all know enough of the law to know that the very fact of your being here this afternoon necessitates an explanation of your movements to the police. The district attorney is coming in this evening, and may want to talk to you here. None of you is bound to talk without the presence of a legal adviser; but I hope all of you feel free—and as my guests and friends I believe you all *are* free— to talk perfectly frankly to Mr. Whipple when he comes. And also, may I add, to Major Heath, who has undertaken to investigate this matter for me. I needn't tell you how very painful all this is to me personally. I have known Blanchard Frazier nearly fifty years, and such ties are very strong. Now I know you will all excuse me, and I'll say good-night to you now. John, when Whipple comes I'm in my study. I'll see you later, Major Heath."

He made us a courtly old-time bow and went out through the library door; and we heard him go down the stairs into his own wing. Those of us who remained were of another generation—even Senator Mellish, who was almost as old as Mr. Radstock. We were separated by æons of custom, manners, and feeling.

"I don't presume to question your authority, Major Heath," Senator Mellish said, after another short interval of silence; "but do I understand that you have, so to speak, no legal right in this matter? I should like you to correct me if I am wrong."

"You're quite right, Senator Mellish," replied Major Heath equably. "I have no legal status whatsoever. Any success I might possibly have in clearing up this matter depends entirely on your good will. My interest is purely personal. Justice Frazier consulted me, and I gave him my word that in such an event as that of this afternoon, I would be on hand. And I'm here—with your permission."

He glanced coolly from one of us to the other, and smiled. It wasn't an ingratiating smile. He might be asking our permission, but he knew perfectly who had the upper hand.

"For example," he went on, after Senator Mellish had granted his and everyone's permission in a gesture, "I wonder if you'd mind telling me just where you were, and what you were doing, at 4:25 this afternoon. I understand from Mr. Radstock that that is approximately the time of Justice Frazier's death. It will clear away a lot of lumber

if you're all definitely placed. And if you don't
mind, may I ask you to be so good as to give me
that information one at a time, let's say in the
library?"

The irony of it struck me, and I almost laughed
aloud. Clear away a lot of lumber indeed; hang
yourself, more than likely! But obviously there
was nothing to do, and I decided that I didn't like
this large Englishman so much after all. He was
too businesslike for me. I was thinking all this
when my eye met that of Caleb Williams, who was
leaning against the door, watching me very
steadily. It was a little disconcerting. It almost
looked as if he were preventing people from leaving.

He had to move just then, however; Sebastian
appeared, ushering in the district attorney. Fortunately John had met Mr. Whipple, and Caleb
and Priscilla of course knew him, as they know
everybody. Their greeting covered up Thalia's
ironic aside to Senator Mellish: "He's been eating
the wrong cakes."

I don't know if the Senator was familiar with
Alice in Wonderland. But Thalia was right; Mr.
Whipple might have stepped out of its pages. His
nose, hands, and brownish hair were long and
thin, his drawling voice was thin, and his clothes
were thin. He seemed the thinnest thing I'd ever
seen, and he had that corn-pone pallor of the pre-
vitamin ages. Caleb's later remark, that his head
was thick enough to make up for the rest of him,

proved not correct, however. Considerable shrewdness, alloyed, or adulterated, with an exaggerated
respect for people who were successful in the world
outside Fairfax County, characterized him. From
the very first he was apparently aware that if he
sat tight and said as little as possible, he would
get himself much further than he could hope by
his own unaided efforts. Perhaps Caleb was right
in saying that this method of his was just natural-
born laziness, and furthermore that as he had just
been elected there wasn't any great necessity for
bestirring himself. But I'm inclined to think Caleb
was a little dazzled by his own Dupin or Sherlock
Holmes.

Norman Vaughan suggested, after a little, that
we have some bridge, until Major Heath appeared
ready for us. The Mellishes of course don't play,
so the Senator got himself a book, and Mrs. Mellish settled down with her knitting by me and
crowed with delight when I had a lot of face
cards, and clucked sympathetically when I had
none; so that my opponents' finesses not un-
naturally worked perfectly and Norman and
Thalia won six dollars from Pericles and me in
two hours.

Mr. Whipple, Sheriff Carter, and Major Heath,
attended by John Radstock and Caleb, meanwhile
looked around, and had a long conference with
Mr. Radstock in his study in the wing. I think
Senator Mellish would have given his right arm
to be in on it, but he had dignity to keep up. So

he sat by the fire absorbed in somebody's life of Napoleon.

Thalia had a series of beautiful hands, bid a series of games, little slams, and grand slams and made them. It wasn't until she let Norman have a bid of four hearts and laid down two honors and eight spades from the Ace-King that I knew anything was worrying her. I was about to make some comment on her bidding when I glanced at her face. My comment died before it was uttered. Her face was a pale olive mask of frozen marble, but her eyes were like flaming points of steel.

She pushed back her chair.

"Want something?" asked her brother without looking.

"No thanks," she replied curtly, but with so controlled a voice that if I hadn't seen her face I shouldn't have noticed she was under any unusual strain. "I'm going up to get a handkerchief."

She rose and went quickly through the hall door. I looked around and half rose myself. Priscilla was not in the room.

CHAPTER EIGHT

IT WAS a little after ten the next morning when Jocelyn and I went downstairs. The papers had got the news of her father's murder, and already the pitiless progress of publicity had started in earnest. I must say for them that they—at least the less yapping journals—were more considerate than we had expected. Priscilla's usual space was devoted to winter fashions, as observed "by a diplomat's wife." But we all had the feeling that they were just holding off, and that the storm would break, and that all the political influence in the world couldn't stop it.

They had moved Justice Frazier's body to Washington, and the autopsy was performed there. The coroner's inquest of course had to be at the Fairfax County Court House, but as it was more or less perfunctory, and considering the importance of the victim, it was all done very quietly.

Major Heath and Mr. Whipple were waiting for us—for Jocelyn particularly, of course—in the library. I thought that both looked as if they had been at work a long time already. I thought too that Jocelyn was going to break down when she shook hands with Major Heath, but she didn't. She managed a pale, brave little smile in answer to his, which was grave and encouraging and understanding at the same time. She was very lucky to have him there. He was a good deal like her father, the same great physique, and giving the same sense of having much in reserve. I think he was more "human" than her father in some way. At any rate he was a great contrast to the lean anæmia of the district attorney. The district attorney must have vaguely felt something of the sort too, for he looked relieved when Major Heath began, without any formalities:

"Mr. Whipple wants you to tell him, Miss Frazier, anything you can that may help us. You came down here yesterday, didn't you?"

We had sat down and Mr. Whipple had closed both doors.

Jocelyn did not answer for a minute, and then, in a calm voice and with a self-control that was the product of centuries of breeding, began her pathetic little tale—which I suppose Major Heath has heard a thousand of in his career.

"Yes," she said. "We had intended coming down before lunch. I was all ready, and Horace—that's our colored butler—was helping Dad on with his coat, when Dad asked him what time he posted the letters. Horace said he hadn't posted any, because there were none. Dad looked at him very gravely and said, 'You'd better take another look, Horace. They're on my desk in the usual place. Bring them here and we'll drop them at the post office.' Horace came right back and said he didn't see any. Dad at once went back to look, and I went along."

She hesitated a moment, and Major Heath more to give her time than to get information, I suppose, said, "Did your father usually leave all of his letters for Horace to post?"

"Always. Letters that he wrote at night he left on the table in the library, and Horace gave them to the postman when he came at nine o'clock. Dad was quite upset. He began turning over papers and looking in drawers.

" 'Are you sure you didn't move them, Horace?' he asked.

"Horace said he hadn't, that there weren't any there. I said then they must be around somewhere. Dad was so disturbed that I asked him if they were very important.

" 'Very,' he said. I knew something serious had happened. After he had looked everywhere he sat down. I was alarmed at him. He'd sort of forgot that Horace and I were there. I motioned Horace out of the room and went over by the door, and waited there until he called me, in a minute or two. He said that if the letters were not found it would be a very grave matter. He told me to call Horace and have him bring in all the house servants. We have two parlor maids, the upstairs maid, cook and kitchen maid. They all came in, but none of them had seen any letters, or anyone in the house or around it, or any unusual signs. Then, after they'd gone out, Dad asked me if I'd mind waiting until after lunch to come down here, and for me to call up Mr. Radstock and tell him that we'd be down later. He said to tell him that he had lost some letters and that he wanted to consult you."

Major Heath nodded without any sign of surprise.

Jocelyn smiled a little, hesitatingly, and went on.

"That's the first time I knew about you. Dad said he thought you would advise him, and that you'd just done something very marvelous for your government."

Major Heath acknowledged this tribute with a grave half-smile. "But he didn't find me," he said quietly. "I suppose you know that?"

She looked at him in alarm. "He didn't? Oh, I thought he must have, because he went out, and when he came back he seemed less disturbed. And he didn't mention the matter again."

Heath shook his head.

"No," he said. "I was out. I didn't get back and get his message until after I'd heard from Williams about—what had happened here. I went back to the hotel when I heard it, and I found this note that he'd left for me. It doesn't say much."

"Then you—you don't know what he was worried about?"

"No, Miss Frazier," he answered gently. Then he looked straight into her eyes and said, "But I'm going to find out. You can count on that."

She closed her eyes, to shield the involuntary pain in their blue depths. "Oh, but I wish he'd talked to you," she cried.

"I do too." Then he added, with a quick smile, "But as he didn't, we'll have to go ahead from the beginning, by ourselves."

"Do you mean, Miss Frazier," put in Mr. Whipple in his thin drawl, "that your father didn't mention the letters again? And you drove down to Monckton Hall together, alone?"

"Yes," she answered shortly, looking at him as if she had not known until that moment that he was in the room.

"When did you get here?"

"A little before four," she replied, frowning a little in the effort to recall each thing that happened. "Sebastian took our things up, and Dad and I went into the drawing room to see everybody. They were all there except John—and you too, Diane—sitting around, and Senator Mellish was giving them some sort of a lecture on the value of the study of the classics. I remember that," she went on with a faint smile, "because when we came in he had to stop and everybody looked so pleased. Mr. Radstock and Dad went out together almost at once, and then everybody melted away. Thalia dragged me out to see the new colt, and Pericles got away and I saw him going down the walk by himself; and I heard Priscilla ask Mrs. Mellish if she wouldn't like to see the knot garden. Thalia and I came back in about fifteen minutes and stopped by the kitchen to say hello to Maria."

"You stayed there a while?"

"Yes. We came in the kitchen door and Thalia took a couple of cookies off a plate on the table and handed me one. Then she went on into the house, and I stayed there talking a while."

"Did she say where she was going, or what she was going to do?"

"No, she didn't. I suppose she went upstairs."

"How long did you stay there?"

"I don't know. Perhaps five minutes. I ate several cookies. It was probably about five minutes."

Major Heath thought a moment. Then he said, "Did anyone else come into the kitchen while you were there?"

"No."

"Very well. What did you do then?"

"I went upstairs to change my shoes. I'd got them muddy down at the stables. Then I came downstairs."

"That would be at about half-past four," Heath said.

She nodded. "I should think so."

"All right, Miss Frazier; you came downstairs at half-past four, or nearly that; who was in the house then?"

"Well," she replied, thinking about it, "almost everybody was there again—except Diane. You came down just after me, didn't you? Mr. Radstock went out to the wing where his study is, just before you came in, Diane. Oh, yes, Senator Mellish wasn't there. He was in this room. I heard him say something to Mr. Radstock as he came through. You know how easily you can hear his voice."

"So that is the situation as you remember it," Major Heath said thoughtfully. "Everyone was in the room, when you and Justice Frazier came at four o'clock, except young Radstock and Mrs. Volney. And everyone left a few minutes later."

She nodded.

"And everyone was here again when you came back, half an hour later—that is, they were there then or came almost at once, as in the case of Mrs. Volney."

"That's right," she said colorlessly, as if that memory brought back all the rest.

"Now then," he continued, and his kindly tone seemed to help her; "you don't know where any of them were during that half-hour between four and four-thirty?"

"I know where Thalia was. She was with me at the stables, and then in the kitchen."

"For fifteen minutes only," Heath rejoined.

"That's true."

"When did you see your father last?"

"Just as Thalia and I went out the garden door. He and Mr. Radstock were just going in the little room across the hall. We waved to him and asked him if he wouldn't rather come see the new colt. He smiled and waved back to us."

Mr. Whipple said abruptly, "Do you know what it was that had been worrying him—as I understand something had—in the last few weeks?"

She turned a little paler, but answered his question steadily. "I know that he *has* been worried, but I don't know what about. My father never discussed his private affairs with me."

Again Major Heath interposed. I suppose it was the difference in his manner that made her respond instantly to him, while resenting Mr. Whipple.

"Have you any notion at all of what it was? Or let me ask this first: what made you realize he was worried?"

"Oh, I knew it in a thousand ways. He wasn't himself at all. I sometimes thought he was even worried about me. He'd never made the slightest attempt to tell me what to do or whom to see and whom not, and then lately he's asked me several times not to go to places with certain people, or to go to other places with people I don't care so much about. He even insisted that I give up a trip that Thalia and I were making to Greece with her aunt. We'd been planning it for ever so long, and all of a sudden he changed his mind and asked me if I'd mind not going."

I was surprised at that, because Justice Frazier and I had talked about it last summer, and he had thought then that it would be an interesting experience for her.

Heath thought about that for a minute. "You

don't know anything definite that occurred to make him change his mind?"

She shook her head. "Nothing," she said promptly. "I've thought about that, too."

Then she went on without waiting for another question: "There's another thing that's bothered me. I've thought once or twice that curious people have been coming to the house lately. No one in particular—just people that aren't our ordinary visitors. For instance, several nights when I've been out rather late I've gone to the library to say good-night to Dad, and I could see that somebody had been there, and I also had the definite feeling that Dad didn't want to have anything said about it. One night there were cigar ashes in a line across the rug in front of the fireplace, as if someone had walked back and forth and just flicked ashes about. Dad's always rather particular about things like that. I said something about it and he smiled and said, 'Politics makes strange bed-fellows, my dear.' That was all he'd say. Then I said something about it to Horace, just incidentally, once, and he said that several times a man had come about 9:30 and left after an hour or so, but that Dad always answered the door and let him out too, so that Horace never saw him. But that's all I know. It didn't seem to me suspicious, actually; but I suppose it is now."

Major Heath thought for a moment again, and then rose to his feet. "Thank you, Miss Frazier," he said. "I think it would be a good idea if you'd find one of your friends and get outside for a bit. I suggest young Williams as the safest—especially if any newspaper people have got in the grounds. And I'd be surprised if they hadn't. And if you wouldn't mind waiting, Mrs. Volney," he added, turning to me, "I'd like to have a talk with you next."

As I lighted the cigarette I'd been holding during the last part of Jocelyn's narrative I recalled sharply the man that Jerry Blaine and I had seen coming out of the house on Dupont Circle. If only I'd been a little closer! I thought regretfully.

"Now, Mrs. Volney. I want you to think pretty far back, if you please," Major Heath began, coming back into the room after leaving Jocelyn in some friendly hands outside. "You know all these people pretty well. What about Justice Frazier, now? Did he impress you as being very much disturbed about something?"

I told him that the night before last was the first intimation of it that I'd had, and I told him about my conversation with Justice Frazier then. I added that I hadn't seen a great deal of him just lately. I'd been quite busy. Even so, I knew him well enough to be surprised greatly at him when he spoke the way he did.

"And he gave you no idea of what it was he feared?"

"I shouldn't have called it *fear*. He was utterly without personal fear. He was disturbed; and he had a very definite feeling, I thought—or it may have been a very definite knowledge—that something was likely to happen to him.

"He was mostly concerned with Jocelyn," I went on, "as far as his talk with me went. He mentioned particularly the crowd she was with last evening. I gathered he didn't think much of them, or of the place to which they were going."

"Did he mention anyone particularly, Mrs. Volney?" Mr. Whipple asked.

"Yes. Mr. Xanthopoulos."

"He had the Greek in mind particularly, did he?"

Having just said so, I saw no reason to say so again. I suppose there was no reason why Mr. Whipple should not have said "the Greek," but it annoyed me intensely. Not that I've ever known Pericles very well. And I was still more annoyed when I caught the slight twinkle in Major Heath's eyes.

"I think he had a typical Southern attitude towards anyone not an American—to some extent, anyway," I said.

I saw Mr. Whipple's sandy eyebrows go up. Whether he thought it was a right attitude, or not a Southern attitude, I don't know. It seemed to me that he had made up his mind about Pericles.

"Well, at any rate, Mrs. Volney," Major Heath continued, with a whimsical shrug, "I take it we're sure of one thing. The letters you saw on Justice Frazier's desk are the ones that were stolen, or that disappeared somehow. And the one you mentioned to me night before last was one of them."

I looked at him with surprise. I'd forgot my *faux pas* and his calm recovery in the presence of our friends.

"Of course it was!" I said. "Of course! It was on top of a neat little pile. I saw the name, and later, when we were leaving I connected it with you. And you stopped me from saying anything about it."

He grinned at that. "Yes. You see the possibilities. Most of the people here were there. Any of them might have heard more than they were supposed to, perhaps."

He looked at me quizzically, but underneath there was a sort of almost sad seriousness. Then he answered my unspoken question.

"Of course, Mrs. Volney. This crime was not done by some casual passer-by. It was planned, and coolly planned; it was executed with a steady nerve and an iron will; and there's no slightest doubt that it was connected with all that business that Justice Frazier was disturbed about. If he had told me— or if I'd been in my hotel that morning, after he found out the letters were gone, and came to see me—or if the letters hadn't been stolen . . ."

He fell into a sort of brown study for a moment. Then he roused himself and smiled at me again.

"So that's why I didn't want you talking about that letter in front of all your friends, Mrs. Volney.

Because I knew something was wrong with Justice Frazier; and I knew also that it was a complicated affair. And what it was I want you to help me find out."

I'm afraid I went a little cold all over; my heart raced, my breath came quickly, and a little shiver ran up my spine. I don't think it had actually occurred to me until then that perhaps someone I knew, whom Jocelyn and her father knew, someone right there that night, perhaps here that very minute in Monckton Hall, had deliberately and in cold blood taken the life of Justice Frazier. After all, murder is murder. Just looking at it from the lowest possible point of view, as a matter of mere manners, it's the sort of thing we don't do. And yet we *had* done it—one of us. And I had no doubt at all, looking at the great figure of the man standing there, perfectly aware, as I knew, of everything that was passing through my mind, that if someone of us had done it he would be found out.

"Yes, it's a bad business, Mrs. Volney," he said quietly. "Now tell me this. And don't get excited, or imagine more than I mean. You say you haven't seen much of Justice Frazier lately. Did you ever hear him mention the importation of liquor—I mean here in Washington—on a very large scale?"

I suppose my surprise was evident again. "No," I said. "I don't think so."

And then an idea suddenly struck me, and I did exactly what he had just finished warning me not to do. "You don't mean that Justice Frazier was . . . ?"

He smiled a little. "No, I don't think that. What about this, now: did you ever hear him say anything about corruption in the government? I mean again, recently, and on a large scale?"

"No," I said again. "I have not."

"Very well, Mrs. Volney. Now you *can* do this. Tell me just what has happened since you've been here. No, I don't mean what people did and so on. Tell me the little social happenings—who looked askance at whom, who made ironic remarks about whom else. That sort of thing. The things you'd notice at once and that Mr. Whipple and I never would.

"For example, or to explain, rather. Let us assume, for the sake of clearness, that a murder has been committed by someone now in this house. Well, I'm a pretty firm believer in what Madame Rosa would call 'plasmic atmosphere,' or something of the kind. All the factors that culminate a little later in an act of violence are already there—in solution, so to speak. If you're among a low people you get one sort of behavior, and among cultivated people another."

He looked at me with some amusement in his eyes, and laughed frankly.

"Does it sound a bit thick?"

He reached in his pockets, brought out an old pipe and an oilskin pouch, and proceeded with great deliberation to fill his pipe.

"But nevertheless it's quite true, you know. What I mean is only this. I could have been here last night, or yesterday noon, and noticed nothing extraordinary, simply because here we're concerned with people of rigorous social training. They'd adhere strictly to the usual pattern of behavior. But you who know them intimately must have seen various tenses and flexes of manner. That's all I mean."

I nodded.

"Well, then!" he went on. "To start you off, now. Just from having casually met these people at Joe's—or whatever he calls himself—that night, I should say that under quite a strain Miss Stone would be excessively garrulous. Mr. Vaughan would be amazingly nonchalant; Senator Mellish would be rather more oracular—I should guess, for instance, that his oration on the classics was longer and more ornate than usual. That's the sort of thing, do you see? I remember once—oh, well, when I write my Trivia that'll be the time for that."

He smiled his whimsical half-deprecatory smile and waited for me to go on. It was very difficult. I tried, however, to describe my feelings that night at Joe's when everything seemed a little—shall I say?—cockeyed. I did say that and he didn't understand and I had to explain. Then I told him about lunch that day when everything, from Sebastian's white cotton gloves, rhythmically serving perfect food, to Norman Vaughan's tale of so many camel-hours in Turkey, seemed to be packed with dynamite. I recalled Senator Mellish drinking his sauterne and setting it down so abruptly when he saw that Mr. Radstock wasn't taking any. That amused Major Heath. I think he regards Mellish as a purely national phenomenon.

I couldn't, when it actually came down to it, think of anything that had *happened*. It was *feeling* that I'd had, and that I'd noticed, more than anything else. Well, then I told him of Thalia and her brother, and what seemed from across the room a very urgent conference under the picture. Then about Thalia's locking Priscilla in her room, and about her going into Jocelyn's room, and about John's annoyance at that.

He was more interested, apparently, in my conversation with John in Mr. Radstock's study. He passed over John's idea of a political "racket," however, without any comment.

"Did he explain why he should be alarmed about Jocelyn?"

"Not at all. He seemed to be about as definite as I am."

"You're not much help, really," he admitted dryly. "In fact, about all I can get is that you thought everything was all wrong without knowing what. Is that it?"

"Just about," I replied. Then, however, I remembered the later events: the little duel between Priscilla and Thalia in the drawing room just before; Priscilla's apparent interest in the Senator; Mrs. Mellish's obvious interest in Priscilla; and all the other little things that I had either observed or imagined.

When I had finished this he said nothing for a minute. Then he abruptly changed the subject.

"You didn't see Justice Frazier at all, out here?"

"No. John and I were in Mr. Radstock's study, talking about Jocelyn. We heard them come, and suddenly I thought I heard the door there click."

I pointed to the cupboard that concealed the door into the hyphen, and Mr. Whipple almost had a stroke.

"Is that a door?" he cried.

He came to life in the most amazing fashion and simply leaped at it. He drew it open, and then it was my turn—and Major Heath's—to be surprised. Coming from the study we heard the flat Middle Western accents of Mrs. Mellish, speaking at the telephone.

"Try again, operator. Have you got the number? Yes, yes! . . . Oh, very well."

We heard the click of the receiver, and Major Heath, moving with a swiftness I shouldn't have thought possible in him, crossed the room and silently closed the cupboard.

We looked at each other in astonishment. What on earth was that woman doing in Mr. Radstock's study?

Without thinking that after all it was none of my business, I asked my question aloud.

Major Heath meditatively filled his pipe.

"I should say she's pretty much upset. And I should venture the guess that she's trying to get advice from her seeress. Now just as a point of curiosity, I wonder what the redoubtable Senator is doing at this moment?"

CHAPTER NINE

MAJOR HEATH stepped to the drawing-room door and opened it. The room was empty. From where we stood in the doorway, however, we could see through the window the large figure of the Senator, who was standing at the hedge, within a few feet of where Justice Frazier's body had lain. He was acting very queerly indeed, I thought. He kept parting the branches of the closely clipped old hedge and peering into it. The hedge, I should say, is about four feet thick and nine feet high, and the lower branches are in unusually full leaf. I couldn't imagine what he was hunting for, if indeed he was hunting for anything, but he proceeded in what appeared to me to be a very methodical manner along the side of the hedge facing us and around the far end. We couldn't see him after that, but I guessed he was going through the same process on the other side—the side towards the river, under which Justice Frazier was found shot to death.

Major Heath went to the window and continued to watch the secret searcher calmly, until he came out onto the path again at the other end of the hedge and walked leisurely down the terrace steps, without so much as a casual glance about, and we lost sight of him.

"Do you think he's hunting for something?" I said, rather obviously.

Major Heath continued to look out of the window. He seemed to be thinking it over. Then he turned back with a smile.

"Mrs. Volney," he said, "I've just learned one of your expressive American idioms that applies to your question. You tell *me!*"

I suppose it was a foolish question.

"However," he continued cheerfully, "without knowing anything at all about it, I should say he was. What do you think?"

"He looked like it to me," I answered.

"Then we'll leave it at that for a while. By the way, Mrs. Volney, did I understand correctly that when you and young Mr. Radstock were in the study in the wing yesterday afternoon you heard a noise that you thought was the latch, or key, of that passage going down to the hyphen door?"

I nodded.

"You didn't *see* anyone?"

"No. The door from the study to the passage was closed."

"Which door did you think you heard? There seem to be several?"

"Yes." I thought about how many there actually were. "There are five. One from the study where we were in to the passage, and one next to it, leading into the front division of the wing, where Mr.

Radstock's telephone and desk are. The steps to his upstairs apartment—that's his bedroom and bath—lead up from there too. Then there's the outside front door leading to the lawn and front garden. That makes three. Then there's the back door, leading to the back garden, and the door at the other end of the passage, concealed by the cupboard, that leads into the library. I think it was one of the two outside doors we heard, because they have the old locks and big keys. The keys are kept in them. At least I thought it was the sharp click that a lock of that sort makes when the bolt is drawn."

"And then there's still another door, as a matter of fact, isn't there?"

I looked at him uncomprehendingly for a second. Then I remembered the door leading to the basement, and added that. It made a sixth.

"When you heard the noise, did you look at once?"

"Not exactly. I said, 'What's that?' and John said 'What?' and then he got up and opened the door and looked out. The passage was empty."

"You didn't try any of the doors?"

I shook my head.

"I didn't look at them at all. They may all have been either locked or unlocked. Not many people go through the hyphen or use either of those doors —I mean the outside ones. But it's perfectly possible to do so."

"Well," he went on, without much interest apparently, and beginning with great care to fill his pipe again, "what did you do then?"

"We came through the hyphen to the house, and I went upstairs and wrote several letters—which I haven't mailed yet, either—and changed my dress. Then I came down again. Everybody except Mr. Radstock and Senator Mellish was sitting around the drawing room here, chatting. I suggested that John and Thalia mix us a drink."

"Have you any idea exactly what time that was?"

"Yes, I can tell you that pretty nearly. When we went in it was just after four o'clock. Sebastian was taking the luncheon coffee tray out, and I glanced at the clock, thinking he was being rather slow about it. When I came down, the clock on the hall stairs struck the half-hour. I noticed as I passed that it read thirty-two minutes instead of thirty. I opened the glass and moved the hand back. We've had some trouble with it because the floor isn't quite level and we've just got it placed now so that it goes. It's a Newport clock with a Goddard case."

Mr. Whipple plainly had no interest in old clocks.

"Where was Senator Mellish when you came down?" he asked.

"I didn't see him until about five minutes later. When Pericles and I went into the library to look at a print or something, he was sitting there with a book. Jocelyn says she heard Mr. Radstock speak to him when he went out to the wing just before I came down."

Major Heath tamped the loose tobacco carefully down in his pipe and lighted it slowly, a slight frown on his high bronzed forehead.

"I've been talking to the rest of your friends here, this morning," he said after a minute. "If everyone is telling me the truth about that half-hour from four to half-past four yesterday, it was unquestionably the dullest half-hour that you people have ever put in in your lives. Which seems especially odd," he added equably, "in view of the fact that during it Justice Frazier was murdered. The contrast seems pretty marked. Here's the list of people's occupations then."

He brought out a small black notebook and read off the summary of what each person was doing.

MRS. VOLNEY:
Upstairs writing letters, 4:00 to 4:30.

MISS FRAZIER:
4:00 to 4:15, at the stable viewing a new colt.
4:15 to 4:25, in the kitchen talking to Maria the cook.
4:25 to 4:30 or a minute before, upstairs changing her frock and shoes.

MISS XANTHOPOULOS:
4:00 to 4:15, at the stable with Miss Frazier.
4:15 to 4:17, in the kitchen with Miss Frazier and the cook.

4:17 to 4:23, going upstairs and coming down again. These times are approximate.

4:23, downstairs in the library.

Stayed there for a minute or so until she heard her brother in the next room and joined him there.

PERICLES X.:

4:00 to 4:25, approximately, walking alone, with no aim or purpose, towards the river and back again.

4:25 to 4:27 or 4:28, alone until his sister joined him in the drawing room.

NORMAN VAUGHAN:

4:00 to 4:28, in his room alone, getting out his ducking kit, until he went down directly to the drawing room and found Miss Xanthopoulos and her brother there.

SENATOR MELLISH:

4:25 to 4:30, in the library, reading. Had been walking before that along the river bank from 4:00. Saw no one, met no one. He was alone in the library.

MRS. MELLISH:

4:00 to 4:10, examining the Elizabethan knot garden copied from the one at Hampton Court, with Miss Stone.

4:10, came back to the house. Went directly up to her room; there till 4:30.

PRISCILLA STONE:

> 4:00 to 4:10, showing Mrs. Mellish the knot garden. The knot garden is at the end of Mr. Radstock's wing.
>
> 4:10 to 4:27, approximately, wandered aimlessly through the front gardens. Came back through the front door and joined Miss Xanthopoulos, Xanthopoulos, and Vaughan in the drawing room.

JOHN RADSTOCK:

> 4:00, left by Mrs. Volney at the foot of the stairs. Seen by Sebastian going down stairs through the doorway under the main front stairs. This about 4:03.
>
> 4:03 to 4:30, knocking billiard balls about, practising bank shots to play Vaughan in the evening. Challenge to a game had been heard by Miss Stone and others.

JACOB RADSTOCK:

> 4:00 to 4:15, in the retiring room, across the hall, with Justice Frazier. They were seen to go in there by Miss Frazier and Miss Xanthopoulos.
>
> 4:15, called to telephone by Sebastian. Sebastian verifies; there *was* a telephone call put through at that time.
>
> 4:15 to 4:30, in his study alone.

SEBASTIAN:

> 4:00 to 4:15, in the pantry washing up the coffee dishes from luncheon.

4:15, called Mr. Radstock to the telephone.

4:15 to 4:30, in the retiring room just quitted by Mr. Radstock and Justice Frazier, listening to an orchestra in which his son plays the saxophone.

MARIA:

In the kitchen all the time.

JEM, the colored gardener:

Coming up at about 4:35 from shooting rabbits in the fields, cut across the meadow at the foot of the terrace. Came up the steps to have a look at one of the box bushes that is being treated for some blight or other. Found the body of Justice Frazier on the flags. Dropped the gun and ran into the house.

JUSTICE FRAZIER:

4:00 to 4:15, in the retiring room with Mr. Radstock. Left when Mr. Radstock was called to the telephone. Seen to go out the garden door by Sebastian.

Major Heath closed his black book and replaced it in his pocket. "The rest," he added with a shrug, "is silence."

I saw the point, and I wasn't surprised when he looked whimsically at me and said, "Does that sound convincing to you, Mrs. Volney? Knowing these people as you do? Would each and every one of them, given half an hour, rush off and spend it—or most of it—by himself?"

It obviously did not sound convincing. They'd all avoid solitude as they would the plague, except Mr. Radstock, of course. But after all, they were my friends.

"It's possible," I said.

"It's not very probable," Major Heath rejoined with a smile. "They all seem to me—except Mr. Radstock—as gregarious as herring."

"In other words," Mr. Whipple drawled, "those alibis are pretty easy to bust up."

"I wonder!" Heath said. "Do you know, I always find them the most difficult sort. It's so damnably hard to prove that the Anglo-Catholic vicar wasn't just walking on the river brim, looking at the wild flowers, when he's alleged to have strangled the Evangelical bishop. I mean, if he hasn't forgot something, and there's a conspiracy of silence. And that's my chief impression here: determined, collective silence."

Mr. Whipple mumbled something that I took to be menacing, and that sounded very funny coming from such an Alice-in-Wonderland-like creature.

Heath shook his head with a quick smile. "It won't work, Mr. Whipple," he said. "We're dealing with intelligent people. They know what you can do and what you can't. All we can do, I think —or rather, I *know* all *I* can do—is to wait until one of them can't be quiet any longer, or until whoever shot Justice Frazier can't stay inactive any longer. It doesn't take long, usually. You've no idea how much intelligence it takes to leave well enough alone. As a matter of fact—you'll pardon me, Mrs. Volney—I have the greatest hopes of one of the ladies."

I thought at once of Priscilla, of course. She couldn't be quiet long if she were paid for it—which is just what she's not. Major Heath seemed to read my thoughts, for he gave me a queer little smile. As it happened, he didn't mean Priscilla at all.

Then we all turned at the sound of the cheery "Good-morning, everybody! It must be almost time for lunch! I'm starving! I've been walking along the path by the river!" and so on, and so on, as Priscilla came beamingly into the room. Her arms were full of long sprays of cat berries.

"Can you use these, Diane?" she lilted on vivaciously. "Wouldn't they look lovely in that tole urn over there?" and so on, and so on. I took the things and went out to get something less decorative to put them in.

I had some trouble finding a pot for them, and I imagine I was gone about five minutes. When I came back Priscilla was just leaving the room to go upstairs. I don't know what they had been saying, of course, but whatever it was it had had a sobering effect on the columnist from the *Chronicle*. I caught a glimpse of her face in the hall mirror as she went up; it looked tired all of a sudden.

Major Heath's face showed no particular elation

at what—if anything—he had learned from her. "One thing more, Mrs. Volney," he said, as he helped me clear a place for Priscilla's wretched berries. "Have you time to show us about the house, so to speak?"

I was considerably surprised at that. I've certainly taken enough people through the old house in my day, but it seemed a curious time to indulge an interest in Georgian architecture and early American furniture.

"Surely," I said; "where would you like to begin?"

"Right here will do." He took a pencil and an old envelope out of his pocket. "Let's have the general plan."

I drew him a rough sketch of the house and grounds, and explained that Monckton Hall was a typical five-unit house of its period, as built throughout this part of the colonies.

"You've probably seen Whitehall and the Brice and Hammond-Harwood houses in Annapolis. This is the same sort of thing, probably done by the same builder. It has two wings, each with its connecting hyphen leading to the main unit, or the 'house,' as we call it."

"Then you weren't just confusing me when you said you and young Radstock came 'into the house' from the study in the wing," Heath remarked with a smile. "Go on, please."

I outlined the arrangement of the house. The main unit is divided into four rooms downstairs,

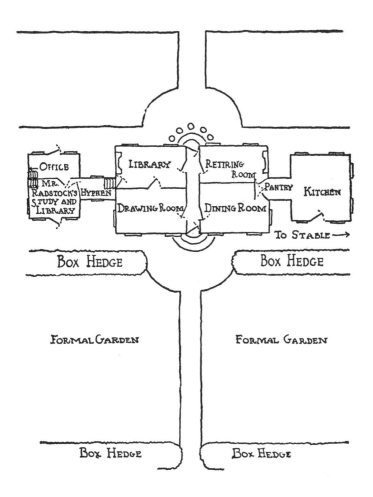

with a central hall running through with a door at each end. The library and the drawing room—it used to be called the Long Room—on one side; on the other the dining room and in front of it what used to be the gentlemen's retiring room. Mr. Radstock uses it as a sort of catch-all; it has the radio and victrola in it, and comfortable modern chairs and a couch, and when you get tired of high-back Chippendale chairs and stiff-back Phyfe sofas you go in there and are comfortable and anachronistic. That's the downstairs.

"Upstairs," I went on, "there are four bedrooms across the river front—which of course formally is the back of the house. Jocelyn and I have the two with a connecting bath—that's modern—at the end to the left of the Palladian window as you go upstairs. Pericles and Norman have the corresponding two to the right, over this room.

"Thalia and Priscilla are in the bedrooms to the front over the library, and Senator and Mrs. Mellish are in the master room, which is normally John's, occupying the rest of the front second floor. The attic has two finished bedrooms. John's overflowing up there, and you're there too."

He nodded, checking off the rooms on the sketch I made for him on the envelope.

"Now what about the wings?"

"Mr. Radstock's rooms are in the old office wing which wasn't originally connected with the house. He had the cupboard in the library made into a concealed door about fifteen years ago after his wife died, and he moved over there. There are two rooms downstairs. One is a study with his law books and so on, looking out over the back garden, and the other is a small front room where he writes. There's a little stairway there that goes up to his bedroom and bath. That's all in that wing. The other wing is connected properly with the house. It has the kitchen and pantries in it, and the hyphen is sort of a butler's pantry. Sebastian and Maria have their rooms over the kitchen.

"Would you like to look around?"

He thought a while without answering my question. "So that upstairs there are four windows looking out over the river," he said finally. "Not including the window on the stairway."

I nodded.

"Those rooms are occupied by you, Miss Frazier, Mr. Vaughan, and Mr. Xanthopoulos," he went on, thinking out loud, it seemed, rather than questioning me. "And you, and Miss Frazier, and Mr. Vaughan, were each one of you in your own rooms for all or a large part of that half-hour yesterday; in fact all of the last fifteen minutes of it, during which Justice Frazier was shot. And each of your rooms has a perfect view of the flagged terrace behind the box hedge where his body was found."

My heart almost stopped beating. I hadn't thought of that, incredible as it may seem.

"But of course," I remembered suddenly, "Jocelyn wasn't in that room then. She was in the front room with Thalia, and Priscilla Stone was there. When her father was shot Sebastian moved Priscilla in with Thalia, and Jocelyn into the room next to me."

"I see." Major Heath tapped the envelope abstractedly with his pencil. "That's different. In fact that's very different. Miss Frazier then *wasn't* there, and Miss Stone wasn't there, either; she was walking about in the front garden."

Then he smiled a little and looked straight at me.

"That leaves two people there, Mrs. Volney. You and Mr. Norman Vaughan. But you were busy writing letters, and Mr. Vaughan was busy getting out his ducking outfit. And you didn't either of you hear anything or see anything. Did you?"

"I don't know what Norman Vaughan saw or heard," I said, "but I didn't see or hear anything."

"All right." He put the envelope carefully in his pocket. "Now for the grounds. I've been around some, but not very carefully. Have you got a jacket, Mrs. Volney?"

I was delighted to find myself included, and not simply dismissed, as I'd expected. I got a jacket quickly and joined them on the garden steps.

It was a gorgeous day, clear and quite warm. The Potomac, when we'd gone down the brick walk past the old box hedge, was like a sea-gray ribbon between its saffron banks. The brilliant leaves were gone, but the old-golds still held and made it all very lovely and mellow.

Monckton Hall is set quite far back, about a city block in fact, from the first slope to the river. The ground is divided by the brick walk from the garden door of the house to the slips, which continue down to the second terrace. On each side of the walk there is a typical eighteenth century formal garden, ending, towards the house, with the box hedge, parallel to the house. The hedge is nine feet high. I imagine its little box trees as originally set out were never intended to make the high wall at the end of the two gardens that they've grown into in a hundred and fifty years. Mr. Radstock had the space just towards the river from it paved with flags when I was a child. It seems difficult to think back to the time when we played there as youngsters. I can only think of it now as the place where Justice Frazier lay dead.

We stood there, at least I stood there, staring about, not very sure of just what I was looking for or supposed to be doing, until I saw what I think Major Heath had tried to hide from me— that terrible brown stain on the gray flags. It made me a little sick. It made my realization of what had happened too clear and sharp.

"I think he must have stood about here," Major Heath said, taking a position near the box, about in the center of the terrace. "And I'm about his height."

He turned, facing the hedge.

"And you see, I can't see any of the windows

from here. Will you, Mr. Whipple, stand over there?"

He indicated a spot farther towards the center of the flags. "Can you see them?"

"I can see the upper panes, and the top of the hall window," Mr. Whipple drawled.

"But of course you're a lot taller than anyone else here. Will you stand there, Mrs. Volney?"

I did as I was told. I couldn't see anything of them except the white trim at the top, and said so.

"You're about five feet five, aren't you?" asked Mr. Whipple. I nodded.

"Then I should say that whoever stood where you're standing and fired the shot that killed Justice Frazier, was pretty well hidden from the house—if he was about your height, Mrs. Volney."

I suppose we all were thinking that almost everyone at the place is about my height. None of the men here that I know well are large, and I'm the tallest of the women. And I suppose we were all thinking, too, that if these measurements were right, one of us was eliminated. Senator Mellish is as tall as Major Heath or Mr. Whipple.

CHAPTER TEN

"YOU were in your room, Mrs. Volney—that's the one on the end at the right—and you didn't hear a shot?—or *did* you?"

"I didn't, Major Heath," I replied positively. "I *had* heard several, during the day. But you're always hearing them in the fall, when the Negroes are shooting rabbits and 'possum, and you get so you don't notice it at all."

"And no one else appears to have heard it either. Very odd—isn't it? Surely some of the men here could distinguish between the report of a shotgun and that of a .38 automatic revolver."

"It wasn't Jem's rifle, then?"

He shook his head. "No, Justice Frazier was shot with a revolver. Which, by the way, we still have to find."

"Well, sir," Mr. Whipple said then, "I'll put those two extra men on that. It ought to turn up before long. A gun is mighty hard to hide in a place like this. Now what I think we can do is let all these people go home to-morrow, or perhaps the next day, and then we'll have more room to look about in."

"I think you're right."

Major Heath was still looking up at the win-

dows, and at the hedge, and down towards the
river. He bent down suddenly and picked up a
minute clump of dirt, which he put in an empty
match box. I thought I saw a slight smile on Mr.
Whipple's face, but he reached down and picked
up another like it for himself.

We were still standing on the flagged terrace behind the box hedge. Just below us was another
terrace, with a low screened summer house on the
right of the steps and on the left a pergola, pretty
bare now but in the summer covered with white
jasmine, roses, and trumpet vines. Below, but only
partly visible from where we stood, was still another terrace, laid out in elaborate flower beds.
There, too, was the old dial that had marked the
sunny hours at Monckton Hall for over a century, on which Mr. Radstock had taught John and
me to tell the time when we were small. Below and
beyond a wide meadow sloped down to the river,
its edges lost in the fringe of willow and poplar
that grew along the old path on the river bank.
The river, still the pale gray ribbon between the
haze of dull gold November foliage, was dotted at
each end with the Radstock duck blinds, and a
boat was tied to the end of the old float down the
stream.

Everything else was wooded. That is, the trees
had never been cut on either side of the area I've
described. The owners of Monckton Hall had
always protected themselves from the sight of their
corn and tobacco fields that lay beyond the woods

on the left, and the stables and garden that were hidden on the right. All the business of the estate, a flourishing plantation in 1800, was concealed behind the strip of woods that ran down to the river on either side of the grounds.

"Of course, Whipple," Major Heath remarked, "a dark object, or two of them for that matter, at after four o'clock in the afternoon would be almost invisible against this box, from the river path."

"I reckon you're right. But I can't see how— and this morning you said the same—two people walking along the river at the same time could get down there and back, in half an hour, without seeing something—even if it was only themselves."

"And I don't see it yet. We have young Radstock's word that he saw Xanthopoulos going down the path quite rapidly about four o'clock, which is what Xanthopoulos said he did. The same person also saw Senator Mellish out this way. How they could have got to the river and back, without seeing either Justice Frazier or each other, I don't see. In fact, it's obviously impossible, unless they were both blindfolded.

"You see," he went on, "we have the fact of Justice Frazier. He was seen last by Mr. Radstock leaving the garden door and coming this way, shortly after 4:15. He could hardly have got past here, one would think, without meeting either Melish or Xanthopoulos. Now Justice Frazier had a habit, we know, of pacing up and down. If I had been here yesterday, I don't think there's much doubt that I'd have found cigar ash that would have shown he was walking back and forth here behind the hedge before he was shot. Whether he came to meet someone, we don't know. When he and Mr. Radstock left the retiring room, at 4:15, they agreed to talk again after dinner. Justice Frazier said—so Mr. Radstock says—that he'd join the party to see the new colt. I suppose that as a Southerner he was fond of horses?"

"Very," I said.

"Doesn't it seem strange," Mr. Whipple put in in his inimitably tired manner, "that he should have come down here to talk to Radstock, and they should then decide to put it off till after dinner, while he went to see a colt?"

At that moment Sebastian came to call him to the telephone and his question went unanswered for the time being. When he had disappeared around the end of the hedge Major Heath turned to me.

"Let's sit down, and you tell me something more about all these people," he said. "I think I understand them less all the time."

"There are some chairs in the pergola," I said.

"Righto. Let's go down there."

We went down the steps; and as we came onto the second terrace we saw—to my surprise, at least —the large figure of Senator Mellish, sitting on the marble bench on the terrace below. He rose when he heard us and picked up the book on the bench beside him.

"Good-morning, Mrs. Volney! Good-morning, Major Heath!" he greeted us heartily. "It's a fine morning. There's nothing like a Virginia autumn morning."

With that, and a cordial wave of his well-kept white hand, he passed us and went up towards the house.

"Mrs. Volney," said Major Heath, holding a match to my cigarette, as we entered the pergola, "is it possible for a complete fool to be elected to the United States Senate?"

I said, "Anything is possible in a democracy, Major Heath."

"So you've said once before this morning. Well, my second question is this: do you think Senator Mellish is one?"

I shook my head. "No, I don't. I thought so when I met him first, but I think I've changed my mind."

"So have I," Major Heath said. He thought about it a minute. "Now," he went on, "tell me something more about Justice Frazier. Or rather, tell me about my host."

"There's nobody I'd rather talk about," I replied promptly. "I'm devoted to Mr. Radstock, as I've probably told you, or you've seen."

I told him the whole story of Justice Frazier, Mr. Radstock, and my father, that fine triumvirate of devoted friends and devoted citizens. About the similarity in their interests and the dissimilarity of their lives, my father and Justice Frazier being two of the great college athletes of their generation, while Mr. Radstock's lameness and his almost abnormal sensitiveness about it had caused him to lead a sedentary and retired existence.

"It was Sebastian, by the way," I said, "who pushed him into the well by the stable when they were boys."

Major Heath nodded, to my surprise. "I heard about that," he said, "from Sebastian himself. He told me about it with a certain mournful pride, as the great tragedy of his existence. He was quite touching about it. And ever since, I gather, he's served Mr. Radstock with even more than the dog-like fidelity you usually get from blacks."

"From some of them," I said. "Yes, he has."

Then I told him about Mr. Radstock's great intellectual power. How his was the keenest and most subtle brain of the three; how he gradually established a consulting corporation and Supreme Court practice without ever going into court, and how he made more money than Justice Frazier or my father, who both went on the bench.

"You've known them both, then, since you were a child?"

"As long as I can remember. We always spent our summers here until I went to college. My father died when I was fifteen, and I stayed here two years then. So Mr. Radstock is almost like a father. He's a wonderful person. He's the best man I know, now that Justice Frazier is dead."

Major Heath nodded. "And John?"

"John's very different. He's got brains too, but he's rather dull. His father hopes that if he stays in his New York office they'll buck him up a bit. Then I think he finds it more peaceful here without John. This is always the sort of thing that happens when John's around."

"What? Is somebody always——?"

"Oh, I don't mean that. But there's always a commotion. A lot of people here, and highballs, and duck shooting, and Mr. Radstock gets tired of it. His interests now are entirely cultivated ones—books, music, furniture, antiques—that sort of thing. John hasn't much interest except in the law and social life. The billiard room in the basement was a dodge to get John's friends off the first floor. They're fond of each other, of course, but there's no sentimentality about it. I suppose that's because there aren't any women about. John's mother died when he was a youngster."

Somehow I didn't want him to know that John and his father aren't very good friends.

"Would you call Miss Stone sentimental?" he asked suddenly.

I recovered quickly from my surprise. "Fearfully, I should say."

"Well, I suppose it does make a difference," he continued calmly. "Now what about Justice Frazier?"

I went over what I'd told him, and tried to think of something I hadn't. That I'd known him, too, all my life, and had been brought up to regard him too as the "compleat gentleman," cultivated, able, and with extraordinary force of character. I even went so far as to tell him what John had told me, the rumor he'd heard that Justice Frazier was to be offered a place in the Cabinet. If I expected that information to be a surprise I was mistaken.

"That's what makes me wonder," he said, "about the cause of his death. I can't feel, you know, that it is any petty little 'racketeering' we're dealing with. He came to see me several times. I got the impression that he was anxious to tell me something but couldn't quite do it. He talked about the liquor ring. I wish you wouldn't repeat this to anybody, by the way. He said he was convinced that the importation of fine whiskies and the rest was in the hands of a few people who were highly placed. Well . . ."

He lapsed into quite a long silence. Then he pulled out his pipe and pouch and began filling in tobacco with his usual care.

"Would you think, Mrs. Volney, that Justice Frazier was the sort of man to have a violent antipathy to breaches of your prohibition law?"

"I don't think so," I replied. "He drank himself, moderately. Senator Mellish's opinion about it was certainly—as far as I know—not his, or anything like it."

"So I would have thought."

"It sounds almost like one of Caleb Williams's stories," I went on. Caleb is always pursuing the "man higher up" who's responsible for excellent Scotch at forty-five dollars a case in the Capital. I asked him once what he was going to do with him when he got him, and he said, "Kiss him on both cheeks."

Major Heath grinned when I told him this, but he was still pondering over something. I began to think it was Caleb more than Justice Frazier who had got him interested. Most foreigners, however intelligent they are, seem to take our prohibition problems too much to heart.

However, we sat there talking about it, or rather with me making a remark now and then and Major Heath sort of reflecting for a minute or two over it, until the luncheon gong sounded and we went in. Even now I couldn't help shuddering when I passed the terrace behind the box hedge where Justice Frazier had lain. I could still see that great inert form sprawled there, so helpless, so undignified! I thought how many times when I was a child he had taken me on his back up that walk in answer to the children's lunch bell at twelve o'clock.

Thinking it over now, I don't know how we got through the rest of that day. There was the undercurrent of investigation going on everywhere. Someone took our fingerprints. I got an unpleasant additional reminder of our situation when I reminded Sebastian to empty the ashtrays in the drawing room and he told me that one of the prosecuting attorney's men had taken the contents of every ashtray in the house away with him, even those from the bedrooms, sealed up in envelopes.

This was all done as unobtrusively as possible, I suppose, but there it was nevertheless. I met Thalia in the hall outside Jocelyn's room and she said with a frightened quiver in her voice that one of the men had taken a pair of her sport shoes that she'd left out to be cleaned, and hadn't returned them, and what did I suppose he was doing with them? She'd heard that Mrs. Mellish had tried to leave the grounds and had been sent back. She said also that Pericles had had to make a private telephone call and had cut across through the woods and got to the little store on the road that supplies the colored cottagers, and there had been ordered back by the sheriff's people. They even threatened to put him under arrest.

She seemed quite alarmed by all this, so I suggested that we get Jocelyn and take a walk. We told a man in the hall we were going, but we'd hardly got outside the house when a couple of newspaper photographers appeared from Heaven knows where and we went back inside. That was worse still; we decided to go up to Thalia's room and found somebody there going through the closet.

The newspapers, however, were the worst of all. Mr. Radstock was getting dreadfully annoyed about them. Mr. Whipple did his best to keep their people away—or said he did—but Monckton Hall can be got at in a dozen different ways. There was a

picture of it from an airplane with a large cross
where Justice Frazier had fallen. There were
other views of the same unpleasant nature.
Priscilla still held off with her column, and Caleb,
covering the case for the *Times,* was as decent as
he could be and keep his job. I don't think there's
any doubt that Whipple and the sheriff were professionally anxious for all the publicity they could
get. They pretended to be trying to isolate us. Perhaps they did to some extent, but I imagine they
were pretty half-hearted about it. One can't blame
them, of course. A political job is a political job,
and this was only the murder of a gentleman.

Norman and Priscilla took it all very calmly, I
must say, and it's the first time in her life that
Priscilla ever did take anything calmly. Norman's
indifference—it almost amounted to that—seemed
natural enough, because he makes a great point of
being blasé. But Priscilla was just the opposite. A
kitten playing with a string could send her into
ecstasies of enchantment, a horse breaking its leg
thrilled her almost into a state of collapse; but her
only reaction to the cold-blooded murder of a man
who had done more to help her journalistic career
than anyone else was what almost seemed to be a
calm, calculating silence. She seemed to be thinking all the time; and Heaven knows that was unusual. She fluttered in something of her old manner when Mr. Whipple or Major Heath was
around, but most of the time she sat curled up in a
big chair in the library, reading Jane Austen,

simply waiting, I thought, until Mr. Whipple said she might go back to town. She even deserted Mrs. Mellish, who wandered about, rather distrait, seemed to me obviously to have been weeping about something, and spent most of the time in her room, writing letters. Major Heath said so many letters had never before been written in one house in so short a time.

The Senator from the Bible Belt gave me the impression, in a queer way, of biding his time. His spirits and optimism were splendid. As Thalia remarked bitterly, "You'd think this was the best possible murder in the best possible world. I don't like that man." But Senator Mellish at least didn't sit about. He was always somewhere, just leaving when anyone came, or just coming when anyone was about to go. He was a perpetual flux. He'd quit talking, however. In fact everyone had, except Thalia.

"I'm getting beastly damn sick of it," she protested to Major Heath. "We might as well be in a Trappist monastery. You say something, and everybody looks at you as if you'd broken a cardinal rule."

"You probably did, dear," remarked Priscilla from her book. "You speak abominable English."

"You're crazy. I spika de beootiful Inglis."

"She's quite right, of course," Major Heath commented to me a little later. "When you think of all these people at Joe's the other night talking a blue streak, you feel their present reserve is a little odd."

"There isn't very much to say, really," I said.

"Or a great deal."

On the next day—Monday—we narrowly escaped a second tragedy, which turned out to have undertones that few suspected at the time. Norman had asked John if Mr. Radstock would object to his going ducking. John was surprised, I think, but he asked his father, who was perfectly willing, and in fact thought it an excellent idea. John wouldn't go; he probably thought Jocelyn would think it disrespectful. Pericles said he would like to go along.

I heard two people set out next morning about four o'clock; then, to my surprise, I heard someone else going out too. I supposed John had decided to go along after all. I couldn't go back to sleep and lay there thinking until about six o'clock, when I dozed off. Suddenly I woke up and sat upright in bed. I'd half heard something, but I couldn't make out what it was until I heard it again. Someone was shouting. I jumped up and ran to my window. I could just see the river and the duck blind, and thought I could make out something moving in the water.

I put on my shoes and a coat and dashed downstairs. There was no use waking the girls or Senator Mellish. Sebastian was in the kitchen and I called to him. Together we ran down the side path that goes straight to the river. I got there first, of course—Sebastian is an old man and has rheumatism. When I got there Pericles, almost on the point of complete exhaustion, was bending over the dripping, prostrate, unconscious body of Norman Vaughan, making a tragic effort, in spite of his own condition, to give first aid. I pushed him aside and began giving the artificial respiration. I thought he was gone.

Jem, who had been bringing wood for the kitchen and had seen us, came running along, and we sent him back for blankets and some brandy. I tried to get Pericles to go on up to the house with him, but he wouldn't.

"I'll stand by till the others get here," he said, with chattering teeth. He was blue with cold. Then we both cried out when Norman's eyelids flickered a little and he took a short gasping breath. My arms and shoulders were aching as they never had before; but in a few more minutes he was quite conscious and breathing pretty regularly. We made him take a big drink of the brandy Jem brought, and I knew then that barring complications he was out of danger. We bundled him up and Sebastian and Jem, with another boy Jem had brought along, got him up to the house.

Pericles gulped down a stiff drink, and together we followed what had just missed being a second cortège to Monckton Hall within three days.

"How did it happen?" I asked. Pericles looked at me a little blankly. He was shivering frightfully, and I think he was hardly aware that of course I knew nothing at all about it.

"Oh, he lost his balance," he said. "We were in the boat, and I guess he must have tripped over something. All of a sudden he sort of pitched out. I shouted and tried to get hold of him, but he went down. Then when he came up he caught hold of the boat, and I was reaching for him on the same side and over it went. I jumped clear just as it capsized and then I did get hold of him. I had a devil of a time. He thrashed about. Then I got him to shore. Have you a cigarette? Mine are all wet."

I had a pack of Camels in my tweed coat pocket, fortunately, and handed him one. He could scarcely light it, his hands shook so. I don't see how he ever did it; I mean get Norman out. He isn't nearly as large a man. He would probably weigh thirty pounds less. Norman isn't tall, but is pretty heavy and much more the sort of person who would do the rescuing.

"Funny he couldn't swim, isn't it?" Pericles said as we got in.

We got them to bed surrounded by hot-water bottles, and I went downstairs, wondering if I ought to call a doctor. I didn't want either of them to develop pneumonia. I started into the library to phone Dr. Perry and ask him what to do, when I heard someone talking in there. I stopped short. I didn't know anybody else was up. It was Senator Mellish. Before I quite realized that I was eavesdropping I heard what he was saying.

"Major Heath, that Greek knocked him out of the boat! I saw it very clearly, with my own eyes. I've been watching that fellow for some time, and this morning I followed them down to the river. I hid in the trees along the bank, and I saw the whole thing. Vaughan tried to save himself, but the Greek dived at his knees like a rocket and threw him off his balance. Vaughan tried to twist around and get back, and the Greek hit him, smashed him in the jaw. I shouted then, and he looked up; and then he shouted and jumped in and staged that rescue."

So it was Senator Mellish, and not John, who went out!

I turned around and went back upstairs without making a sound.

CHAPTER ELEVEN

I MET Sebastian at the head of the stairs coming from Norman's room.

"He's goin' to be all right, Miss Diane. Don' you worry 'bout him," he said kindly. "Now where is you goin' to have your breakfas'? The Senatuh an' Majuh Heath is havin' theirs in the dinin' room now. I guess they's plenty hungry. They was both out an' aroun' befoh five o'clock."

"Both of them?" I asked.

The old darky nodded his kinky gray head. "Deed so, Miss. Ah guess they hunts duck without no guns. Ah was gettin' up to make some coffee fo' Mistuh Vaughan an' Miss Tolly's brothuh, but they was too soon fo' me, 'cause Ah heard them an' Ah looked out the window, and saw the Majuh goin' down toward the stable. Ah thought Ah'd better get up anyway, an' so Ah went down an' made some coffee, and them other two came down then."

"Did you tell them that Major Heath was already out, Sebastian?"

"Deed Ah didn', Miss. They didn' ask me an' Ah didn' tell 'em nothin'. But when they got done Ah looked out the window an' Ah saw the Senatuh

151

come out the house an' follow them. That was mighty funny, Miss."

I agreed with him. "Is Mr. Radstock up?"

"Yes'm. Ah was jus' goin' to take his tray ovuh," he said, consulting his enormous silver watch. "It's jus' eight o'clock."

"Tell him I'd like to have breakfast with him, will you please? I'll be over in ten minutes."

"Yes'm. An' don' you let these goin's-on worry you none, Miss."

"I wouldn't let anything at all worry me, Sebastian."

Major Heath was in the hall when I went down a few minutes later.

"Sebastian tells me you're having breakfast with Mr. Radstock in his study," he said. "Think I might come along?"

"Surely," I replied, thinking that he looked astonishingly fresh for having been out since before five o'clock.

Mr. Radstock was sitting in front of the fire in his study, the gleaming breakfast service on the low table in front of him.

"Nice of you, Diane; come in." He greeted me with that rare charm of his that quite covered up the fact that he hated people to disturb him early in the morning—and especially, I imagined, when they brought detectives along. "Good-morning, Major Heath. I suppose you've heard that Whipple has arrested Jem. It's an outrage."

"I *didn't* know it," Major Heath said placidly.

"But I can't say I haven't been expecting it, rather. Mr. Whipple feels he has to have somebody tangible. You don't think the Negro shot Justice Frazier, of course?"

"Stuff and nonsense!" Mr. Radstock said sharply. "It's not only absurd on the face of it but there isn't one tittle of evidence to support it. I'm convinced that Frazier was murdered as the result of a deep-laid scheme. And if Whipple or any of the rest of them think they're going to railroad a poor half-witted darky to the gallows to save their political hides, or to let the criminal go scot-free—well, they're mistaken. I've seen that happen in Washington too often these last ten years, and it's not going to happen now."

He brought his stick down sharply on the hearth. It was the first time I'd seen him stirred from his polished urbanity. He seemed to realize what I was thinking, for he settled back in his chair and cast me a whimsical and deprecatory smile.

"I'm glad to hear you say that, Mr. Radstock," Major Heath said quietly. "I wasn't quite sure what your attitude would be. Senator Mellish, by the way, says he saw young Xanthopoulos 'in earnest conversation' with Jem early Saturday afternoon."

"And why not?" said Mr. Radstock with a little amusement. He was quite himself again. "Jem usually goes ducking with my son's friends. I'm inclined to think Mellish is an alarmist. I only wish he wouldn't accuse my guests of murder while he's also under my roof."

"Has he?"

"Well, not exactly, perhaps. He's been inquiring so stubbornly into the life history of all of you that I'm almost in trepidation. I saw him and Whipple in what he calls 'earnest conversation' yesterday afternoon. Some toast, Diane? Sebastian says you've already breakfasted, Major?"

"Yes, thank you. What I came along here with Mrs. Volney for, Mr. Radstock, was to find out what you think of all this—and then I'll promptly clear out. I might as well confess I'm a little bewildered by it myself. I think it's by national types as much as anything else. I find—for instance— Mr. Whipple's arresting the most defenseless person in the place a little—distressing. His theory, if he bothers about anything so intellectual as a theory, seems to be to make an arrest, then trust to luck that something will turn up."

"Mr. Whipple will find that Jem is far from defenseless," Mr. Radstock said quietly. "As for this affair, there are always clues, Major Heath. I'm not a criminal lawyer, but I'm interested in human behavior. There are *always* clues, sir. They may be material, and if they are, they're easy enough for a man like Whipple to get hold of. If, on the other hand, the thing has been done cleverly enough to leave no tangible evidence, there's where you come in, or so I'd thought. The psychological clues are inevitable. They can't be removed. The consciousness of guilt is so bound to influence every action of the guilty person as to make every act, every evasion, just one more bit of evidence for the psychological investigator."

It was a terrifying picture that he drew so calmly and urbanely across the low breakfast table. The gleaming silver threw back the dancing flicker of the yellow flame, and I shuddered, wondering what stark wastelands of guilty knowledge someone was staggering through—perhaps someone still at Monckton Hall.

"I've been wondering, Major Heath," Mr. Radstock went on, with the slightest hint of steel in his voice and in his clear blue eyes that regarded us calmly across the table; "—you'll forgive me, I hope, but I believe in plain speaking—I've been wondering if you had been in this country long enough to be affected by the—standards, if I may call them that, of our detective system."

I didn't at first realize what he was saying, and I think Major Heath didn't either. Then we both did at the same time. A strange look of whimsical incredulity came into his face.

Mr. Radstock continued calmly and relentlessly: "I have asked your pardon if I'm doing you an injustice," he said; "and I think I am. But I've seen many men, Major Heath, who could not resist the offer of a large sum—as much, even, as fifty thousand dollars—especially when they were in no way involved, as you are not. After all, justice and corruption are social matters, and in a foreign country it's easy enough to say they are 'relative' terms. Frazier and I have watched the gradual dissolution of law and order in Washington for a good many years. Frazier was a fighter. I never was. He was hot-headed in defense of his ideals. I have always lived apart. But I'm involved now; first because my friend is dead, and second because one of my men is wrongfully accused of his murder.

"Well, Major Heath, I can see I was mistaken about you. You have an honest face. So I'm getting afield. Now what have you done?"

The question was abrupt, and I almost trembled, for a moment, at what Major Heath might think of Mr. Radstock's "frankness." But he replied at once with great placidity, and only that one queer look told me that he had understood what Mr. Radstock was saying.

"I think you're right about psychological clues," he said, "at least in the large. Only," he continued with a faint smile, "here there's too much 'static.' I don't know what's the matter with everybody. Even Mrs. Mellish seems anxious to conceal something. I have the feeling, furthermore, that it's all off the track, in some way. I prefer material clues, if possible, for that reason. And I have some of them, too, if I can just fit them together."

"For example?" said Mr. Radstock. "Diane, have you anything to smoke?"

I nodded and Major Heath went on:

"I was out very early Saturday morning—you

remember it was dark when I got here the evening
before. It was easy enough, even the next morning,
to trace some of the things that had happened outside there. I found some particles of earth that
were obviously from shoes that had walked in the
stable yard. They had approached the terrace from
the kitchen side. And on the turf in front of the
hedge, to the right of the walk, I found some very
important material evidence: four footprints. Not
very clear-cut, but distinct enough. They were the
prints of a man's shoes, medium size. The heel is
not marked nearly as distinctly as the ball; the
man was either going on his toes or running. The
footprints lead away from the walk, towards this
side of the house. He was leaving the spot where
Justice Frazier's body lay, and I suppose he was
running. Now, if he entered the house, he had to
do it through the hyphen door just here, or go
around and come in the front door. If he came in
the hyphen door, he could have entered the house
through the library door. Or second, he could have
come in here. Or third—well, you know the alternative."

There was a silence. We both knew the alternative. Mr. Radstock took a neatly folded handkerchief out of his pocket and blew his nose. Major
Heath sat gazing into the fire.

"Let me understand you, Heath," Mr. Radstock
said at last. "I take it that you mean that a man
came running across the garden directly in back of
this room, and that he must either have gone

around to the front of the house, or have entered the door of this hyphen. And if he entered this hyphen door, he must have gone through the library, or come in here, or—this, I take it, is your alternative—gone through the other door there down into the basement."

"That is the way it appears to me," said the Englishman deliberately.

"In other words, sir, I'm to understand that you think it's perfectly possible for my son to have been the person whose footprints are out there on the turf?"

"*Were* out there." Major Heath corrected him with a smile. "They'd been obliterated by ten o'clock that morning when I took Whipple out to see them. Your boy Jem had just mowed the lawn. It seems," he went on gravely, "that Miss Thalia had asked him to do so the day before. It was necessary to use it as a putting green. It seems she brought along a sort of garden-golf arrangement—very ingenious affair."

There was no irony in his voice, but I caught a twinkle in his gray eyes. Very ingenious indeed, I knew. I wondered where he had found out—or if he had found out—Thalia's aversion to miniature golf in all forms. Norman Vaughan will only give her four strokes on the Chevy Chase course.

Mr. Radstock's blue eyes twinkled too. I think the idea of an impudent wisp of a girl calmly destroying an important set of clues under Major

Heath's eyes and the prosecutor's very nose amused him greatly.

"So they don't do you a great deal of good," he said dryly.

"On the contrary," Major Heath returned soberly. "They are almost enough to send some-one to the electric chair. I don't mean in them-selves, but in what they tell me to look for. They were the prints of a man's foot, medium size—about eights—and they were the prints of some-one coming this way."

He looked directly at Mr. Radstock, and I thought there was a challenge in that very clear steady gaze. Then he hesitated a moment.

"What I want, you see," he went on then, "is—well, cases of this sort are so much better settled if—if the person concerned, or if someone who is concerned, naturally, perhaps, in sheltering him, will just come forward and tell about it. That's why I've kept taking so many people here along with me—I mean into my confidence. A confes-sion, in other words. Don't you see? There may be mitigating circumstances—the inevitable judg-ment is likely to be so much less severe."

He stopped there and looked at us. "I wouldn't tell this to everybody," he continued. "Of course it might be taken as an indication of weakness. Well, what do you think of it, sir?"

Mr. Radstock shook his head dubiously.

"Well," Major Heath went on, cheerfully, "so

much for that. Now there's one question I want to ask you again, to be sure that I've got the answer right. You left the retiring room at 4:15, and came here to answer the telephone. And you saw, and heard, no one."

"No one. That is correct," Mr. Radstock said. "I came out of the house through the library. The telephone is in my other room, not in this one. I closed the door when I went in. I talked with Mr. Raymond Carson, an agent of the Treasury Department, who has been interested with Frazier and myself in this importation business. I talked to him—I should say—about ten minutes. I then went up to my room above this one, and came down in a few minutes. Then I went over to the house to give Sebastian some order or other."

"That would be at 4:27, or thereabouts."

"Yes."

"Just eight minutes, or so, before the body of Justice Frazier was found."

"Yes."

"You heard no shot, Mr. Radstock?"

"No, sir."

"Not even a silenced—I mean partly silenced— report, that would sound like the report of a gun at a considerable distance; or rather more like a sharp cough?"

Mr. Radstock looked quickly at him, and thought a moment. "No," he said at last, with decision; "I can't recall that I did."

Major Heath nodded. "And then, after you saw Sebastian?"

"I then came back through the drawing room and stopped to speak to some of my guests who were there. That must have been almost exactly at half-past four. Then I excused myself until dinner. I had some work to do here. I'm still a consultant, and I'm advising a group of New York attorneys in a Radio Corporation case before the Supreme Court in January. I wanted to get it in shape for Frazier's opinion that evening. Mellish was in the library, reading, and I spoke to him and came on out. The hyphen door was closed. You'll have to ask Sebastian if it was locked. If it was not, then you'll have to find out who unlocked it, because it's usually kept locked. No one ever comes out here except my son and Mrs. Volney—they've no respect for privacy. And Sebastian, of course. And now a word of advice, Major Heath. I know you have to consider every possible person, but I think you're wasting your time on my son."

"No doubt," said Major Heath lightly. "I merely wanted to let you know that there is such a possibility. I have heard, for instance, the vaguest rumors to the effect that Justice Frazier was opposed to your son's interest in his daughter."

A little cloud passed over Mr. Radstock's serene face.

"That's true," he said. "The reason, however, was quite simple, and it certainly was nothing that would make even the most desperately infatuated person take such a step. Frazier thought that because Jocelyn has known John a good many years, and because they've practically grown up together, she was simply drifting into a marriage with him without really thinking very clearly what it was all about. In a sense I quite agreed with him. I don't think, in addition, that a twenty-year-old girl is the proper wife for a thirty-year-old man. And certainly a man in my son's position was in no state to marry. I thought that if their attachment continued, they should wait five or six years, until John was ready to come to Washington, possibly to go into the diplomatic field.

"Frazier was afraid that Jocelyn might marry my son simply because all her crowd were marrying somebody. I think, too, that he wanted something better for Jocelyn. He was romantic, incurably so. He fell in love some years after he had married Jocelyn's mother, and I think he wanted to protect her against a marriage out of simple friendship. But especially, Major Heath," he continued, coming out of a half reverie, "that John has not the temperament required for such an act."

It *was* amusing to think of John in such a rôle; yet who knows?

"I may be wrong," Mr. Radstock went on thoughtfully. "I know very well the intense, bitter despair that can torture a human soul under an ordinary workaday exterior. I think that is the thing that surprises me most about people. How they can go on as if nothing were happening, while their hearts are breaking with a sick hopelessness that no one else can ever realize, I can't see. Perhaps my son is one of them. They are the legion of the damned. It's no wonder that they break now and then. I only wonder that they don't break oftener."

Neither Major Heath nor I said anything. It seemed to me then—and he agreed with me when I mentioned it later—that Mr. Radstock was just then for the first time thinking of his son as an actual, thinking, feeling human being. He seemed to have forgot us momentarily, thinking of the possibilities of his son's being involved. I wondered what he would do then. Which loyalty would be the greater—to friend or to son? Here was another battle in the secret places of the heart.

"I'm afraid I'm taking up your time," Major Heath said, looking at his watch. "But there's one other thing I want to ask you."

Mr. Radstock brought himself back to the present. "I'm quite at your service, Major Heath," he said.

"About Senator Mellish. Can you give me any information at all?"

"Very little, I'm afraid. He is a wealthy man, he is a puritan reformer of a school that I have no patience with, and since he's been here—in Washington, I mean—he's managed to get his nose into everything. What his game is exactly, I don't know; but I'm pretty sure he has one. He spends money lavishly, and effort, too, in uniting various elements to himself. I think he's a complete egotist, and a shrewd one."

"Where does he get his money?" Heath asked.

"That I can't tell you."

Mr. Radstock looked at Heath with a slight smile. Then he continued, "When you've been in Washington a little longer, sir, you'll discover it's wiser not to ask such questions. The important thing is not where it comes from, but where it's going. If you're really interested, however, I imagine Miss Stone could tell you."

He smiled again, with that pleasant fleeting smile, always faintly ironic.

"What about Miss Stone, by the way?"

"Priscilla?" Mr. Radstock replied. I could see that deprecatory, tolerant expression that men always had when they talked about Priscilla. "Priscilla's father was Secretary of the Treasury in the Nineties, had a breakdown, and died, leaving his family in very bad straits. Priscilla grew up in Washington society, poor but with enough relatives and friends to keep her going. I was very proud of her when she decided she'd be a journalist. She failed at reporting, and then in some way dropped with extraordinary ease into the sort of thing she's doing now. She makes a good living at it and has a good time doing it. I'm a firm believer, of course, in women's being financially independent, and knowing how to do something."

"Had she any connection with Justice Frazier?"

Major Heath stuck to the point if Mr. Radstock wouldn't.

Mr. Radstock frowned. I had a sudden intuition —let me call it—that that question brought something to his mind that he'd half forgot.

"None that I know of. Frazier got her her first job on the *Chronicle*. She'd written chatty articles for the Junior League magazine. I think he was helpful to her in many small ways."

"Then just one more matter, and I'll be getting along," Major Heath continued, apparently unaware that Mr. Radstock was leaving something unsaid. "Do you think Whipple is honest? I can understand your distrust of me, because, as a matter of fact, I feel the same way. I haven't the foggiest notion what constitutes honesty and dishonesty in your public life. I hear the strangest stories of 'privilege' that sound to me like plain bribery; and I don't know where one ends and the other begins."

"I'd have to have notice of that question, Heath," Mr. Radstock returned. "I don't think Whipple would steal my silver. I don't think he'd forge my name to a check. But I'd hate to have my neck at the mercy of his political ambition. Is that clear at all?"

"Well, vaguely," said Major Heath with a smile. "But perhaps it's clear enough. And now I'll apologize for taking up so much of your time."

I stopped him as he was taking his leave. "By

the way, Major Heath," I said, "I overheard your conversation with Senator Mellish this morning, quite inadvertently. I wanted to tell you that I had."

He looked at me as if he hadn't a notion what I was talking about. But I had no intention of letting him out of it, whatever his purpose was.

"I heard Senator Mellish tell you he'd seen Pericles attack Norman Vaughan and throw him out into the river."

"Oh," he replied, exactly as if it didn't really matter in the least. "I think Senator Mellish was a little excited. I wouldn't mention it to a soul, if I were you. I'd hate, for one reason, to think of the things Miss Xanthopoulos could say to Mrs. Mellish and the Senator if she thought she had *reason* to dislike them. Good-morning; I'll be seeing you later on."

We heard him unlock the door of the hyphen and go out towards the back garden.

I told Mr. Radstock, who was considerably surprised that neither of us had ever mentioned Norman's accident, about the whole thing, including what Sebastian had told me about Major Heath's being up and in fact the first out. He lay back on the sofa, his eyes closed, gently tapping the carpet with his stick. When I'd finished he sat up.

"Don't let it disturb you, my dear," he said. But I could see he was thinking seriously about it, and was a little worried himself.

Then he waved his hand as if brushing the incident away. "There's another thing that bothers me a little," he said. "I mean John. I don't know what it is, but he's seemed rather strange. Last night, in the side garden about 11 : 30, I saw him talking to Priscilla. I'd stepped out to smoke my cigar before I went to bed. They disappeared when they heard me, but I'd already seen them."

I was about to say that there was nothing particularly mysterious or alarming about that, when Sebastian came in for the tray and handed Mr. Radstock a note.

"Miss Tolly done ask me to bring you that from Miss Priscilla. Miss Priscilla wasn' feelin' very well las' night, so she gone back to town 'bout nine o'clock, suh. She didn' 'sturb nobody, and she's goin' to come back this noon."

Mr. Radstock tossed the folded note into the fire.

"If that's what she says, there's not much use in my trying to make out her writing," he said. I've often wondered since if that wasn't a very great mistake—as it turned out.

Curiously enough, neither of us mentioned the obvious discrepancy. If Priscilla had gone to town at nine o'clock, she clearly couldn't have been talking to John Radstock in the garden at half-past eleven—or vice versa. Nevertheless we were both equally aware of it. As it turned out, what Priscilla did the previous night between nine and half-past eleven—or rather what she didn't do—came to have a very special significance.

★   ★   ★

From the Washington *Chronicle*

BY PRISCILLA STONE

The tragedy at Monckton Hall last Saturday was a great shock to us all. Justice Frazier was one of the best-loved men in the Capital, and those of us who knew him realize that his place can never be filled.

He was of a generation that is passing, when a great heart and a great mind could dwell together in the same noble frame. Sometime I'm going to write a book about Blanchard Frazier. His was a charmed life compounded of Romance and Tragedy. His love of justice was the Achilles heel; his going when he did, on the eve of his greatest battle, was Sophoclean irony. Those of us who remain know now how insecure and shifting are the footprints on the sands of Time.

How few of the fine figures of Justice Frazier's generation are left! How changed is our political scene. Who can match them? Who can match the great triumvirate that were a power in Washington twenty years ago? Whose houses can compare in influence with the Curtis mansion on Massachusetts Avenue (the younger generation know Diane Volney, not her father), or the Fraziers', on Dupont Circle? They were open sesame to a more exclusive circle than the Adams house.

Monckton Hall down the Potomac carries on, now that Death has closed those two.

Mr. Radstock's lameness has kept him out of the swirl that made his two friends more publicly known. But it needn't have. His ability has made him a power in the legal world. And now that his old friends have passed one likes to think of him as an Emerson or Thoreau, the Sage of Monckton Hall.

REQUIESCAT IN PACE

★   ★   ★

When I came back to town I found the town had left me a little behind, so I went at once to Madame Rosa. I'd forgot about her. Of course I know a great lot of people who go to her for advice because she knows the ropes in Washington. Especially political ladies who are newcomers. Mrs. Mellish, the wife of the Senator, was telling me about her the other day, so I went around.

But she's too discreet. She wouldn't tell me a thing. I did learn something while I was there, though, but not from her.

Adèle d'Acosta is going back to Madrid or Paris. Diplomatic changes are responsible, I understand.

I also heard that a certain somebody is out just exactly $20,000.

I'm sure I'd be glad to go to Paris, or Timbuctoo for that matter, for $20,000 cash.

CHAPTER TWELVE

I STAYED talking with Mr. Radstock about an hour after Major Heath went out. We talked about a lot of things, avoiding the subject uppermost in the mind of everyone at Monckton Hall. I don't think I realized how deeply it had hurt Mr. Radstock until he said what he had about John. Sitting here now I felt what I so seldom felt with Mr. Radstock—the difference in our ages. He seemed moving in another world, in which I didn't belong, divided by a gulf of years that I couldn't cross. What is it that Matthew Arnold or somebody says about the eternal note of sadness? I had the feeling that that was about all that was left now for Mr. Radstock.

"Major Heath doesn't seem particularly worried, or even interested, about Pericles and Norman," I said after a little.

"He's waiting, my dear. After all, Vaughan is alive and able to make his own accusation—if Mellish is right. It worries me, a little. I don't understand it. I'm going to have a talk with Vaughan. I'll admit, Diane, that I've never trusted young Xanthopoulos, but I've always thought Vaughan was a gentleman."

He said it placidly, but I felt rather sorry for Norman. He is a gentleman, and I know he would be sorry to have been the cause of still more trouble around Monckton Hall.

There was one other point that I simply had to ask Mr. Radstock about. "What *is* Senator Mellish doing?" I said.

"I don't know what to think of him, Diane. I don't know very much about that kind of person. But I'd say, offhand, that he's playing some kind of a game that's deeper than he is. A man of his kind, in his position, is bound to be suspicious. He thrives in politics, but he's constantly on the alert for enemies, frame-ups, anything of the sort. Such people are a constant equation in our public life. What do you think of them—the Mellishes, I mean?"

Which showed that Mr. Radstock was a shrewder judge of people than I'd known. I'd regarded Mrs. Mellish as nothing but a sounding-board for her luxuriant husband.

"I don't know," I said. "That's the trouble. Thalia asked him last evening if he'd found it yet. He was quite nonplussed for a minute, and then asked her what. She said she didn't know, but she'd been watching him crawling around the terrace like Nebuchadnezzar. Major Heath broke in with a funny story about the Grand Llama of Tibet, and Pericles gave Thalia a violent kick under the table."

Mr. Radstock smiled. "She's a very nice girl,"

he said. Then he picked up the morning paper that Sebastian had brought and glanced through it.

"I see Priscilla's back on the job," he commented. He read through her column, and tossed me the paper with a sardonic smile. "I didn't know she was such an admirer of mine. These columns of hers are the strangest mixture of good writing and illiteracy, and triteness and pungency."

I read her column for the day.

"She has to make a living," I said, and he chuckled.

"Oh, I suppose so. And I suppose that's why she left last night—to get her stuff in in time. After all, she could have said more. Priscilla's a very clever woman. I only hope she's not too clever. That's usually the trouble with you women. The funeral's at three to-morrow at Arlington, by the way. Shall you go from here?"

"I think not, if you don't mind," I replied. "I haven't done anything with my mail, and I've got to go to town and have a look at the shop, and do up some letters. I'd thought of going in this afternoon."

We talked of a few other things, and I left in a moment or so and walked into the very center of the Mellish situation.

Mrs. Mellish was in the drawing room when I came back into the house. She was knitting and I sat down to talk to her a few minutes. It occurred to me when I came in the room that I'd hardly spoken ten words to her since we'd been here, and that whenever I'd seen her Thalia and Priscilla had been present. Here she was alone, and she was obviously not very happy.

"What are you knitting?" I asked, sitting down on the sofa opposite her.

"Some sweaters for a Kentucky mountain welfare center," she said, smoothing out a little blue garment.

I expected her to add something about idle hands, but she didn't. In fact she didn't add anything, and we lapsed into silence.

"It's a lovely day," I said next. "Why don't you get a coat and let's go for a walk?"

"I'd rather stay here. I want to finish this today."

"Very well," I thought, and had about decided to take myself off, as she obviously didn't care to talk to me, when I noticed a newspaper on the sofa beside her. It was the *Chronicle,* and I guessed what the matter was.

"Have you read Priscilla Stone's column this morning?" I asked, watching her pale face and growing beastly sorry for her.

She nodded, and looked around furtively.

"I'm afraid my husband will see it." she said in a frightened whisper.

So she *was* afraid of him!

"Don't you want him to?" I asked gently.

"Oh, no! No!" she cried, a plaintive, hurt little cry, and looked around again. "You see, when we came, I didn't know what to do. His position is so hard, and I've always lived in a little town—I didn't have a secretary, and somebody told me about this woman, Madame Rosa. That she gave people advice and had a lot of people that she had helped. So I went. I didn't want anybody to know I went, so I got Mr. Williams to take me. I didn't tell him why. He thought it was a great joke, but he took me. And she knew so much about my husband, about his past life. I asked her how she knew and she said from her crystals. She seemed so kind, and told me so much I didn't know about his work, and what people thought of him here, and how they admired him so much. Then I began to tell her things. I was so lonesome here! My husband was so busy, I hardly saw him, and she used to tell me what fine things he was doing. So I told her things too."

She spoke in broken little leaps, clutching her knitting bag closely in her lap, glancing still furtively at the hall door between her faltering sentences.

"Then I learned one day what a terrible woman she really was."

I gazed at her in wonder. To think she was capable of such duplicity as her earlier defense of the woman!

"One day she said the stars were against him. Everything was black, and in a chaos. If I could find out what was worrying him, she could help to clarify things. So I went home and—I went through his papers, as she suggested. I told her some things I'd found out in them. He'd been going to see Justice Frazier, for one thing."

Her thin voice sank to a whisper when she mentioned Justice Frazier's name.

"She said it was too late. There was a commotion in the stars already. The very next day my husband was bitterly attacked on the floor of the Senate. He said someone had been spying on him, and was trying to discredit him. I was so frightened, I went to Madame Rosa, and she said she had certain influences, and I was to give her a thousand dollars so that she could exert them. And since then—I've been paying her all the time. I've paid her out of my own money, but if my husband ever finds out I've been to her, then he'll know it was me. That I gave them the information. And now she wants five thousand dollars—she says the stars are all in commotion, and he's in trouble again."

The poor woman was shaking like a leaf as she told her story, incredible except that it came from just such a person. She looked at me imploringly out of terror-haunted eyes.

"Did you tell Priscilla this?" I asked.

"Oh, no! I told her about Madame Rosa because I wanted to find out what she thought of her. Oh, Mrs. Volney, what *shall* I do?"

"Tell your husband the whole thing, at once," I said, frankly, and I suppose a little brutally.

"I can't, I can't! He'd be so hurt!"

"Not as hurt as he's going to be if you keep on, Mrs. Mellish."

She shook her head with dull finality. "I'm afraid," she said simply.

"My dear woman," I said, "don't you see that you're being blackmailed by a malignant fortune teller? Whatever harm you've done, you haven't committed any crime, and you're just doing more harm by not making a clean breast of it. If, instead of telling Priscilla that you think Madame Rosa is wonderful, you had told her the truth, she'd drive the woman out of town, by threatening her with publicity. Caleb Williams could have done it. And it wouldn't cost anybody a cent."

"Oh, no!" she repeated pitifully. "It's my husband's political enemies. I've played into their hands, and he's ruined!"

"That's absurd on the face of it," I said, knowing very well how easily it could be true. "And anyway, you have a better chance to fight if you know what you're fighting. You aren't giving your husband a dog's chance. If I were you, I'd go to Madame Rosa and tell her that you intend to expose her, no matter how it affects you."

Mrs. Mellish shrank back as if I'd struck her. She was on the verge of a collapse.

"Then I'll do it for you."

She was almost on her knees in an instant.

"Oh, would you? Would you?" she cried beseechingly. "Don't tell her that—tell her I can't pay any more until January. I haven't any more money, and if I sell my bonds my husband will find it out."

"He may have to find it out anyway. It's best for him to. I know: why don't you let me tell Mr. Radstock? He's a lawyer, and he'd know what we ought to do?"

"Oh, no," she cried again. "You go to see her about 5: 30 this afternoon——"

She stopped abruptly, and I looked around. I hadn't heard anyone come in the room, but there in the doorway stood Major Heath and Pericles.

We both rose quickly and a little guiltily, I suppose. Mrs. Mellish's knitting bag slipped from her lap and struck the floor with a dull metallic clang. With a choking gasp she stared helplessly down at it, her body frozen into stone. Major Heath was across the room in a stride, picked up the bag and held it open. Among the balls of blue yarn and half-finished garments for Kentucky babies lay an automatic revolver equipped with a silencer.

Major Heath took it out, laying his handkerchief over it first.

"This," he said simply, "is the gun that killed Justice Frazier."

With a low gasp Mrs. Mellish sank, a crumpled white heap, to the floor.

We collected our startled wits and did the proper things—I mean I collected mine, for nothing ever seemed to startle Major Heath. He telephoned Mr. Whipple and I put Mrs. Mellish to bed. She was in a bad way, running a temperature, and out of her mind. She carried on about Madame Rosa, imploring me hysterically and disconnectedly to go see her. We called a doctor, but he couldn't get out until after lunch. Jocelyn and Thalia, who'd been in Jocelyn's room all morning, took charge of her while I went back downstairs.

Senator Mellish wasn't in the house, and I think Heath rather hesitated about finding him until Mr. Whipple came. On the other hand, the man's wife was ill, and our duty was clear. Major Heath was clever about it; he sent Pericles after him. He thought that was safe, considering what the Senator knew about Pericles, and what Pericles now knew about the Senator.

I wanted to tell Mr. Radstock, but Major Heath didn't give me a chance to get away. I wanted especially to tell him about Mrs. Mellish and Madame Rosa, in spite of her injunction, because I knew he was the man to advise me about putting a stop to the wretched business. It would have saved a lot of trouble later if I had told Major Heath right then and there; but in view of the affair of the gun I felt it would not be quite fair to Mrs. Mellish. I think I understood a little of the terror that she lived with.

Pericles came in with Senator Mellish. He said later that he hadn't told him anything except that his wife was ill, but he thought Mellish sensed something wrong at once. He asked where Major

Heath was; Pericles said at the house; and they came up together without saying a word to each other. He found the Senator sitting in the summer house on the lowest terrace.

Mellish saw Major Heath and me sitting in the drawing room and came in at once. Major Heath stood up, and their eyes met in a steady challenge. I suppose he felt there was no possible use in beating about the bush. He picked up Mrs. Mellish's bag and held it open so that the ugly little weapon was visible. Mellish took a step forward and sat down, his elbow on his knee and his head in his hand.

"Poor little Emily," he said. "Poor little Emily!"

It was theatrical, but it was effective. It took the blame off someone, somehow. I don't know whom, or just how, but it seemed to. Major Heath did not seem much impressed, however.

"Can you explain this, Senator Mellish?" he said. "Your wife's knitting bag here slipped off her lap when she got up suddenly; it was quite accidental. This is almost certainly the gun that killed Justice Frazier. I'm perfectly aware that you don't have to tell me anything about it, if you choose. I think I needn't tell you that it is illegal to carry a weapon equipped with a silencer—although I've no doubt you can explain it satisfactorily to Mr. Whipple when he comes. I've telephoned him."

Senator Mellish thought a moment. Then he

said, "I'm willing to tell you what I know about all this, Major Heath, from the beginning, in the presence of these two witnesses. I shall tell Whipple nothing until I've seen my lawyer. First I wish to see Mrs. Mellish."

He strode out of the room, his rather fine leonine head held high. I was proud of him, in some way, until Pericles remarked cynically, "Wants time to think it over."

He lighted a cigarette. Major Heath looked at him. I wondered if he would have smoked so indifferently if he'd known what we both knew about the early morning river sport.

In a few moments the Senator reappeared.

"Miss Frazier tells me you've called a doctor?" he asked in a perfectly matter-of-fact fashion.

"He won't be here until this afternoon," I said. "I didn't think it was necessary to call anyone from Washington—do you?"

"No."

He turned to Major Heath.

"That gun is mine," he said simply. "At least it came down here in my possession."

His straightforward story I thought was a revelation of much more than we had seen in him. It was far removed from his usual highly mannered, very florid style that he used even in ordinary speech.

"I don't ordinarily carry a revolver. In fact I don't even own one. This was given to me several days ago by a—by an acquaintance of mine. His name is Harry Mello. I accompanied him to a roadhouse outside of Washington, near Upper Marlborough, to investigate a tip I got from a friend on a Washington newspaper. Before we went in he said 'Got a gun?' When I said I hadn't he handed me that and said, 'Stick it in your pocket. You got too many birds after you to take a chance.'

"I wanted to return it but I couldn't very well. It was a gift made in the best spirit. I felt that only a difference in point of view made it unwelcome. I said 'Thanks' and put it in my pocket, thinking I'd throw it in the Potomac the first opportunity I had. When I got home I put it in my suitcase and forgot it. I didn't think of it again when I was near it until I packed to come down here. I thought then that the only thing to do was keep it with me. I know how open to misinterpretation such a thing would be if it were found in my rooms or could be traced to me.

"So I brought it down here in my suitcase. My wife took it out of my coat pocket—a coat that was in the suitcase—Saturday evening, and it's my guess that she's carried it with her in that bag ever since then."

"She hasn't spoken about it to you?" Major Heath asked.

"No."

"Suppose you tell me, Senator Mellish, just what you know about Justice Frazier's death from the beginning."

Mellish nodded in acquiescence. "That would be better. I came here hoping to talk to him, thinking we could work together on the matter that interested us both. He said he'd meet me at 4:15 in the summer house down there, with a third—whose name he did not mention. I went down there and waited for him. I waited ten minutes. He never came. I thought he was detained by Mr. Radstock, and I was getting chilly. I came up the steps on my way to the house. I saw him. He was lying on the terrace as you found him later. I started to raise a cry, when, to my horror, I saw that revolver, with the silencer on it, lying not a yard from him. I looked at the wound in his forehead, and saw at once that it was not suicide—there was no discoloration or burning. And I made my great mistake right then."

He stopped and looked from one of us to the other, his handsome face set grimly.

"I have political enemies, Major Heath, whom I know; and I have others I don't know. I've been attacked from strange quarters. And I saw this thing at once as a plot, a serious plot, against me. Because I did not shoot Justice Frazier, and I had no idea that that revolver was not in my suitcase. I had no notion how it came to be beside Justice Frazier's dead body but I realized how serious my position had become. Well, I guess I'll have to admit I showed the white feather. But I know too much of politics and justice to think that innocence is any shield. If that gun had been found beside Justice Frazier's body and its ownership traced to me, my political ruin would have followed, no matter how innocent I was afterwards found to be. I couldn't risk it; I dared not. I picked up that gun and put it in my pocket and came into the house through the garden door and went to the library. There I sat down with a book."

He looked from one of us to the other again, rather longer at Pericles than at me, and then turned his gaze to Major Heath again.

"I sat the rest of the afternoon with the gun in my pocket. Jem brought the news of the murder, and when it was first announced I watched the faces of all the people in the room. And I swear to you, Major Heath, that three people there, besides myself, knew it already."

"Who were they?" Major Heath asked.

"Miss Xanthopoulos, Mr. Xanthopoulos, and John Radstock."

Senator Mellish's answer came without hesitation. We all turned to Pericles, who was standing by the window, regarding us with a cool smile. He inclined his head politely and said, with great calmness, "I'm sure you're mistaken about my sister, Senator Mellish."

Major Heath looked from one to the other of them.

"Just a minute," he said. "Let's stick to your story, sir."

"There's no more of it, Major Heath," Mellish

replied. "When I dressed for dinner, I thought the safest place for my gun was in my coat pocket, until I had a safe way of getting rid of it. My wife must have found it. She said nothing about it to me, and it didn't occur to me at any time that that was what was on her mind. When we went to our room that night, I found that the thing was gone. Since then I've waited for it to turn up. I may say I expected it to turn up in different hands. And that, Major Heath, is what I know, and all I know, about Justice Frazier's death. As I said, I shall have a lawyer present before I say one word to Whipple. I think you understand my motive."

"Yes," Major Heath said quietly. "One other point. What were you and Justice Frazier to talk about, and why was it important to do it at once?"

"I'm sorry, sir," the Senator replied promptly, with a return to something of his old Chautauqua manner, "but that is a question I'm not at liberty to answer. If you'll excuse me now, I'll go to my wife."

He went out. Major Heath reflectively lit his pipe before he turned to Pericles, still standing dark and.calm in front of the window.

"And you, Mr. Xanthopoulos," he said. "Are you not talking until you have a lawyer?"

"I have nothing to say, with a lawyer or without one," Pericles said. "I'm inclined to think, however, that the Senator is what my sister calls 'touched'—or rather 'teched.' He's simply a preposterous fellow. He followed us ducking this morning, and shouted violently from the bushes when Vaughan went overboard. I expect to hear any moment that he's told Whipple I shoved Vaughan in and then pulled him out when I saw Mellish. The man isn't responsible."

Major Heath smiled.

"He's certainly not responsible for what he saw this morning, Xanthopoulos," he said, lighting his pipe again with great deliberation. "I saw it too, you know."

Pericles said nothing. I waited breathlessly for one of them to speak. They still stood there, looking steadily at one another, the cool smile still on Pericles's lips.

Then Major Heath said, "That will be your doctor, perhaps, Mrs. Volney. Whipple drives a Nash."

I hadn't even heard a car drive up, much less any particular sort of a car, but then the far-away lilt of a bell came to my ears. I went to greet the doctor. But it wasn't he. It was only Caleb Williams.

CHAPTER THIRTEEN

I LET him in. He'd come to see Major Heath, he
said, and as I wanted to go upstairs I left him with
Sebastian, who had come from the kitchen to answer the bell. Major Heath must have recognized
his voice, because he came out into the hall just
as I started up.

"Going to have a look at your patients, Mrs.
Volney?" he asked pleasantly.

"Somebody sick?" Caleb demanded with a start.

"Not exactly," Heath said, and turned to me
again.

"Will you do me a favor?"

"Surely. What is it?"

"Don't let your curiosity run away with you. It
might be dangerous."

With that cryptic admonition he turned back to
Caleb.

"Shall we go in here? How did you get on?"

He motioned to the door of the retiring room
across the hall from the library. I was still standing on the second step, my hand on the mahogany
banister. Major Heath glanced back at me as he
followed Caleb through the door. I smiled lightly,
but there was no answering twinkle in his eyes. He
was deadly serious. So I went on upstairs, consid-

erably perturbed, wondering what he meant by that very definite, if enigmatic, warning, and which of my patients, as he called them, he was thinking of. I wondered, too, how much of Mrs. Mellish's conversation he'd overheard, and what he'd think of my promise to her. Because I intended to go and see Madame Rosa, and more than that, I intended to get Mr. Radstock's advice before I went. Whatever our attitude towards the Senator was, this poor inexperienced woman was certainly not to blame for what had happened. She was as innocent as a gnat in a spider web.

As for Madame Rosa, I'd never seen her myself. I'd heard of her, as everybody who lives in Washington has, and as a matter of fact I'd been vaguely curious about her. I think I'd have gone to her, too, except that I was afraid Caleb or Jerry Blaine, or even Priscilla, would find it out. I'd never have heard the last of it. I could imagine Priscilla taking a dig at me in her column some day, if she ever found it out—which she would as sure as fate. Madame Rosa's initial fee was twenty-five dollars, so she's not in the class of ordinary practitioners. Her clients made dignified appointments, and invariably, so I'd heard, went back for more. It was all very discreet. They went in at one door and out at another. It was carefully arranged so that no one ever met anyone else. Not that it was clandestine at all—merely private. If her clients wished to tell their friends, well and good. Madame Rosa made a great point, people said, of emphasizing the fact that an interview with her was a closed secret. I'd heard, too, that the place was luxuriously furnished and dimly lighted, especially the consulting room, and that the whole atmosphere was strictly confidential.

And undoubtedly Mrs. Mellish was exactly the type of person who went there, and certainly just the sort who'd get involved when they did go. But at that, most people, women particularly, are amazingly credulous—almost eager to be duped. I imagined, from all I'd heard, that this woman was a shrewd judge of character, besides knowing perfectly all the tricks of the trade.

But I'm getting ahead of myself.

Norman Vaughan was still in bed. His head ached and he looked pretty much all in. I was dying of curiosity, of course, but I curbed it. Major Heath's warning was still in my ears. I rang for Sebastian to refill his ice pack and left him in peace.

The two girls were in Thalia's room with the door open, listening for any sign from Mrs. Mellish in the next room.

"She's been quiet for half an hour," Jocelyn said. "I think she's asleep."

"She kicked up a frightful row at first," Thalia added, much less solicitously. "John came down to see what it was all about, and went back upstairs. I think he's avoiding everybody."

"He's not, either, Thalia."

A faint flush mounted Jocelyn's fair pale face.

"He has a lot of work to do. He was supposed to go back to New York last night. He's working on an important brief."

"Rot," said Thalia. "You'll notice that John never comes home without an important brief. And either it's all hooey and an excuse to see you, or it's a brainy scheme to get Mr. Radstock's opinion for nothing. He looks it over. If they sent it to him through the mails it'd cost them five thousand dollars."

"Well, why shouldn't his father help him?"

"He should, my child. But John shouldn't retire to the attic and work on a brief when the rest of us have to sit about jumping every time we hear a footstep lest it's Sheriff Carter coming to arrest us. Oh, I'm sorry, Jocelyn!" she cried penitently, when the quick tears came to Jocelyn's eyes and she turned away.

"It's all right," she said with a wan smile. "Who was that downstairs, Diane?"

"Caleb."

"Caleb!" Thalia cried, delighted. "Where is he, Diane?"

She danced gayly down the stairs, calling, "Caleb! Caleb!" It was the first merry note that had sounded through those halls since Justice Frazier's murder.

Jocelyn smiled. "I don't know what I'd do without her, and you, Diane," she said wistfully.

"And John," I added.

She shook her head sadly.

"He's not much help. I've hardly seen him, Diane. I don't know what's the matter. It almost seems as if he's avoiding me. I don't know why. He and Dad had a long talk a few weeks ago, and ever since then he's been different. Of course I don't care. I don't care at all."

"Has it occurred to you that your father may have asked him to—change, Jocelyn?" I said, sitting down beside her on the chaise-longue. "And then aren't you being—well, let's say awfully nice to Pericles and Norman Vaughan, and rather cavalier with John?"

"I'm not going to let him think I care, if he wants to——" She stopped, with a tiny catch in her breath that was almost a sob.

"Don't be silly, dear," I said gently. "You'll learn, my dear, that the minute you fall in love with anybody you refuse to give him the benefit of the smallest doubt. Maybe John is just as upset as you are—probably a good deal more."

"I'm not upset in the least about John, Diane," she said primly. "I just don't think he's being very—very thoughtful. That's all."

"Of course not," I agreed. "But men never are."

My excellent advice was interrupted by the return of Thalia, who came up the stairs and into our room with elaborate stealth.

"Sssh!" She tiptoed in with her finger at her lips.

"Caleb's giving Major Heath the lowdown on everybody! My dears, it's killing! I *didn't* listen,

Diane, you do me an injustice. Anyway, I'm a Greek and we don't have the same ethics about eavesdroppers that you Nordics do. But I didn't really listen, because Caleb'll tell me all about it anyway. But he *did* say that Norman Vaughan has no visible means of support. Lord, when he starts on us! I can't remember which of my aunts paid for my last meal."

We stared at her.

"It's true, I swear it is! If I didn't get ten thousand a year from my grandmother in Philadelphia I'd starve, that's the situation *I'm* in. And they'll find it out! And poor Norman, who's got more money than anybody I know, has no visible means of support! Ha, ha!"

"They mean they don't know where he gets it all," I put in.

"Whose beastly business is it where he gets it, I'd like to know?" she demanded hotly. "I think Caleb's a rotten busybody and I'm going to tell him so."

"But not now," I said firmly. "You stay here with Jocelyn. And when Mrs. Mellish wakes up take her temperature, or something. At least stay around until the doctor comes."

"O. K.," she groaned, and collapsed on the chintz arm of her chair with a cigarette in one hand and a bar of chocolate in the other.

I thought for a moment I'd go up and tell John what a stupid person he was, and then changed my mind. It wasn't, after all, any of my business. I decided that Thalia would do it with a more brutal hand and with greater effect. I was quite right about that; on the other hand, if I had seen John just then I might have saved a great deal of trouble.

Downstairs Sebastian told me that Priscilla had phoned to say she wouldn't be back for lunch but that she'd try to get out for dinner. It was part of Priscilla's faculty for making herself invaluable. She appreciated social problems, the business of dinner-table conversation with difficult people, and the rest of it, and she never shirked. I was particularly grateful to her then because I knew she'd rather stay in town to Nancy Foster's coming-out party at the Mayflower than come clear back to Monckton Hall. It was quite unnecessary, too, for her to come back—she didn't, as it turned out—because Mrs. Mellish would still be in her room and the rest of us could manage very nicely.

I asked Sebastian if he'd told her anything about Norman or Mrs. Mellish, and he said he hadn't. He gave you the uneasy feeling that if one's best friend were dying he'd never bother to mention it. A close-mouthed servant is rare, and I suppose Sebastian's discretion was all the more remarkable because he'd been at Monckton Hall since he was born and was as much an integral part of it as Mr. Radstock himself—and more than John, somehow.

I've wondered since what difference it would have made in all our lives if Sebastian had told

Priscilla that Norman Vaughan and Mrs. Mellish were confined to their rooms. Or for that matter if I'd called her up as I started to do as I passed the telephone on my way to see Mr. Radstock. Instead, I decided to wait and telephone from my shop in town that afternoon.

I was still thinking mostly about Mrs. Mellish and Madame Rosa. If she had an appointment with the woman at 5:30, the best thing for me to do, obviously, was to keep it, and come to some understanding with her before Senator Mellish found the whole business out.

Obviously something would have to be done at once. With the best political will in the world they could hardly keep Jem in jail any longer. If Senator Mellish admitted the "death gun"—as the papers say—as his own, as he had done to Heath, Mr. Whipple would be bound to arrest him. Even if Whipple were anxious to keep the Senator's name out of it, and even if he acted in collusion with the Washington police, there were still too many reporters whose papers were aching to "get something on" Mellish. It was humanly impossible to keep it quiet very long. But of course, Senator Mellish hadn't yet admitted to Whipple that the revolver was his, and he had told us that he didn't intend to do so without legal advice.

I don't know very much about the theory of criminal law, but I do know that in Washington (and I see no reason to believe Fairfax County, Virginia, is any better), a bad loophole is better than none. Perhaps that was Senator Mellish's idea too. If he was safe as long as he didn't tell Mr. Whipple what he'd told us, then he was safe at least for the time being. Major Heath was not in a position to give out information, and I wouldn't. I suppose the Senator felt he had enough "on" Pericles to make him keep still. So until he talked to Whipple he was safe; and if he refused to do that until he got a lawyer, he was safe until the next day anyway; and if Whipple didn't get around to talking to him right away, then he was safe until Whipple did. Procrastination is a great thing, and sometimes invaluable.

In any case I'd have time to see Madame Rosa, and maybe, if necessary, talk to Senator Mellish before the storm broke.

I was planning to leave just after lunch, so I went over to the wing and talked to Mr. Radstock about it.

"I think you're very wise, Diane," he said, with an approving smile. "I think you ought to tell Major Heath. He was just here to tell me about finding the gun. I can't help admiring Mrs. Mellish, if she's kept that thing in her bag, under our very noses, probably terrified lest one of you women might pick it up or touch it. I didn't think she had that much pluck."

"But she begged me not to tell him," I objected. "After all, her position is slightly different."

"You're right, I suppose," he agreed. "You can tell better after you've seen the woman and talked to her. Maybe that will be enough. Blackmail is cowardly business, and tricky business. Perhaps Mrs. Mellish hasn't done anything, or said anything, of any importance. The woman has probably simply worked on her fear of her husband until she's beside herself. It's been my experience with that sort of thing, my dear, that it's hardly ever as bad as the victim thinks it is. I wish I could see the woman for you—but you'll manage it. Decide after you've seen her whether it's necessary to tell Heath."

"What about taking Priscilla, or Caleb, along, to make her think she's going to be exposed?"

A barely perceptible twinkle came into Mr. Radstock's calm eyes.

"You might. Priscilla's column was a little thin this morning; I expect she'd be glad to pick up something. I imagine she could give Madame What's-her-name a hard jolt, too, if she put her mind to it. You've never been to her, yourself?"

"No indeed. I can't imagine anything that's going to happen to me that's worth twenty-five dollars—in advance—to know about."

"Wise girl, Diane. How's Vaughan making out?"

"Pretty rocky, and not very communicative. By the way, John is in his attic and won't come out, and Jocelyn is almost in tears. Thinks he's treating her very badly and all that."

"They're both old enough to take care of their own affairs, Diane. Or John is."

A shade passed over his face. He hesitated a moment and seemed about to tell me something. Then he shook his head a little sadly.

"Well, Heath says young Williams is here. What's he after?"

"I don't know. Thalia says she overheard him giving Major Heath the 'lowdown' on everybody. All she got before she retired with her hands to her ears was that Norman has—as she put it, or as Caleb put it—no visible means of support. She got the idea Caleb was supplying a financial summary of all of us, past and present. I don't think John knows he's here."

Mr. Radstock seemed to be hardly listening to me. He was thinking of something else. After a little he said, as if just coming to a deliberate and rather unpleasant conclusion, "By the way, Diane, there's something I might just as well tell you, though I'd planned not to. John came in to see me this morning, before breakfast. I didn't tell Heath, for obvious reasons, and I didn't want to bother you. It's different, I think, in light of what you have told me about Mrs. Mellish."

He hesitated again, then continued with an expression of gathering pain:

"John wanted me to lend him ten thousand dollars. He declined to say what he wanted it for, and I declined to give it, or lend it, for that matter. Ten thousand dollars is still a lot of money; too much, I told him, for—anybody's silence."

I looked at him open-mouthed, I'm afraid.

"Mr. Radstock! Not——"

He nodded. "I'm afraid so."

He brought his stick down sharply on the floor. I looked at him in what must have been a comical consternation. His face gradually relaxed into his charming, urbane smile.

"I'm afraid it is. Do you suppose Jocelyn has done something indiscreet?" he added whimsically. But underneath he was not whimsical at all.

"Because I can't imagine John being indiscreet himself, or if he was, not being willing to confess it. I told him, Diane, that it wasn't a matter of ten thousand dollars merely, but of the later demands that were inevitable. That silence was a matter that one bought and kept on buying, without end. I offered him any other service I could give him; but not that. Now when you see Madame Rosa, remember what I've told you. There's the lunch gong. If you'll wait a moment I'll be with you."

He picked up his stick and limped into the other room. In a few minutes he came back with a check in his hand.

"I've changed my mind, or what I like to call my mind," he said with a smile, and handed me the check. "Will you be my agent? If you find that John is in Madame Rosa's hands—for some reason that I'm confident is not connected with him only—and this is needed to tide him over until some legal action can be taken, use it. John was disturbed this morning; perhaps I was too hard on him. Now I'm not certain it's the same thing; but coincidences like this don't happen very often; things have a way of being connected. When is Mrs. Mellish's appointment?"

"Half-past five. I'll be back for dinner. I was going to stay in town, but I'll come back and tell you about it."

I folded up his check for ten thousand dollars, wondering about all this—doubting, yet forced to believe—and put it in my pocket.

"Thank you. Shall we go over to lunch?"

We went out, through the cupboard door into the library.

"We must do something about this hyphen, when we do the house, Diane. I've never liked that cellar entrance here, and I like it less now."

The rest of them were waiting for us in the drawing room, except, of course, Mrs. Mellish and Norman Vaughan. I didn't notice that John wasn't there until Sebastian came in and said to Mr. Radstock, "Mr. John says he wouldn't be in to lunch, suh. He says to say he's gone to town, an' he's not comin' back till late."

I couldn't help hearing what he said, and I glanced at Mr. Radstock. His control was perfect. Only the barest tightening of his jaw showed that he realized that this announcement might have a deeper meaning than was apparent.

"Very well, Sebastian," he said quietly. Then he turned, perfectly collected, to the rest of us. "Shall we go in?"

"I hear you're going to town this afternoon, Mrs. Volney," Major Heath said when we were seated. "Are you coming back this evening?"

"Yes. I intended staying in until after to-morrow, but I think I'd better get back. To look after Mrs. Mellish."

"May I go with you?"

"I'd be charmed."

Our eyes met and we both smiled.

CHAPTER FOURTEEN

WE LEFT Monckton Hall about two o'clock. Caleb decided he'd go with us. He left his car behind, saying that if he didn't get back for it we could give it to Jem for Christmas.

"Not that he'd be found dead in it," I remarked.

"Like a woman," he retorted. "Just because I'm not a beastly plutocrat, and have to work for a living. You've got me on two counts, Diane. I never had a husband die and leave me a cool million, and nobody's ever going to pay me five cents to tell 'em what rotten taste they've got. As a matter of fact you've got to drive a Lincoln. If your foolish clients met you in a Ford they'd think you weren't so hot and you'd be back living on the dole—in a manner of speaking. Now if anybody saw me in a Lincoln they'd know I was the liquor ring, and they'd put me on the spot some high noon on G Street."

"Aren't you afraid they will anyway?" I asked maliciously. "Pericles says you've got a bet with your city editor that you'll get the head man in the Washington ring before New Year's."

"Don't let it surprise you if I do," he said, more seriously than I'd expected. I looked at him in surprise.

"What do you mean, Caleb? You're not serious?"

"Of course not," he said with a shrug. "I haven't got very dangerous yet. A thousand's the biggest offer I've had. That's what gets me. I know a couple of birds that pull down that much a month —regular."

"Cheer up," I said. "Some day you'll get a bullet in your head, and you'll die happy. You'll make the front page with headlines. Death, Not Bribe, Shows Correspondent's Fine Integrity."

He grunted and lighted a cigarette.

"Well, I fancy that's about what happened to Justice Frazier," Major Heath remarked imperturbably.

Somehow that brought it unpleasantly close to home. I stole a sideways glance at Caleb, sitting next to me. His face was set and he was looking straight ahead. I couldn't think of anything but Thalia's joy at the mention of his name, and I wondered with a little pang if he was the next, and if another tragedy to blight another young life was waiting for us around some corner that we had to pass. We must all have thought something of the sort, because none of us said anything until after we'd come to Pohick Church. I stopped to get some gas.

"Are you going to find out who killed Justice Frazier?" I asked Major Heath point-blank, when we'd started again.

He smiled wryly.

"That's hardly a fair question, Mrs. Volney," he evaded.

"Do you know now?"

"No. Quite frankly, I don't."

"Is Mellish in on it?" Caleb said curiously.

Again Major Heath smiled.

"Can't you two be more discreet?" he said. "Still, I might as well be frank. I did think the Senator was involved in some way until I found it was his revolver that did the work. Now I'm not so sure. It has all the appearance, do you see, of the put-up job. And on the other hand—well, the Senator may have acutely figured all that out, and maybe—merely maybe, you understand—maybe that's why we found it."

I scoffed at that. "Don't be absurd! Mrs. Mellish wasn't play-acting this morning."

"Perhaps not. But granted it was pure accident as far as she was concerned, I still have a feeling that we would have found that gun some way or another before we left Monckton Hall to-day. I've been waiting for it for two days. Would you believe that this morning I *knew* we'd find it to-day? I don't *look* psychic, do you think?"

"No one less," I said promptly.

"Well, I am," he said with a grin. "Some of my most marvelous successes have been due to sheer feeling and intuition. Well, I knew it would turn up. And so did the Senator. He's been going over his story for some time—in front of the mirror, probably."

"He may have done," I said; "but she didn't know it, I'm sure. I'd swear she didn't; and he'd never let her carry that gun around knowingly, and then some fine day have her just bring it out and say, 'Is this by any chance what you're looking for?' She's been almost demented."

He smiled again at that. "Well," he said, "there are still three points to clear up. And when they're cleared up . . ."

He shrugged his great shoulders, and was silent. I wondered then if he knew about Madame Rosa, and started to ask him. Then I changed my mind. I didn't want Caleb to know about it, because it's the sort of thing he can't resist to save his soul. It's occurred to me so many times since then that it might have made all the difference in the world if I'd spoken up and said I was going to see her for Mrs. Mellish that afternoon. Then I wonder if it would have. If perhaps in the long run it wasn't just as well I didn't. It isn't a question to answer easily; it's all so mixed up with so many things. Anyway, I didn't tell him, and our talk shifted from the Mellishes.

Caleb was delighted with the idea of anyone's bashing Norman—whom he hates—over the head, and insisted that the only bad thing was that Mellish had raised an alarm, so the job couldn't be finished.

"It's what any decent person would do," he said positively, "if they had him off by himself."

"Why, Caleb!" I said. "What have you got against Norman?"

"Not a blessed thing, except that he was born and didn't die."

"You're jealous of him, Mr. Williams."

"Not a doubt of it, Mrs. Volney. Listen! What I want to know is this: what's the matter with old John?"

"Nothing," I said.

"What's he wintering up in the attic for?"

"He's working, stupid, on a brief."

"Yeah? I think he's gone off the deep end somewhere. I was looking out of the library window before lunch, and I saw him going down the front steps. I dashed out to see him, but he'd gone, and a second or two later along he came down the drive in that old machine of his, doing sixty or more."

"Really?" I said. "I wonder where he was going."

"Probably to the Congressional Library to work on the brief," said Major Heath. "Now I'm going to the Frazier house, Mrs. Volney. Is that anywhere near where you're going?"

"Yes. I'm going to my shop, and it's quite near. I'll give you the address and you can come back when you're ready. About six, say? You're going back to Monckton Hall, aren't you?"

"Or what do you say to our going with you?" he said. "I'm meeting Whipple and Lieutenant MacKenny of the Homicide Squad at the Frazier house at four o'clock. It's three now. If you've nothing to do we'll go with you. I'd like to see your shop."

"Oh, let's go see La Garbo instead," Caleb protested. "There's nothing in Diane's place but rags and junk. Have you got the Tudor room from Marl Castle up yet? That'll make Heath feel swell. Fine old paneled room lifted up bodily and brought over from Cornwall to sell to a profiteer."

Major Heath shrugged his shoulders.

" 'The old order changeth'," he said. "We sell them, you buy them. As a matter of fact Lord Leighton had to sell Marl Castle to pay death duties. Which room have you? Has it got the Leighton arms carved in the stone overmantel?"

I nodded. "Do you know it?"

"Rather. Leighton was in my form at Winchester. I spent several holidays there. That was long ago."

"You make me feel like a vandal," I said weakly. "I'd much rather you'd go on to Frazier's and not come in at all. But here we are if you insist."

"And we do insist. But this isn't a *shop*."

"Not really. It's an old house, 1780, that I've restored and furnished in period. I don't sell chintz by the yard over the counter. But it's better to call it a shop than a studio."

"And clients, not customers," Caleb put in.

We went in. Miss Arthur, who's my secretary and assistant, came to meet us. I introduced her.

"Miss Stone telephoned, Mrs. Volney," she said.

"I didn't know you were going to be in. I told her you were at Monckton Hall. She said she'd called there but you had left. Shall I get her for you?"

"Please do." I turned to my two friends. "Would you like to go around? The Marl Castle room is upstairs. Miss Arthur will take you over as soon as she phones Priscilla. If you'll excuse me I'll get at some work I have to do."

I left them—Caleb making scurrilous remarks about a priceless mantel garniture in the drawing room—and went back to my office, which is the old kitchen of the house. Here Miss Arthur informed me that Priscilla had left her office, and that she'd left a message for her.

"That's good. Now take those two people through the house. Be tactful about the Tudor room—Major Heath played in it when he was a child. Is this all the mail?"

I sat down to look it over and make memoranda for Miss Arthur's use. My mail was not very exciting: several requests from manufacturers to use their soap, furniture oil, or wax in return for free advertising, the usual requests for advice and the loan of pieces for exhibitions. However, I got the letters I came for especially and put them in my bag.

Meanwhile Miss Arthur had showed Major Heath and Caleb over the place and they came back to the office. We chatted a moment about the things, and then Major Heath looked at his wrist watch.

"We'd better be getting on, Williams," he said. "I'll be back for you at six, Mrs. Volney? Good-bye."

I went to the door with them and watched them set off down Connecticut Avenue towards the Circle. Back in my office I talked over some details of our business with Miss Arthur. I left her finally working at the typewriter while I went upstairs to have a look around.

The room from Marl Castle I've got set up in the back room on the second floor. It's the pride of the shop, of course, although it is rather odd to come up a Georgian staircase and find yourself in a Sixteenth Century room perfect in every detail. I sat down by the fireplace and lighted a cigarette. It was just 4:30. I had another forty minutes or so and a lot of thinking to do before I tackled Madame Rosa. I took the letters out of my bag, read them desultorily and burned them in the fireplace, conveniently there in front of me. Somehow I had no interest in anything, just now. I decided suddenly that I'd go abroad for six months and get away from the whole atmosphere of Washington. I sat there planning what I'd do on the Riviera instead of what I'd say to Madame Rosa until almost time to leave.

She lived, I discovered, in a very ordinary brownstone house, period 1880, on O Street. It's the sort of house that's entirely unobtrusive. A limousine or a butcher's cart could stop there without being noticeable. A faint light glimmered through the transom. I lifted the iron knocker and let it fall. My heart was beating like a trip-hammer but I pulled myself together and tried to adopt the manner I use with rich customers whose business I don't want.

I waited interminably. Then I knocked again. I was sure she was home, because Mrs. Mellish had a definite appointment. I waited and waited. Still no one came. Finally it occurred to me that perhaps when one had a definite appointment with a fortune teller one was supposed just to walk in. I tried the door very tentatively. It was not locked. I decided it was proper to be firm about this, so I simply opened it and walked in.

The hall was an ordinary Victorian middle-class entryway with a hat tree and a majolica umbrella stand, with carpeted stairs going up on the right and double doors hung with heavy green portières opening to the rooms on the left.

I rapped gently on these double doors and waited. Again no answer. Again I tried the door knob, and again I walked in. This, I gathered, was the reception room. It was gorgeously furnished; incredibly luxurious, with heavy Persian rugs, long velvet hangings, soft deep chairs. It was dimly lighted, and a curious, faintly seductive and mysterious odor, like that of sandalwood, seemed to move through the air. It was prosaically wicked, in some way—as if it had been planned to break down Middle Western inhibitions.

There was a door to my right as I came in. It

was slightly ajar. I went over to it at once and knocked on it. I had the most strange feeling, as if I might have been an infinite distance from the doorstep with the light faintly glimmering through the transom. I'd come probably forty feet. It might have been a thousand miles and a hundred years, all seemed so remote, and so removed from the dusky fact of O Street.

Again no answer. I pushed open the door, and stood gazing into a half-darkened room. At first I saw only a table with two great crystals on it, one a deep living red, the other silver, which kept going on, repeating themselves, each reflecting the other into the very center of each globe. Then I saw something. Behind the table was a woman.

The rest of it is still very hard to remember.

I saw a swirl of red hair, over a black velvet gown. Two long white hands, contorted and twisted like claws, lay on the velvet lap. Two eyes staring, hideously bulging; a tongue . . . O God! I looked and closed my eyes; grasped the velvet curtain, and clung to it for a moment that seemed interminable. There was a sound behind me. I was terrified, but I couldn't scream. I couldn't even make a sound. I opened my eyes; it was Major Heath. He was standing beside me in the doorway. He brushed me aside without a word, as if I'd not been there, and stepped across the dark little room until he was behind that table where Madame Rosa lay, horribly strangled, with her frightful hands folded in her lap. I was hideously fascinated. I couldn't go, but I thought I'd go mad if I stayed. I tore my eyes from her terrible figure and looked at Major Heath. He was standing there looking down at her; a little pale himself, I thought. Gradually the expression on his face changed to a bitterly twisted tragic smile— if it was a smile. He took a step to the chair and laid his hand gently on that ghastly red head. I almost screamed. His hand moved, and in it was the red wig. I looked at it and then back at Madame Rosa, and saw one thing before I fainted. The figure in the chair was not Madame Rosa. It was Priscilla Stone.

CHAPTER FIFTEEN

WHEN I came to I was lying on a divan in the outer room. Major Heath was bending over me. My first blurred vision was of his rugged face, concerned and kindly. The other thing came back with a rush. I closed my eyes again to blot it out, but it was still there, hideously branded on my very soul. No mere physical closing of the eyes could rid me of it. It still comes back sometimes in my dreams, and I struggle to get away from it. But now I sat up and pulled my hat back in place simply as a reflex action.

"That's better!" His solicitude gave way to a half-encouraging, half-mocking smile. "We haven't time to faint, you know. Will you be all right here for a while? I've got to get the police, and I want to have a look around before they come."

"Then can't I phone?" I asked, a little hysterically. He shook his head.

"The phone's probably in there, and you'd better keep out."

So I sat there. He went back into the little room where Priscilla Stone sat waiting. I tried to think what this meant, I wondered what had happened to change everything so suddenly. Here we'd gone on for years, a civilized, cultivated group of people, never very concerned with anything not perfectly decorous and polite. What had come to throw us into a mad jungle of elemental passions? How had Murder so come to stalk our path? At what point in the smooth stream of our life had something changed the even current into a swirling, seething whirlpool of disaster and death? It was fantastic, incredible. It couldn't be Priscilla in there with Madame Rosa's wig on. It wasn't possible! I must have dreamed it! But then it came back again, and I closed my eyes to let it move on past me, like some insane emanation.

I could hear Major Heath moving briskly about, if I listened. He sounded far away, and when he spoke his voice was indistinct. The heavy curtains and rugs made the place almost sound-proof. He was calling Caleb and the police, but I didn't hear just what he said.

After that I imagined him examining everything in the room. I tried to follow him around in my mind; but I kept relentlessly coming upon the thing in the chair and trying to realize—or not to realize—that it was really Priscilla.

Suddenly I heard a low buzz. I thought it was the door bell. I got up and peered out of the front window. It was quite dark; the street light showed through the bare branches of the elm trees. The street was deserted. There was no one on the porch. I thought it was too soon to expect the police. Then I heard Major Heath say "Hello!" and it flashed into my mind that it was just as well that the person at the other end of the line couldn't see that room into which he was speaking.

"Hello!" I heard again, this time a little louder. Then silence. In a few seconds I heard him ask the operator to trace the call that had just come in, and explain that it was an emergency and he was acting for the police. Pretty soon I heard him say "Thanks very much," and put the receiver back. I went and sat down in a deep chair by the front window. I had the most curious feeling of apathy, and yet I was acutely interested in what they were going to do. I wanted to go, to get away from the place; at the same time I wanted to stay. I *had* to stay, somehow. So I sat there in my chair, waiting.

In a few minutes Major Heath came back. He was entirely businesslike. A cold shiver went down my spine. There was something very hard about him that rather frightened me. Someone was going to pay the last full measure for that horrible deed. I simply sat where I was and watched him. I didn't quite dare to ask him anything. He gave me a kindly, encouraging smile.

"Not very pretty, is it? Murder isn't, you know. Ah, that must be the police. If you think you can stick it, you might wait until we see what they're going to do. Then I'll take you home."

They came in. Lieutenant MacKenny of the Homicide Squad and two detectives. They impressed me at that moment, and later, too, as most of their sort that I've seen do. Simple men in a complex environment, who've learned the ropes by heart and get around very well as long as nothing varies from the norm. Hardboiled and basically sentimental, they respond to a touching tale with curious naïveté. Major Heath and MacKenny had met before. They shook hands all around before they went into the next room.

In a minute or two one of the detectives came out and eyed me doubtfully.

"You'd better get out of here, Miss. This ain't no place for you."

I said I was waiting for Major Heath and he grunted.

"We gotta have more light in here." He hunted for an additional light for some time and finally took the shades off the lamps on the table. He looked around in the harsh barren glare of the denuded bulbs.

"Now we can see something. Pretty swell layout. Wonder how Miss Stone got in here?"

That was what I'd been wondering for some time. How had Priscilla—prim, vivacious, clever Priscilla—got herself murdered in that other room, all rigged up in Madame Rosa's trappings? It seemed tragically preposterous.

"D'you find her?" the man asked. His name was Blake, I learned later on.

I nodded, and he whistled. "Must of given you a jolt. Friend of yours?"

"Yes. A very dear friend."

He whistled again. "She was a mighty nice little woman." Then he added cheerfully, "I guess that'll be Doc Martin. Sounds like his bus."

It was Caleb, however. People are always mixing him up with doctors, apparently.

"Hello, Williams. Leave it to you guys to get here before the corpse is cold," Mr. Blake greeted him, and then remembered me with great consternation and begged my pardon clumsily.

"Good God, Diane, what are you doing here?" Caleb said.

"Waiting," I answered. He went to the door of the room.

"Good God!" He turned back, and his face was the color of putty.

Another man came in; it was the doctor this time. Blake pointed discreetly to the inner room and wagged his head in my direction. He sensed in a clumsy sort of way that this meant something different to us from what he'd thought, and he was acutely embarrassed. I remember now how I wondered at the time that he would be.

Caleb went back into the room with the doctor. I waited still. The reception room was strangely vulgar now in the glaring light—like an over-dressed woman with purple powder and green fingernails on Fifth Avenue at high noon. But Mr. Blake preferred it light, and I didn't like to protest.

Soon more official-looking people came in with cameras and other paraphernalia. Lieutenant Mac-

Kenny appeared, to give them directions. Major
Heath came out, after they'd gone in the dark
room, and he and MacKenny talked in low tones
in the bow window. I heard something about calling the Police Commissioner, and somebody else
came in to say that he'd be here shortly. I hoped
Major Heath would be ready to go before he
came. I know him a little, socially—he's an army
man—but I felt that meeting him under the circumstances would be a strain.

Caleb came out with the doctor. Dr. Martin
was shaking his head and rubbing his jaw vigorously. "Two hours at least," he said. "No doubt
of it. Neat job, that."

"There's bedside manner for you," Caleb whispered, coming over to my chair in the corner and
making a futile effort to be himself. He was shaking like a leaf. He and I, in fact, seemed to be the
only ones who didn't take it as all in the day's
work. The rest of them seemed to get a certain
amount of satisfaction out of it, as if it were their
turn now to do something clever. I don't mean
Major Heath. Of course it *was* different for us.
They thought of that hideous thing in there as
another crime, the murder of a Washington newspaper woman. We thought of it as Priscilla Stone,
good old Priscilla, with a whole background of
good-natured jokes, and constant helpfulness and
kindness to people she liked. She was an original
if there ever was one.

I was thinking that when the man with the

camera came out and asked us to go into the hall-way so he could get some pictures.

"It's so damn dark in this hole," I heard some-one complain. The doctor departed, and Major Heath wandered off down the hall towards the back of the house, and I followed him.

The whole place was dark. We went into the dining room, very well furnished in good repro-duction Sheraton. Major Heath looked around.

"What do you think of this, Mrs. Volney?" he asked, indicating the place generally.

"Not bad," I replied. "It just looks as if nobody ever lived in it. It's never been used."

He nodded assent, and we passed through an-other door into the pantry. Here again the place was furnished. The cupboards were full of rather good china, but the dishes hadn't the gloss that indicates Ivory soap and hot water. There was a Frigidaire in one corner, and Major Heath, cov-ering the lower part of the handle with his hand-kerchief, opened it. A bottle of cream, a small stick of butter that had been used once or twice, a couple of pots of *paté de foie gras,* a container with the remains of fresh caviare, and a few oranges were its contents.

"Madame Rosa had a delicate appetite," the Englishman remarked, closing the box.

The kitchen was spotless and unused. The cup-board shelves were well stocked with staples of all sorts. The tea canister was half empty, and there was only a little coffee left. On the shelf at the bottom of the cupboard were some dozens of bottled wines—Sherry and Madeira chiefly—and liqueurs. There were two burnt matches in a pottery jar on the back of the gas stove. The shade at the window was drawn to the bottom, and the back door, which had a formidable-looking Yale lock, was double-bolted.

Major Heath looked around minutely, without any comment until he opened one of the two doors on the other side of the cupboard. It opened on some dark steps leading down to a basement. The other door led upstairs.

"Shall we go up or down, Mrs. Volney?" he asked, rather as if we were doing an entertaining puzzle. "Shall we make it up?"

We went up. We went through bedrooms and bathrooms on two floors. They were like the rooms downstairs, furnished but not lived in. Only one bedroom, the front one on the second floor, looked as if it had been occupied at all, and that only occasionally. Major Heath picked up the comb from the dressing table, very cautiously taking it by one edge, and looked carefully at it, turning it this way and that in the light. Then he examined the hairbrush there.

"Red hairs and black," he said. "The red ones dead, the black alive. What do you make of that?"

I had no faintest idea, and said so.

"What about these, then?"

He pointed to the two jars of powder on the table. I looked at them. One was a normal daytime powder for brunettes and the other an almost indigo evening powder. I explained, and he nodded. Not very much interested, I thought, in women's cosmetics.

The closet was next. It was empty, but in the bathroom opening off to the left, over the lower hall, there was evidence of use. We could hear the others moving about downstairs, but the floors we were on were heavily carpeted, and I don't think they could hear us. We paused a moment on the threshold of the bath, thinking we heard a footstep; but no one came, and we stopped inside.

On hangers in a built-in wardrobe were six long velvet gowns—purple, deep wine, mulberry, and blue. On a shoe rack beneath them were some exotic-looking sandals. Madame Rosa's garments were unusual, to say the least, but certainly all in her manner.

Hanging next to them were some other more conventional clothes. I started, and looked aghast at Major Heath: the first one of them was a green wool crêpe Molyneux that I'd bought in Paris in August and sent to Priscilla Stone. Major Heath met my stare without a trace of surprise.

"Mrs. Volney, has it just occurred to you that Priscilla Stone *was* Madame Rosa?" he asked gently.

I sat down on the bench in front of the little Louis Quinze make-up table, and tried to understand. Major Heath moved my hand and put it in my lap. I was barely conscious that he'd touched me until I saw him wipe the edge of the table with his handkerchief. He answered the question in my eyes.

"They aren't convinced yet, downstairs, that Priscilla and Madame were the same person," he said quietly, putting his handkerchief back up his sleeve. "They're going to start a search for her. They'll never find her any more than they've got her this minute. Then they'll go all over this place. And they'll find that it's covered with two sets of fingerprints. One is Priscilla Stone's; the other I suppose is the maid's. And while they're doing that, we're going to find a man who wears medium-sized shoes—say eights—and who left the marks of them on the black rug in that middle room, especially where he stood behind Priscilla and strangled her. And we're going to find out who telephoned from a pay station in the Union Station and hung up without speaking when I answered. And when we know that, Mrs. Volney, we'll know who killed Priscilla Stone; and I *think* we'll know who killed Justice Frazier."

I was beyond the power of being surprised at anything. I simply looked at him dumbly.

"The footprints on the black velvet rug are about the same as those on the grass at Monckton Hall," he said cheerfully. "Miss Xanthopoulos removed those before we could use them very much. The police have trampled these beyond recognition. But I saw them first. They were like this, Mrs. Volney. That velvet, for a while, was as good as an inch of snow."

He took a pencil and an envelope out of his pocket and made a rapid sketch.

"There's the table. Priscilla Stone was sitting behind it. The man came in and stood in front

of her table for several minutes. Those marks were deep in the pile. Your own high heels were just behind them. Then they move lightly, barely distinguishable, to the right. They stand for some little time just behind Madame Rosa's chair. A scarf or something was tightened around her neck. Strangulation isn't very hard, Mrs. Volney. The victim may struggle frantically for a few seconds; then unconsciousness comes very quickly; then you collapse. Your hands may beat about a little, feebly, but it's all over with you. Then our man detached his scarf, folded her hands—there's an ironic touch; no vulgar criminal would have done it—walked around the table to the right and out the front door. Simple."

I stared helplessly down at the diagram he'd finished and was holding in front of me. It was so cold-blooded!

We heard the sound of voices approaching us. "Well," said Major Heath, "there you have it. I suggest we go to your shop and wait there for MacKenny. He'll have to take your evidence and he might as well do it this evening. Maybe we can save you the coroner's inquest. Hullo, what's this?"

He'd opened the drawer of the dressing table and was glancing over its contents, odds and ends of elaborate antique jewelry that Priscilla must have used in her rôle of Madame Rosa. He picked out a Yale key. I caught the glint in his eyes as he looked quizzically at me.

"Would you like to be an accessory before and after a burglary, Mrs. Volney? If this is the key to her apartment I'd like to have a look at it before the police wreck it. Do you feel up to coming with me, or shall I take you to your shop?"

"I'll go with you," I said, without much enthusiasm.

"Then let's move."

We went downstairs. Major Heath stopped to speak to Lieutenant MacKenny, who was still waiting for the Commissioner.

"He won't be sorry, 1 guess," 1 heard him say. "She was always taking a crack at him, one way or another."

It was cold and drizzly outside. I started the car and missed every green light out to Priscilla's apartment house. I couldn't stay at twenty-two, so we sat at every corner interminably, it seemed. At last we got there. The doorman hadn't heard about it, of course. He told me Miss Stone was out. I said I'd go up anyway and he touched his hat and opened the door for us.

I was sure we'd find Priscilla sitting there when we went into the charming drawing room where she had presided with so much gayety and newspaper offices were forgot. The place was like Priscilla as I knew her; I couldn't reconcile it with the sybaritic luxury of that other place. This was delicate, intensely feminine and intimate, and perfect of its kind; exactly the sort of place Priscilla would live in, one always said. The terrible feeling that this wasn't the real Priscilla but a sham, a counterfeit that she had built up consciously, kept recurring to me, and I now began to be aware, painfully, that I wasn't so much shocked as simply mortified that I'd been Priscilla's dupe, as much as anyone. How she must have laughed up her sleeve at all of us, and at our patronizing amusement at her vivacity and naïveté. It was a ghastly thought, and one that needed a good bit of going over.

Meanwhile Major Heath was very much interested in the place. He strolled around in each of the six rooms and looked into closets, drawers, and chests.

"Doesn't she keep a maid?" he said, coming back from the kitchen.

"Surely. But she's probably off to-day. I think her housekeeping was pretty spasmodic. I know the maid doesn't live in."

"Probably more convenient," he said. He stopped in front of the mahogany desk in her room that she used as a study of sorts, and looked at it a while. Then he opened it. I heard him give a mutter of satisfaction as he pulled out of one of the drawers a large blue leather folder.

"I think we'll just take this with us, Mrs. Volney," he said. "We can return it later."

"What is it?"

"It's a collection of clippings of her column, beginning—let's see . . . ah, it's for the last two years. I think there's a lot to be got out of this."

Again the possibilities of Priscilla's dual existence struck me speechless. Of course! How much of what had appeared in her column had come across that table with its two crystal balls? But I think that even then the whole enormity of her deception didn't dawn on me.

Major Heath looked through the rest of the

desk in a matter-of-fact way. Then he looked at his watch, and got up at once.

"Look here!" he said, apologetically. "It's 7:30. You must be starving. Let's telephone Monckton Hall and tell them we'll be late, and get something to eat."

He picked up the phone and gave the number, then handed it to me. When Mr. Radstock came to the phone I told him baldly what had happened, and that we'd be out later. Then I added, half mechanically, "How is Mrs. Mellish?"

"All right, Diane," he said, after expressing his astonishment at my news. "But your other patient's gone."

"Who?" I said in surprise. "Not Norman?"

"Yes. We've had a quiet afternoon. Mellish has just got back and Vaughan hasn't turned up yet. Jocelyn and I are here alone, in fact. I guess this is John coming now. Pericles and Thalia went off down the river and we've decided not to wait dinner for them any longer."

I was silent a second, thinking that over.

"You'll be back shortly, won't you, Diane?"

"Not until late, at any rate," I told him. "I'm in excellent company."

Major Heath was looking at me with a little smile on his face, as I started to go.

"You're not going to tell me what he said? Well, how's this for a guess? Norman Vaughan has left and isn't back yet. Thalia and her brother weren't at the house, and—let's see: John and the Senator had just arrived. That it?"

I nodded weakly.

"Thought so," he said with a grimace. "Well, let's go eat. How about the Mayflower?"

CHAPTER SIXTEEN

HAD anyone been listening to our conversation at dinner—in fact from the time we left Priscilla's apartment until we went to my shop about nine o'clock—he would never have got the faintest notion that either of us had heard at any time of murder in the abstract, let alone just finished seeing so concrete a one. He would probably have thought we were travel-talk artists with a concealed microphone. It was exasperating at first, until I discovered that my companion hadn't the slightest intention of discussing the events of the day. He skilfully and blandly eluded and evaded every reference to Priscilla or to Madame Rosa or either of their—or her—places. To pay him back I said nothing about the Mrs. Mellish business. Although I suppose anyway he wouldn't have allowed me to mention it.

Still I must admit he's a very engaging person. He's been many places and certainly has had many amusing adventures—or at least, to be malicious, has many amusing stories. He is apparently one of those people whose minds can work, when necessary, in compartments to be opened or closed at will. And during dinner the compartment con-

227

taining the affairs of Monckton Hall and its friends was entirely closed and sealed. The blue portfolio was the only apparent reminder of the afternoon—that and my haggard face and trembling hands.

As we went in my shop Heath stopped, and looking at me with a smile said, "You know, you must be exhausted. I don't know why I always expect so much endurance from you. Let's call it a day. I'll phone MacKenny."

"No," I protested. "I'm all right. Let's get it over with. The storm will break soon enough, and Heaven knows I'm going to retire to Monckton Hall and *stay.*"

"All right, then. Let's go up to Marl Castle."

"It's more comfortable down here. There's nothing but Tudor benches to sit on up there."

"But it'll be jolly. American crime in front of Tudor fireplace. Jolly good title for something or other. I can write to Leighton about it. Buck him up no end."

So we went up.

"Hullo!" he said. "The fireplace works!"

"Why not?" I said, smiling, with a glance at the ashes the maid characteristically hadn't cleaned up before she went. "Didn't it always work?"

"It used to smoke most horribly, sometimes, as I remember it." Then he told me a very amusing story about an encounter they'd once had in connection with the fireplace and a sweep. They built a fire to burn some paper in June, quite forgetting the sweep, halfway up inside the great old chimney. The sweep was very funny, but his account of the trouble they had explaining it to the old Earl, who was deaf as a post, was funnier still. He told it perfectly and I laughed till the tears came to my eyes.

Caleb came in a few minutes. He said Mac-Kenny was with the commissioner and would be delayed.

"Gad, can you really believe it, Diane?" he burst out. "Damned if I can! It's just unthinkable. She must have been crazy. She might have known she'd get caught sooner or later. To think of the way she pulled the wool over my blasted eyes, too! I *interviewed* her not two months ago! She sat there, perfectly straight, with that red hair and unearthly face above a purple robe of some sort. I knew it was a wig, of course, but good Lord . . . ! She had a French accent that sounded O. K. to me, and she said she was from Quebec. She even told my fortune, and when I was about half convinced in spite of myself that she wasn't a fake, she leaned forward suddenly, right over that table, and nearly scared the wits out of me. She said in a whisper, 'Meester Weeliams, you mus' not belief me, *non!* I know all about you long before you come. I know you lof'—er—somebody—and I hope you be happy someday. I hope you get many front-page story. I help you some day. I gif you front-page story.'

"Gad, she must have laughed at us! Poor old

Priscilla, I don't care what she did. Some dirty hound's going to get it."

He put his head in his hands and stared into the cold fireplace. I looked at Heath. He was lighting his pipe with his usual deliberation, one eyebrow slightly raised.

"If Priscilla *qua* Priscilla had just been a journalist, or if Priscilla *qua* Madame Rosa had just been a fortune teller," he said slowly, "I shouldn't mind. I think it's rather jolly that all of you thought she was a fool and she knew you all were. It's remarkable that she had control enough to keep from telling you. That's almost as remarkable in a woman as refraining from overdoing it, being too much of a fool. I don't know how long this has gone on, or what decided her to do it. I don't know yet when this dual rôle became actually criminal."

Caleb looked up at him sharply, with amazement written plainly on his features.

"Because it was criminal. As Madame Rosa she got more information than she ever gave, and as Priscilla Stone she published it—unless she was paid not to do it."

"What's that?" Caleb said.

"Blackmail, my young fellow. Even in the short time I've been here I've heard from half a dozen women that Priscilla was dangerous because she always naïvely hit on the wrong thing for her column. I can hardly imagine anyone less naïve than Priscilla was. There aren't many women who like their little foibles paraded in the daily press, you know, especially if those foibles happen to be scandalous."

"I can't believe it," Caleb said despondently. "She was so damn decent to people. You know she'd give you the shirt off her back, Diane. She turned in a feature one Sunday, I remember, and Clem Burns brought one in the same time. Old Potter decided to use Priscilla's. Well, she heard Clem had a sick wife and she took hers away. She knew they needed the money. Potter was sore as hell but she wouldn't let him have it. Said he'd have to use Clem's. She'd help you every time, and she'd never take assignments when she was a reporter if she knew somebody else wanted them badly. Simply refused. Said they could fire her if they chose."

"How do you feel about her treatment of Mrs. Mellish, then?" Major Heath asked, with an amused glance at me.

"What's she done to her?"

"Drove her half mad. Wormed the Senator's personal and political secrets out of her—as many as she knew. Turned a decent Middle Western woman—is that the right term?—into a snooping liar and charged her a good sum of money for doing it."

"Oh, what the hell do I care about Mrs. Mellish," Caleb muttered.

"Ah, well, Heaven only knows how many other Mrs. Mellishes there are inside of a mile or two of us. Hardly daring to call their souls their own, in embassies and drawing rooms and Congressional boarding houses. No, Williams, I haven't any sympathy for Priscilla Stone. There are too many like her around. We're lucky they aren't all as ingenious."

The bell rang.

"That's MacKenny," Heath said. "I'll let him in."

Caleb and I were alone for a moment.

"I don't believe it yet," he said, shaking his head.

"I'm afraid I do," I said. "I'm beginning to remember many things, now. I wonder who could have killed her."

"Mellish, probably."

"Or John." I told him about the ten thousand dollars, and showed him Mr. Radstock's check, which I had still neatly folded in my bag.

He whistled. "For God's sake don't let Heath see that. I'll see John, the beastly ass! Does he think it's connected with Frazier?"

I nodded.

"We were over at the house on Dupont Circle this afternoon," he said, in an undertone. "He went over the library as if he was hunting a pin point. MacKenny was with us, and he thought Heath had gone gaga. He didn't find anything that I could see, but he seemed satisfied when he got through. He looked at the windows, servants, everything. He wouldn't say what he was after.

Whipple showed up just as we were leaving and said he'd just seen Mellish going in the Senate Office Building on a dead run. Do you suppose that old bird could have bumped Priscilla off? Did he know who she was?"

Lieutenant MacKenny appeared with Major Heath and they sat down.

"Well, you were right about Miss Stone being Madame Rosa, Major," he began. "Anderson fingerprinted the whole place and found the maid's prints all over the kitchen and Miss Stone's everywhere else. No others except in the reception room. And several women had left prints on the mahogany table and the cigarette box. Guess they hadn't been wiped off for some time. The crystal globes were clean, though. Guess she never touched them. Or perhaps she just hadn't to-day."

Heath nodded and handed MacKenny his tobacco pouch. He took it, then handed it back and got a cigarette out of a battered package in his pocket. He was a very worried policeman.

"We traced that call. One of the fellas went down to the station. There's just a stream of people going in and out of that booth. Counted eight in fifteen minutes. None of the redcaps could remember anybody. We've got a call out for a taxi that picked up anybody around there, but with all these thirty-five-cent cabs there's not so much check on them unless it just happens. Nobody next door saw anyone."

"How about the maid?"

"Nobody knows her. They've seen her, that's all. The servant on the right is new, and the one on the left is an old darky who's been with the family thirty-two years and doesn't associate with the other servants on the street."

"Well," said Major Heath, "she isn't important. She'll turn up at her usual time to-morrow morning and not know a thing. I can't imagine Miss Stone's being so foolish as to give any secrets away to a colored servant."

"I guess you're right there. Now will you tell me all you know about it, Mrs. Volney? I don't want to keep you any longer, and I'll try to keep you out of the inquest."

I thanked him very sincerely for that, and told him all I knew from the beginning. Mrs. Mellish's fears and my promise to interview Madame Rosa for her; my going there and no one's answering the bell; my going in and seeing that horrible thing; and Major Heath's coming and taking off the red wig and my seeing Priscilla Stone, who was an intimate friend of many years' standing.

"How old was she, by the way, Mrs. Volney?" Major Heath interposed.

"About thirty-eight, I should say. I'm thirty, and I remember she always seemed out of my age class, although I knew her very well. She was a young lady when I was a kid. I've known her best from shortly after the war, when I started this shop for something to do. Since then I've seen her almost every day, or talked to her on the phone if I didn't see her."

"And you never suspected this business?" Mac-Kenny asked.

"Never, indeed."

I was sure he didn't believe me.

"Did it never occur to you, Mrs. Volney," put in Major Heath, "that she had more money and lived in better style than most newspaper people?"

"No. I'm not in the habit of wondering about people's incomes and expenditures, for one thing, and for another I knew she had a good job, and that she got almost everything she wore or used at about a tenth its regular price, just because she had a woman's column. I haven't this minute the faintest idea what she got as a columnist. I know she got a big raise last year when she decided she'd go live in Cuba."

"She sure did," Caleb said. "They almost gave her the Monument to keep her. They gave her a dinner and asked her to reconsider, and she sort of wept and said of course she'd stay if they really wanted her. The bosses wept on each other's shoulders. Devilish touching. I wonder if she was laughing at all of us that night. I went home with her and gave her a lecture about how she ought to be more hardboiled, and not let people impose on her."

Major Heath chuckled.

"What did she say? Do you remember?"

"She said, 'Do you think so *really*, Caleb? Because I couldn't bear to be imposed on!' Lord, Lord! But say, how did she get back and forth without anybody ever knowing it?"

"There's a back way, of course," Major Heath said. "But the simplest way would be to walk calmly in the front door, and when she was through walk calmly out the front door, and drive away. The assumption would be, of course, if anybody saw her, that she was a client. She made her appointments almost always quite far in advance, so she could arrange her own time; and I needn't point out to you that as a columnist she was complete master of her time. All she had to do was get the column in—and she wasn't likely not to do that. However, we'll know more about it in a few days. Eh, MacKenny?"

MacKenny agreed, with some hesitation.

"I don't know where all this is going to lead to," he said, with a curious glance at us. "The Commissioner's going around to her apartment with me to-morrow morning. I was going to go to-night, but he said to wait."

I stole a glance at Major Heath. His face was as calm and as expressionless as Gibraltar.

"Maybe his wife is one of the clients," Caleb suggested callously, and MacKenny looked over his shoulder to see if anybody had heard him. As a matter of fact she does go in for that sort of thing and might very well be. I remembered Priscilla telling me once that she was going to a séance at the Commissioner's house. Of course it may have been entirely in the nature of novel entertainment.

I noticed that Major Heath said nothing about connecting this with Justice Frazier's death. Caleb started to say something about it, once, but I thought the Englishman cut him off in the middle of a sentence, and Caleb retired discreetly.

It was almost ten o'clock when Caleb said he guessed he'd be shoving off, he had a story to get in before midnight. Poor kid, it must have been the hardest story he ever wrote. He was sincerely fond of Priscilla Stone.

"Coming, MacKenny?" he said as he tossed his cigarette stub into the fireplace of Marl Castle. He wouldn't have dared to do it if it had been properly cleaned out; it's one thing I'm particular about. We all got up and I got my coat and we went downstairs and out into the wretched cold drizzly night. We said good-night, and Major Heath and I set out in my car.

I was dead tired. The drive to Monckton Hall seemed interminably long. We lapsed into lengthy silences. Then one of us would say something, always about Priscilla or Justice Frazier. At least there was a certain comfort in not pretending; we didn't, it seemed, have to talk about travel in Indo-China.

"What makes you think there's a connection between this and Justice Frazier?" I asked once.

"Too much of a coincidence not to be. Too many of the same people involved. For instance,

Priscilla Stone was at Monckton Hall when Frazier was shot. Two people, if not more, at the Hall have a definite connection—professional, I mean—with Madame Rosa."

I looked over at him.

"Who besides Mrs. Mellish?"

I felt that he was probably smiling, although I couldn't see his face.

"Well—let's say Miss Xanthopoulos."

"Thalia?" I was genuinely amazed this time.

"You had someone else in mind, I take it."

"Why Thalia?" I insisted. I simply couldn't tell him about John.

"Wasn't it Thalia who upset Mrs. Mellish so, when you women were discussing Madame Rosa after dinner the night of Justice Frazier's death?"

"How did you know?"

"Thalia told me that Mrs. Mellish was 'hipped,' as she put it, on a certain fortune teller and she'd bet anything it had something to do with the murder. Miss Xanthopoulos, it seems, is clearly convinced that we don't need to look any further than the Senator. Well, of course it seemed a bit far-fetched to me. I asked her why she thought it. She told me then that Madame Rosa had driven her mother out of Washington some years ago, and that her mother was frightened to death of the woman. And Miss Xanthopoulos then added, in her splendid way, 'Mother's nobody's fool if she *is* a Philadelphia Adler—so what chance would that prairie rose have?'—All of which was very shrewd of Miss Xanthopoulos."

I began then to wonder about something else. That evening when Thalia had locked Priscilla in the bathroom came back very clearly. It was a curious business, and I began patching two and two together and getting nine or ten, I suppose. Anyway, I kept it to myself.

"Then there's young Radstock, of course," Major Heath remarked imperturbably.

"John?" I said.

"Yes. I thought you knew. There must be some connection there that I've got to find out about. He was barging up and down O Street hunting for her number when I came up in my taxi. He saw me and tried to get behind a tree. I don't think he knew she was dead. He didn't look like it. Nor did he know when he telephoned from the Union Station."

"Was that John?" I said quickly.

"I think so. He's the only slow-witted person on the scene. Nobody but a half-idiot ever telephones and then hangs up in a panic when he hears the wrong voice. It's a dead giveaway. D'you think Priscilla—for instance—would have done it? Not in a lifetime. No, I'll bet you most anything it was John Radstock. You knew he was interested, didn't you?"

"Yes," I admitted. "But I didn't know you did."

"I know a good deal about things," he said blandly. "Will you have a cigarette?"

We turned off the highway into the dirt road that goes through the three miles of road to Monckton Hall. I'm sure Jefferson when he came out in a coach and four was never so glad to see the five white pillars of the portico.

"We'll leave the car out here," I said. "I'm too beastly tired to take it down."

"Let me do it," he offered. I've got the feeling about him that he never makes useless suggestions, and I was satisfied provided I didn't have to go along.

"I'll take your book inside," I said. "Would you like a drink before you turn in? I would. I'll mix it and take it to the library."

The house was perfectly silent, yet alive with the curious suspended vitality of an old house that has always been lived in. The hall lights were on. I put Priscilla's portfolio on the table and went into the dining room to get a bottle of Scotch. Sebastian had left a tray for us, however, with a decanter and siphon, some biscuits and a thermos jug of coffee. I took the tray across to the library. I turned on the light, sank, so glad to be safe home again, into one of the deep leather chairs, and dropped my hat and gloves on the floor beside me. I was glad that everyone was in bed. I don't think I could have stood Senator Mellish's fine heartiness, or Jocelyn's blonde solicitude, or John's appalling inability ever to understand anything not in black and white and one syllable. I'd have staged a Russian scene, I'm afraid, and rushed screaming out of the room. Gradually I felt the load of that dreadful afternoon slip off in the peaceful security of the house that was more my home than any other place in the world. But my quiet was not for long.

I had hardly decently relaxed when the dead silence of the night was split by the sharp report of a gun. I jumped up and ran out into the hall. The front door was still ajar, as I'd left it. There was no sound. I suppose it was subconscious fear, perhaps subconscious knowledge, that caused me to dash out, as fast as I could go, and rush down the drive towards the garage. I knew, with a deadly conviction, that something terrible had happened. Down halfway to the garage Major Heath was lying face downwards in the road. I knelt down beside him and raised his head.

Then I went sort of limp. I was trembling violently as he gave me a twisted smile. "It's you, is it?" he said. "I'm all right; it's nothing much."

"For God's sake, what happened?" I said.

He grinned again.

"Two guesses for Mrs. Volney," he said. He kept looking about steadily, and when I began to speak again he motioned me to keep still.

"Thought I heard something. I guess it's all right now. Give me a hand, can you?"

I helped him to his feet, too much overcome to say anything. I tried to call for help then, but I couldn't make myself, someway. I could have wept when I saw the upstairs windows of the house spring into being as someone turned on the light. In a moment Sebastian came hobbling towards us, followed by Senator Mellish, John, and Thalia.

I heard only dimly Major Heath's statement that he had been shot at from the trees by the roadside, just after he had put my car in the garage, and that the bullet had grazed his chest on the left side. Senator Mellish and John got off his coat and shirt and we put a temporary pad of handkerchiefs over the wound, which as he'd said was not serious.

"That came very nearly being a good shot, sir," Senator Mellish said, looking at him seriously.

"So it did," Major Heath said.

He declined any help, and we set off towards the house. Mr. Radstock and Jocelyn were waiting on the porch. I looked around for Pericles and Norman, but I didn't see them. A minute later Pericles appeared out of the dark and said he'd heard a shot and asked what had happened. I noticed Mr. Radstock looking queerly at him, but I was too tired to tell him, and the rest of them were too excited.

And suddenly—and it's almost the only thing I remember of these events that evening; I suppose it shows how beside the point one can get—I noticed Senator Mellish's feet as he went up the steps beside Major Heath. For a man of his size they were almost grotesquely small.

That was going round and round in my head when Mr. Radstock came and put his arm around my shoulders. "Heath says to get you off to bed, and I think he's right. Thalia will go up with you. Good-night, Diane."

CHAPTER SEVENTEEN

I WAS awakened the next morning by Sebastian, bringing in my tray. He deposited it on my lap and drew the venetian blinds. For a brief instant I wondered if I'd had a terrible nightmare. Then he handed me the paper he always brought up in his jacket pocket, and I caught a glimpse of the headline:

COLUMNIST SLAIN AT FORTUNE TELLER'S.

"How you all feelin', Miss?" the old darky said, pouring my coffee into the delicate china cup in front of me.

"All right, Sebastian. How's Major Heath?"

He shook his gray head.

"That man's powerful foolish. The doctor come las' night an' tol' him to stay in baid a week. He los' a lot of blood. That there bullet didn' come so far from his heart, Miss. He's lucky he ain' daid this minute."

"He's in bed, then?"

"No suh, he ain' in no baid. He was outside lookin' roun' befoh six o'clock this mohnin', soon as it was light. Ah heard him come down, an' Ah tol' him to go back, and he said he been shot a lot an' he didn' min' it one bit."

"He'll probably catch cold," I said. "Then he'll

244

get pneumonia and die. Have they found out who shot him?"

"Ah don' think so, Miss. He was powerful quick on his legs. Ah didn' see nobody when Ah come out the back doah of the kitchen. An' he must 'a' been right there somewhere. Is you-all goin' get up, Miss, or is you stayin' in bed? Miss Tolly asted me."

"I'll be down in half an hour."

Alone, I opened the paper and read about the murder of Priscilla Stone. The police were at a loss to find a motive, I learned, for the brutal attack. A wide search was being made for the woman, and the police were confident of finding her within forty-eight hours.

And the *Chronicle,* with its genius for the macabre, had run Priscilla's column on the front page at the left. It was headed "Priscilla Stone's Last Comment on Washington Society." A heading that I daresay a good many people read with heartfelt relief.

I read the column with horror. How neatly she did it!

I was surprised to learn an hour ago that Norman Vaughan is leaving for South America. I met him coming out of Cook's. I was astonished at how low he looked. He wouldn't discuss his plans except to say that he'd be gone indefinitely and expected to get in some good shooting in the spring. I should think he'd had enough lately to last him for a long time.

Miriam Franklands is going abroad next week—to

Rome this time—to visit her sister, who married a papal nobleman. I've forgot his name.

And speaking of papal noblemen and forgetting things, I hope Lady Joan Wilton hasn't forgot our meeting last spring in Tripoli. We had so much to discuss. A native fortune teller—but that would be telling!—and I imagine Sir Arthur would be very cross.

I hear indirectly, by the way, that other guests at Monckton Hall are departing. I suppose Mr. Radstock is rather glad to get rid of them, under the circumstances. I understand that Mrs. Mellish, who is devoted to her husband's political career, is returning to town for important engagements. Never having any important engagements myself I can't ever understand the consequences of missing them.

And somebody said the other day that Prince Pericles Xanthopoulos and his charming sister Thalia are sailing the first of the week for Delos, where the Princess—you remember Mercedes Adler—has a stunning Villa. I wonder if Jocelyn Frazier will go along?

So Norman was off to South America, and Pericles and Thalia to Greece! How closely they'd guarded their secrets! And the quiet subtlety of Priscilla's innocent little remarks; the warning to Mrs. Mellish, the veiled threat to Joan Wilton. It was hardly conceivable that this was the Priscilla that I'd known. And now, I thought, Sir Arthur would never be cross—about that fortune teller, at least—and Mrs. Mellish would have no more unwelcome appointments to keep.

I finished my breakfast and got up, with that empty, weary feeling of a great disillusionment. I supposed without being very clear about it that the shooting the night before was just another part of the whole affair, so to speak; it seemed just a logical step in the fatal progress we were forced into. It seemed to disturb me very little. I had the conviction that Major Heath, I learned later, himself had, that the shooting was a confirmation of his theories—whatever they were. Someone was afraid of him; his death was necessary for someone's safety. I wondered what it was that someone knew he had found out.

I dressed and went downstairs just as the clock struck ten. Major Heath and Thalia were in the drawing room. He was a little white around the mouth, I thought, and he was sitting down.

"Good-morning, Mrs. Volney," he said with an amused, deprecating grimace. "I hope you had a better night than I did."

"I had a longer one," I said. "Sebastian tells me you were up before dawn."

"He's unreasonable enough to want to know who took a shot at him," Thalia put in.

"Surely that's reasonable?"

"Not at all. It's obvious that whoever did it felt you were better out of the way than in it. Therefore you're in somebody's way. Therefore this is a testimonial to your success—and why not announce the fiend without delay? He thinks, by the way, Diane, that it's Pericles."

I looked at her and him in consternation.

"I didn't say that."

"You might as well. A rabbit could make out a case against the idiot. Even the prosecuting attorney couldn't help get a verdict on it. Point Number One: he's a Greek, he's a furriner. Second: What was he doing dressed at midnight on the lawn when decent Americans were in bed in their pajamas, Senator Mellish lilac, John roman stripes, Jocelyn outing flannel, myself canary dimity—all the legs as spick and smooth as the second they were ironed—not a dewdrop nor a burr on them—only Pericles, the Greek lad, with wet feet, as though he'd been plopping about in a river, jittering about repairing duck blinds. Point Third: The defendant, ladies and gentlemen of the jury, was born in Cyprus and has criminal ears. I ask for death. Then he was probably in love with Priscilla, too. Heaven knows she hounded him enough.

"Well, that's that. I won't claim the body and I'll bet my aunt won't." She ended with something like a sob.

Major Heath looked steadily at her. She was talking rapidly, her eyes flashing, her long slim hands making futile gestures of despair. She was ready to burst into tears. I'd never seen Thalia really perturbed before. It was the measure of her devotion to her brother that she was afraid, desperately afraid for him.

I glanced at Major Heath, wondering if he

realized that this youngster was simply torturing herself in her anxiety for her brother. He looked at her as steadily as before, but now he wore an expression of kindly concern that I'd seen once before, for an instant.

"Well, you know," he said, shifting a little with a grunt of pain, "one of your points against your brother would be my chief point for him—if he were to be tried for shooting at me."

"What do you mean?" she said quickly. The thin curtain of nonchalance was dropped.

He grinned at her. "Well, if he had taken a pot at me as you're trying to make out, he'd hardly have strolled in three or four minutes later, obviously the only person in the house who'd been out of it. Would he? You see, it's so much more difficult to explain why you aren't in bed than to put on a pair of pajamas—even if you do forget to wrinkle them up a bit. Ordinarily you don't expect observing young women to notice you haven't slept in them, and by morning you have. Of course, if your brother had come in and said he saw a prowler and took a shot at him, I'd wonder if he really thought it was a prowler.

"No, Miss Tolly," he went on, with a tolerable imitation of Sebastian's pronunciation of her name, "your brother, on the contrary to your elaborate and—may I add?—ingenious case, is almost the only person I don't suspect at all. Mrs. Volney here is the other one. She was too tired. No matter how much she'd like to see me on the lone prairie, she couldn't have got up the necessary energy last night."

I saw that Thalia was on the point of tears. "Don't be absurd, my dear," I said. "Nobody suspects Pericles of anything. Even if he is a southern Slav."

She managed a smile. "He's *not* a southern Slav," she said. Then she grasped Major Heath's great brown hand.

"Thanks!" she said. "That's awfully decent of you. I feel better now. As I can't do anything for you that Diane can't do better, I guess I'll go up and see Jocelyn. She's still upset because John isn't playing his guitar under her window. I wonder if he has a guitar?"

With that she went out—to tell Pericles, I was certain, rather than Jocelyn. Major Heath gave me a grin and I saw he had the same idea of it.

"Are you hurt badly?" I asked.

He shook his head.

"Just a scratch. It's uncomfortable, though, and inconvenient. I've got a lot of things to do. I wanted to go to town and see MacKenny, but that's out of the question. Perhaps you'll take me in to-morrow?"

"Surely. Have you seen the paper?"

He nodded.

"That's one of the reasons I'd like to go in. I know Joan Wilton. I'd like to find out from her how much of what I suspect is true. I fancy she's not going to be cut up very much about Miss

Stone's demise. You know, I often think the murder of a blackmailer adds so much to the total of human happiness that it's too bad it doesn't happen oftener. There ought to be a complete immunity for it—after reasonable proof. Or even a bounty."

"Dear me!" I said. "Aren't you rather more harsh than usual?"

Mr. Radstock interrupted us then.

"How are you feeling, Heath?" he said. "Sebastian tells me you were up and at it early this morning. That's very unwise, I think. Didn't the local practitioner tell you to stay in bed for a few days?"

"He did," Major Heath said with a smile, "but I can't afford to. In fact I was just wondering if I could make it to town this afternoon. I'm not sure I can."

"You'd better be quiet a day or two. Diane, I think, if you don't mind, you'd better stay this afternoon, just to see that he doesn't get into more trouble. We'll be back by dinner."

He smiled pleasantly as he said it, but there was a trace of sadness in his voice. I remembered with a pang of sorrow and shame that this was the day of Justice Frazier's funeral. The new tragedy had made me forget it completely. It seemed centuries since Saturday—three days ago.

"I think Jocelyn will understand—I'll speak to her when she comes down. Now, Heath, what's this terrible business about Priscilla? What's the connection between her and the fortune teller?"

Major Heath told him briefly the whole ghastly story. How we went through the house and found no evidence but that pointing to Priscilla and Madame Rosa as the same person. He explained then how he had become convinced that Priscilla had used the information collected as the fortune teller to conduct her column, or at least a part of it, for the purpose of blackmail.

"Had you suspected that?" Mr. Radstock said.

"No. I'd investigated Miss Stone's finances and found she was comfortably fixed but not wealthy. I had no reason to suspect a secret income, or a dual existence. But, oddly enough, I'd heard about this Madame Rosa several times, from almost the day I came to Washington. Then I discovered that Mrs. Mellish was distressed about something, and in trying to find out what it was I came across Madame Rosa again. I decided I'd call on her, and I did."

"Have you any idea who shot her?"

"She wasn't shot, she was strangled. No, I haven't yet. I have three 'suspects,' as your police call them. I should say that of the three one is highly improbable, one is almost impossible, and the third is completely impossible. I won't tell you who they are, yet. Whipple is getting me certain routine information that may help. In the meantime all I can do is agree with the police and say, that it's a puzzling case.

"Oh, by the way," he added, "Whipple has also stationed a couple of his men around here somewhere on guard. They're prowling about the grounds. Don't be alarmed, Mrs. Volney, if you see them."

Mr. Radstock nodded his approval.

"We shall start off soon after lunch, Diane," he said. "Some of Jocelyn's relatives are meeting us at the house on Dupont Circle. I suggested to Jocelyn that she stay with them, or go to Kenworthy with her Aunt Laura. But she says she'd prefer to come back here."

Poor man! I could understand that he'd prefer that she'd go to Kenworthy with Aunt Laura. I think this was much harder on him than on the rest of us. He was a prisoner at Monckton Hall, to a large extent, and then I had no doubt he was worried about John. And about Norman Vaughan too; for he said, a little irascibly, tapping his stick on the floor, "What's this about Vaughan's running off out of the country?"

Major Heath shifted a little painfully.

"I suppose he's tired of all this. As a matter of fact, I doubt if he's gone. I've been in touch with the sailings and with Cook, and he had a passage on a boat leaving New York to-night at midnight. I think we'll see Vaughan before he goes. Depends on Whipple," he added, with a barely perceptible twinkle in his blue eyes.

"I can't imagine anything being very satisfactory that depends on Whipple," Mr. Radstock said, getting up. "Well, if I can be of use to you I'll be in my study until lunch. Diane, I won't try to go upstairs; when you see Jocelyn send her over, will you? Thank you."

"Now, Major Heath," I said when he had gone, "won't you go upstairs and lie down? You're awfully uncomfortable."

"Does it bother you?" he asked with an exasperating grin. "My dear young woman, I'll tell you something out of my long and extremely interesting life: I once sat in a Bengal swamp with six bullets in me and nothing to eat or drink for twelve hours. I'm perfectly happy at this moment. Sorry if you're not. Would you like me to be entertaining?"

"Oh, of course not. Don't be absurd. I just hate to see you in pain."

"That's very sweet of you. Do you know, it's rather nice to have somebody worry about you."

"Hullo! I think he's making love to you, Diane!" Thalia came in in her normally exuberant manner.

"Have a cigarette, Diane, and beware of him. He's just planning to hang you."

And she began to sing dramatically

> *"She was poor but she was honest,*
> *Which you couldn't say of 'im;*
> *Now she lies beneath the willows,*
> *Victim of——"*

Pericles came in before she'd finished. "Shut up!" he said fraternally. "You make such a beastly racket."

"I'm repressed and inhibited constantly," she declared. "If it's not my aunt it's my brother, and if it's not him it's my dearest friends. I can't understand why somebody didn't murder me instead——"

"Give them a chance. And give me back my last pack of cigarettes you swiped this morning. Look, Diane; are you going to Arlington this afternoon?"

"No. Mr. Radstock thinks I'd better stay with Mrs. Mellish and Major Heath."

"Mrs. Mellish is going herself," Thalia put in.

"What?" I asked incredulously.

"Fact. She's been her own sweet self since the Senator got home last night—looking a bit grayish, he was, too, just as if he'd been having tea with a supposed fortune tell—— Oh!"

She stopped and looked at Major Heath, her great dark eyes shadowed with horror.

Pericles patted her on the shoulder. "Buck up! Nobody's going to take your chatter in earnest."

But I saw the glance he shot at the Englishman, who sat smoking imperturbably, quite unconcerned with Thalia's indiscretions.

It was just as well that we went no farther with that. Both the Mellishes were coming down the stairs. By the time they came in the ordinary decorum of the drawing room was quite restored.

"You're looking much better, Mrs. Mellish," I said.

She looked at me intently, trying, I thought, to read on my face some answer to the question that must have come to her a million times since she heard of Priscilla's death. I wondered if she knew that Madame Rosa was also dead.

I left them talking, after a moment, and went out to see how lunch was getting on. When I came back from the kitchen I went directly upstairs. I stopped in my own room to get a handkerchief before I went in to talk to Jocelyn, and I found, very much to my surprise, that Mrs. Mellish was waiting there for me.

Neither of us said anything for a moment. Then I said, "Yes, Mrs. Mellish?"

"Madame Rosa," she said. "What did she———?" Her voice trembled and faltered, but the look in her eyes and the lines of her mouth didn't falter.

"She's dead," I said shortly. "She was Priscilla."

"What did you say?"

"She and Priscilla were the same."

Then the surprising thing happened. "I knew it!" she cried, in a sort of terrible triumph. "I knew it all along!"

"What!" I said. "What do you mean?"

She seemed to feel then that she had been horribly indiscreet. But it was too late.

She hesitated only for an instant, and then went ahead with vindictive eagerness.

"I knew Miss Stone was Madame Rosa. I knew

it that night after dinner here. She was asking me about Madame Rosa, and all of a sudden I saw the same look in her eyes that Madame Rosa had when she asked me to get her a letter of my husband's. Like they say a snake charms a sparrow. I was terrified, Mrs. Volney! Then she wouldn't let me alone. I thought I couldn't ever get away from her."

"Didn't you tell your husband?" I asked, looking straight into her pale blue eyes.

She stared at me, fascinated. She must have been like putty to Priscilla.

"Oh, no!" she cried.

"*When* did you tell him?"

"Yesterday—after I talked to you. I told him everything I'd told you; and I told him that about Priscilla Stone."

CHAPTER EIGHTEEN

HALF an hour later I went to Jocelyn's room to
talk to her. She was lying all curled up on the rose
damask chaise-longue, in elaborate black velvet
pajamas. I thought for a moment that she was
asleep, until I saw her slim shoulders quiver convulsively.

"What's the matter, Jocelyn?" I asked, sitting
down beside her.

"Oh, Diane! Diane! I can't bear it!"

"What?"

"Oh, everything—nothing!"

"Listen, Jocelyn," I said firmly. "You've got to
buck up. You've got to pull yourself together.
Don't you see you can't go on like this?"

"Oh, I know it, Diane!" She sat upright and
seized my arm with both hands. "Diane! Do you
think John killed Priscilla? Thalia's just told me
about her, and John wasn't here yesterday afternoon—he went to Washington. Be honest, Diane!
You've been talking to Major Heath—tell me
what he says."

"He doesn't think John did it, my dear," I said,
hoping more than I'd ever hoped anything that I
was right, and that he really didn't think John
had done it.

She looked intently into my eyes, trying to find if I was telling her the truth.

"Does he *know* who did it?"

"I don't know that, Jocelyn. I can't tell what he thinks—he hasn't said that. Surely, my dear, *you* can't think John——?"

Her eyes dilated with sudden horror.

"Oh, how *could* I, how *could* I? I know he didn't. But he's been acting so strangely—I don't understand him. Since the other night he's hardly spoken to me, and he stays upstairs all the time. Thalia says it's because he doesn't like Mellish, but it can't be that. Oh, Diane, won't you go see him? And tell him I—— No, no! Don't tell him anything! Oh, Diane! It was so easy to be brave at first, but not now!"

I was beginning to be alarmed about the girl. She was on the point of hysteria.

"Listen, Jocelyn," I said. "I'll see him now, and then I'll come back and tell you what he says."

I thought I might as well do it and get it over with, so I left her despondently lying there and went upstairs. I knocked on John's door.

"Come in!" he said gruffly.

I went in and sat down. We stared at each other.

"Well?" he said coldly. Then I saw that he had been weeping.

"John!" I said. "Jocelyn is terribly upset; she thinks you've been treating her terribly. She's got enough trouble without your adding to it. Can't I tell her something from you?"

He looked at me in the utmost misery.

"Yes," he said. "Tell her that—— No, there's nothing to tell her. I haven't a right—— Oh, I guess that's all over."

He buried his head in his hands and sat motionless for a moment. I noticed his books and papers, unopened, piled up on the table in front of him. Then he got up suddenly and began to pace the floor.

"Are you still in love with her, John?" I said. It was an unpardonable impertinence, but having got myself into it I thought I'd go through with it. "It's so absurd for you both to be torturing yourselves like this."

He sat down again. His face was white with pain; but he looked me steadily in the eyes. I thought he was more of a man and a human being than I'd ever known him to be.

"Diane," he said simply, "I tell you I have no right to love her now. Don't ask me why, please; I can't tell you any more. Can't you let it go at that?"

"If you've done anything that puts you outside the pale as much as that," I said, "I don't want to hear it. But you owe it to Jocelyn to go and tell it to her. And I don't think anything you've done would make any difference to her, John. Go tell her you killed Priscilla, if you did. She asked me if I thought you had."

"She asked you that?"

"And everybody else in the place is asking the

same thing. Come, John! Take my advice. Come
out of your attic and act like an intelligent man
instead of an idiot. Can't you at least write her a
note, if you won't go down and see her? You're
going to Justice Frazier's funeral this afternoon;
did you remember that?"

He hadn't remembered it. I got him to write the
note and left him with his head in his hands, looking unheedingly at the center of his table. I went
downstairs with a sort of numb fear gnawing at
my heart, a fear that I was afraid even to think of.

I took the note to Jocelyn, explained to her as
best I could without telling her what John had
said that he was as much in love with her as ever,
as far as I could see, and left her, a little reassured,
to go back to my own room.

It was a warm day, and I went to the window to
open it. I saw Major Heath sitting in the sun on
the second terrace. With him was Pericles Xanthopoulos, and they were deeply engrossed in conversation, Pericles talking earnestly, Heath bent
over, looking at his omnipresent pipe. So deeply
were they engrossed that they did not seem to hear
the light footsteps of Senator Mellish, who stopped
pacing on the first terrace, turned quickly, and
went towards the house when I opened my
window.

I had a great deal to think about. What was going on? What were these people doing? Who was
it who had committed the terrible crimes that we
seemed to be hopelessly involved in? I felt that

these were problems that were beyond my understanding; almost every new incident, and even almost every new conversation, added to my perplexity. I'd thought of getting off some letters I'd had to write for a long time, but the atmosphere of the house and our situation in it made it impossible to settle down to any work; so after a few minutes I went over to the wing to talk to Mr. Radstock. It was undisturbed and peaceful there; just now it seemed the only place I could go where conflicting emotions and temperaments weren't openly at war.

We talked until Sebastian sounded the luncheon gong. I told Mr. Radstock about poor John and the call they'd traced to a pay box in the Union Station.

Mr. Radstock listened attentively. When I had finished he shook his head. "John may be foolish, Diane," he said, "but he'd never strangle Priscilla Stone."

Those of us who were going to Arlington started off about two o'clock. Mr. Radstock, Jocelyn, and Thalia in the Packard, Pericles and John in Pericles's Cadillac. I looked around for the Mellishes. They were nowhere to be seen. I went back to the house. They were sitting in the drawing room; she knitting—for Kentucky orphans, I supposed—and he reading the New York *Times*. They looked so smug and satisfied with themselves that I was intensely annoyed. Unreasonably, perhaps, but I was.

"Aren't you going to Justice Frazier's funeral?" I said, probably rather abruptly.

The Senator cleared his throat and looked both impressive and embarrassed.

"I'm sorry that we can't, Mrs. Volney," he said. He took off his gold-rimmed pince-nez and tapped his front teeth with them. "I'm forced to consider that the less my name is connected with Justice Frazier—for whom, however, I had the greatest respect—the better it will be"—I knew with perfect conviction what was following—"for all concerned."

"I don't understand you, Senator Mellish," I said as coldly as I could.

"Justice Frazier and I represented very different political views, Mrs. Volney," he said blandly. "We had, furthermore, some rather severe altercations. I regret them exceedingly; doubtless there was intolerance on both sides. I don't think I can say anything more than that, while I have every desire to act in a manner respectful to his memory, I'm forced to remain at home this afternoon. May I add that Major Heath has advised me to stay away?"

"I see," I said. "I hope you'll excuse me; I have a number of things to do." I couldn't bear to stay in the room with those two people.

Major Heath got up as I was going out. "Oh, Mrs. Volney!" he said, and followed me out into the hall. "May I come along? Let's take a walk. You really haven't anything to do."

"That's right," I admitted, smiling in spite of myself. "All right! Let's."

I was still annoyed, however, at the Senator's explanation of why he would not go to the funeral. It seemed very "small." I didn't think for several minutes that Major Heath might have had some reason for wanting Senator Mellish to stay at Monckton Hall. If I'd thought of it I would have seen that appearing in a big way at a political opponent's funeral was a rôle after the man's own heart. Perhaps that wasn't fair, either. I wasn't in a mood to be fair just then.

I got a coat and we strolled down the garden walk. The scene was a fearful contrast to the terrifying foreboding that I couldn't rid myself of. It was a gorgeous, cool, but sunny day. The Potomac lay before us calm and brilliant. A fishing boat chugged up to our dock and unloaded a couple of barrels of oysters. I explained to Major Heath that Mr. Radstock got his sea food directly from fishermen who kept him supplied all year around. We watched them casually from the terrace and after a bit made our way around to the stables.

Old Joe the coachman and one of his sons were there. Joe was as obsolete as the brougham he still kept shining like silver, but he was a fixture. One son tended the garages and washed the cars, the other was the chauffeur.

Joe hobbled out, taking off his ancient tattered cap as we came up.

" 'Deed, Miss Diane, you ain' been out here for bery long time! 'Deed, it's nice to see you, honey. Won' you take a cheer?"

I introduced Major Heath and they started to talk at once about horses like old stable-cronies. I wandered off to see the colt and on up to the garage about a hundred yards off to have a look at my car. After a bit I strolled back, just in time to see Major Heath slipping a bill into Joe's hand.

"Yassah!" he was saying. "Mastah John he'd already gone right fas' in his cah, an' othah gennel-man he come down about quahtah of three an' drove out like he had the debil at his coat-tails!"

I gathered that my companion had combined duty with relaxation, or vice versa, on our little walk. He was looking a little pale and tired. I suggested that we go back, and he agreed with so much alacrity that I knew he'd got what he had come for.

"By the way, Mrs. Volney," he said suddenly, as we came back toward the garden stairs, "Miss Xanthopoulos was telling me again before lunch how much she disliked Priscilla Stone, yet how Priscilla was always nice to her. She says it used to frighten her rather, because she always felt that Priscilla—as she put it—was going to get her pound of flesh some day when Miss Xanthopoulos was off her guard."

"I know," I said. "I think Thalia really did her an injustice, in spite of what you say about her."

"Perhaps. I'm not so sure. Of course Priscilla

was a strange mixture of the two personalities she affected. I don't think, however, that it was any love for Thalia that influenced her."

"I don't either. It was entirely her devotion to Caleb."

"Precisely!"

"And that's almost as strange as the rest of it," I went on. "Priscilla's love for Caleb—because that's what it was—was maternal, I think, in the best sense. She helped him in all sorts of ways. I suppose the only reason she tolerated Thalia was because she knew Caleb loved her. You'd expect her to be jealous, but it wasn't that sort of thing. Personally, Major Heath, I don't see how she ever put up with that girl's impudence. I'd have cut her throat years ago."

"Shows you haven't Priscilla's self-control," Major Heath remarked casually. "Well, Thalia says she's rather ashamed of herself now."

"I didn't know she could be."

"She was telling me one instance that alarmed her particularly," he went on, with a glance at me. We had sat down on a stone bench in the formal garden, not very far from where Justice Frazier had fallen. "That was a rather strange thing that's puzzled me no end. It was the evening Frazier was killed. You were all in the drawing room with the door closed, when the men came in with Frazier's body and carried it upstairs."

I remembered it very well. We were all on the ragged edge just then.

"Suddenly, Thalia tells me, almost like lightning, Priscilla was at the door listening. And stood there for some seconds. Curious thing, wasn't it?"

"Very. I remember we all thought so, until she explained it."

"So Thalia said. She made some impudent remark, and she says that for a split second, so brief that she really almost didn't know whether she imagined it or not, Priscilla turned on her like a fury. Then she was her old sweet self."

"I didn't know Priscilla 'turned on' her, I thought she was amazingly forbearing."

"Why didn't you tell me about that?" he asked, looking at me quite suddenly.

"I don't know. I suppose I didn't think it was important. I hadn't thought of it till this moment. You see, I had no reason at all to know that Priscilla was two persons."

"That's right, of course. Still . . . Well, you see I've got in the habit of expecting you to be inhumanly observant."

He grinned boyishly and I laughed. "It's Thalia you're thinking of," I said. "Do you think that scene of Priscilla's is important?"

He looked at me very seriously. "I don't know. Many things become important when something important happens after them. In view of her murder almost everything she did is important—or may be. But the thing about this is that I can't understand it. I've been racking my brain all afternoon to try to fit it in somewhere. It's just some such thing as that little episode, Mrs. Volney, that's apparently meaningless, that's going to make this whole thing as clear as glass."

He sat there for a moment intently studying the toes of his heavy brown shoes. Then he shrugged his shoulders.

"Well," he said without enthusiasm, "there's another job to do. Like to help me?"

The Mellishes were in the room across from the library, listening to the radio and playing backgammon. It was a very homely scene. Major Heath and I retired across the hall and sat on the sofa with the clippings of Priscilla's column for two years between us.

Looking back over that whole terrible week in which Justice Frazier was shot and Priscilla strangled so horribly, I think it is the hour I spent reading her columns that comes back to me most vividly. I'd read it before, of course, almost every day. Sometimes, as I've said, it seemed malicious, a little; but we were all so convinced of its author's naïveté and ingenuousness that we never believed it was meant to be. But as I read now, with the new background, her little paragraphs wove themselves into a web of the most terrible ingenuity and cruelty. She had marked one item with a red cross. It struck me with the suddenness of a blow.

I saw Alexa Peterman and John Coffey dancing together at one of our more exclusive clubs the other night. They're so perfectly matched that it's a pleasure to watch them.

How pleasant, how harmless! Six months later Frances Coffey divorced John in one of the most unsavory suits that ever stained the front pages of the Washington papers, and Alexa left town and hasn't been heard of since.

There was another item, equally harmless, that brought back a host of memories.

Raoul Tardieu's interest in Russia doesn't seem to be confined to going over there every summer. I saw him last night in very deep conversation with Natalia Komroff.

Raoul blew out his brains in his bath the next morning. Nobody ever connected that with Priscilla's chatty little item. I remember her mentioning it herself, in great surprise and almost with tears in her eyes. How could she know that he'd been selling secret military information?

So it went on. The cumulative evidence was devastating. How many of her sprightly little comments were as innocent as they looked, I don't know; undoubtedly a great many of them. But —just of those I could pick out—there was Rosemary Howe's divorce and Jane French's hasty departure for London, and Janet Shipley's broken engagement to Horace King. Those were only a few that I could recognize. I wondered how many of the people mentioned so chattily had paid heavily never to be mentioned again. And how much of her information so artfully hinted at had come to Priscilla Stone across Madame Rosa's

table. There's no doubt that she worked it mostly
that way, and got most of her money as Madame
Rosa, too. Serious things appeared in her column
only when she had a great deal to gain and a very
strong hold. The odd thing is that I'd never heard
a breath against Priscilla. Many people disliked
her, or were frankly afraid of her, but I've never
heard deliberate malice attributed to her, far less
blackmail.

We looked through that record of clever
malignity for an hour, perhaps longer. At one
point Major Heath handed me two clippings that
seemed to interest him. One was mostly concerned
with the coming-out party the Woodruffs gave
for Anne. It was a particularly elaborate affair,
which surprised everybody because Anne was
practically engaged to Derry Steiner, who was
rolling in wealth. Most of the Washington mam-
mas felt it was a sheer waste of money. There was
another item just below it that was about me. The
Erders, she'd heard, were remodeling their place
in Florida and paying me ten thousand dollars for
directing it.

The other was an account of Margot Gulick's
escapade in Rock Creek Park. She was unusually
discreet about that, because nothing ever came out.
Then she mentioned that Thalia's mother was reported to have lost five thousand pounds at one
sitting at Wiesbaden.

"She doesn't spare her friends," I said, giving
them back to him.

"Or her enemies. Do you get the point?"

I looked at him. "No, I don't."

"Well, I find them very interesting," he said. His eyes were shining. His pipe had gone out, but he held it gripped firmly between clenched teeth, and puffed away as vigorously as before.

"What *do* you mean?"

"Just a minute," he said, with more excitement than I'd ever seen him show. "Let's get down to date."

He turned over the clippings until he'd come to the last one. Not the one, of course, that appeared this morning, but that about Justice Frazier's death.

"She filed this before she went off to O Street as Madame Rosa. Orderly woman, at least."

He read it with great care. Then he read it again, and handed it to me. Then he got up and began pacing about the room. I read it, and I was just starting to read it a second time when I heard a loud snap and an exclamation of mingled disgust and exultation. I looked up quickly, to see that Major Heath had bitten through the stem of his pipe. The bowl lay on the rug, and he was removing fragments of hard rubber from his mouth.

"Got it!" he mumbled. "Damn it, that's my best pipe.—I *beg* your pardon! But I've got it!"

I looked at him steadily.

He picked up his pipe and returned to the sofa, as calm and imperturbable as ever, took Priscilla's

columns and put them carefully back into the
portfolio.

"There was just one point needed, Mrs. Volney,
and we've got that now. What a woman—clever,
damnably clever."

The bell rang, and Sebastian showed Lieutenant
MacKenny into the library. I had to suppress the
questions that were on the tip of my tongue. And
later I didn't have to ask them; everything was too
terribly clear.

MacKenny's astonishment at Major Heath's
wound took some time to calm, which was a little
annoying, as we were both anxious for the news
he'd brought. And it took us some time to get that
he'd built up a good case for Priscilla as the mur-
derer of Justice Frazier, only to have it pretty well
shattered the moment he came to Monckton Hall.
Priscilla had been carrying on her deception since
1920. In that time she had amassed a large fortune, probably larger, MacKenny thought, than
they would ever know.

"I've traced four accounts in Washington, and
Millington says she dropped about fifty thousand
in the November crash."

"Find any correspondence?"

"Not a line. Found this, though. Funny such a
wise woman would have this."

"This" was a sheaf of onion-skin foolscap pages,
which Major Heath looked through cursorily.

"It's certainly the cream of the social register,"
he said, without great interest.

"I'll say it is."

"This is a list of her clients, and the amounts they've paid, Mrs. Volney," Major Heath said, handing it back to MacKenny. "I won't show it to you; you might find some of your friends in here."

"That was in a safety deposit box at the Farmers' Deposit & Loan," MacKenny added.

"Well, you've got a fine list of suspects there— a little too large for practical use, perhaps. Which one of them are you going to arrest?"

"I dunno."

Lieutenant MacKenny scratched his head. "I got a hunch this is going to be one more of the unsolved crimes of Washington. That won't be so bad. I can't see anybody getting heated up about hanging some poor woman who was off her base, she was so scared. I don't mean to say that they'll condone the crime."

"Of course not," Major Heath said gravely. "And I fancy there'll be a lot of people in Washington who'll sleep better if you can persuade the *Chronicle* to admit that Priscilla and Madame Rosa are the same."

"The other papers'll be *glad* to. That's what I told the Commissioner. They'll come to it. The maid and Miss Stone were the only people ever used the house."

I decided that I was in the way here, so I went out to make a highball for them. When I came back they'd finished their business and Lieutenant MacKenny was on the point of leaving. He did leave when he finished his drink. Major Heath went to the door with him. Then he came back to the library and came over to where I was sitting.

"Mrs. Volney," he said, sitting down across from me and looking very steadily and gravely at me, "is it possible that you don't know—will you swear to me that you don't know—who killed Justice Frazier and Priscilla Stone, and tried to kill me?"

I met his look just as steadily.

"I do not know, Major Heath," I said, slowly —and truthfully.

There was an expression on his face that I'd never seen there before. It was pity, and something more than that. "No, I don't think you do. And for your sake I wish I didn't. I thought you did, for a while, you know."

With that he got up a little brusquely and looked at his watch. "I've got to phone Williams," he said. "MacKenny tells me they're holding Norman Vaughan in New York."

CHAPTER NINETEEN

I WAS upstairs when I heard the cars enter the drive about half-past six that evening. I waited a few moments, thinking that Jocelyn and Thalia would come up and I could speak to Jocelyn before I went down. But they didn't come, and I decided not to wait any longer. I think now that if I'd known what I was going down to, nothing could have hired me to put my foot on those stairs.

John and Pericles were in the hall talking to Caleb Williams. I asked them where the girls were. John said that Jocelyn had decided to go to Kenworthy with her aunt and Thalia had gone along. We all went into the drawing room where Mr. Radstock and Major Heath were talking to the Mellishes. I remember thinking that if Mrs. Mellish would go somewhere I'd be a lot happier —or at least if she'd only quit knitting baby-blue sweaters. She had changed completely since the morning her husband's revolver had been found in her bag. Fear certainly reduces people to their elements, and their elements are sometimes much less objectionable than their compounds.

We had dinner early. Everyone was subdued; we missed the vitality and wit of Thalia, who al-

ways managed to put sparkle into the atmosphere
no matter how heavy it was. Everybody seemed to
be waiting, either fearfully, or despairingly, or
defiantly, for something. I ought to except Mr.
Radstock, whom nothing ever seemed to move
from his calm urbanity, and Major Heath. But
apart from them everyone seemed to partake of a
feeling of foreboding. There was a vague undercurrent of tenseness that broke sharply up to the
surface when Pericles dropped his fork, and again
when Mrs. Mellish started violently when Sebastian's white-gloved hands appeared suddenly to
take her plate.

Major Heath and Mr. Radstock managed with
very spasmodic help to keep conversation going.
Some people can discuss food by the hour. I suppose at many dinners it's the safest thing to talk
about. Mr. Radstock knows all about oysters, for
instance; he can tell from the shell the exact spot
along the Atlantic seaboard where it was born. He
and Major Heath engaged in a brisk tilt about the
respective merits of American and European
products. Major Heath was forced to give up
when we all agreed that English oysters were completely inedible unless you liked the taste of
copper.

After dinner Mrs. Mellish and I left the men
to their port. This was one of the invariable cus-
toms; I don't suppose Mr. Radstock would have
done without it if he had known we were all going to the electric chair to-morrow. He'd sent

Sebastian for the last bottle of his eighteen-eighty-something. I thought it was in a sense a farewell glass to Blanchard Frazier, sleeping so quietly now in the cold night at Arlington.

I'm afraid I must have been rather rude to Mrs. Mellish. I poured our coffee and said I was afraid I had to go upstairs, if she didn't mind, and I went without waiting to see if she minded or not. She apparently doesn't care much about solitude, for she followed me in a few minutes and went to her own room. I stayed up until I heard the chairs pushed back from the table and knew the men were going to the drawing room. Then I went down again. John and I took Caleb and Pericles on for a rubber of contract. Senator Mellish was on the last chapter of the Life of Napoleon.

It was a curious game of bridge. We played with set determination to keep our minds off other things, and we made a good many mistakes. We had just finished another seven-hundred rubber when the clock struck ten. John added up the score.

"Plus fifty-two, Diane," he said. "As I need money more than you do I'll collect from Pericles."

Caleb managed a smile. His retort was cut short by Major Heath's entering. He came in from the library without saying anything. I suppose all of us knew as well as if cannon had been fired and the castle bell tolled that the moment had come. He sat down on the sofa and there was a general cessation of activity. I could hear the clock on the stairs beat the incessant pulse of time.

"I find it very difficult," he said at last in his firm clipped speech, "to tell you what's been going on around here. But you have all been under suspicion—some justly, some unjustly—and those of you who are guiltless are entitled to an explanation of my actions. So I shall begin at the beginning, without any preliminaries.

"You all know, I suppose, that Justice Frazier was engaged in running down what he believed was the controlling genius of a highly organized attempt to put your laws at defiance—particularly your Volstead Act, with which, I may say, he was entirely out of sympathy. He believed that somewhere in the Capital there was a force that not only had made vast profits out of traffic in liquor, but also—and it was here that his interest began—was bringing about a widespread corruption in all branches of the government. Justice Frazier had come to believe that this force had to be put down, for the safety of the nation's institutions. He set out on a lonely crusade, not openly, but subtly, with full knowledge of all the tricks and devious scheming of political life in Washington.

"And at the same time Senator Mellish was conducting an open campaign against the same enemy, but, I take it, with a different end, at least a different primary end. Justice Frazier was opposed to political corruption; Senator Mellish was opposed, primarily, to prohibition violations. It was impossible for these two men to work together: for Senator Mellish, working politically, courted publicity, while Frazier, working secretly, and knowing the ropes, if I may use the word, better, avoided it as much as he could.

"Senator Mellish had an interview with Justice Frazier in which Justice Frazier said just what I have told you. At this interview there was so definite an intellectual clash that it ended in heated controversy and harsh language. Each of them then continued on his own way; and Mr. Radstock undertook to bring them together again. They came down here. Justice Frazier came, if you remember, after luncheon, and for two reasons. It was not entirely because he had lost some important letters. He was a man of what might be called old-fashioned punctilios, and he refused to take food at the same table with a person he believed to be a criminal. For by that time Justice Frazier had found out, I now have no doubt, who it was who was at the head of the liquor ring in Washington."

Senator Mellish sat rigidly in his chair without moving a muscle, his eyes fastened steadily on Major Heath. Caleb gave a sudden, half-stifled exclamation.

"Senator Mellish knew that. He knew that Justice Frazier was sending a detailed account of his investigations to me, and to a certain Treasury agent, by post that night. As you all know, those letters never reached the post. They were stolen

by someone to whom it was a vital necessity to
know how far Justice Frazier had got in his investigations. As soon as he found they were gone
Justice Frazier tried to get in touch with me.
When he gave up hope of doing it that morning he
came directly here. I telephoned him later, learned
about the letters from his butler, and came here at
once. I didn't then realize that I myself, by a queer
chance, had seen the letters. In fact, I missed my
first clue in the most childlike fashion."

I thought as I looked at him that I had never
seen anyone less childlike in my life. He looked
about as innocent to us sitting there as Madame
Rosa must have appeared in retrospect to Mrs.
Mellish.

"And Justice Frazier was dead when I got
here. I explained myself to Mr. Radstock and told
him I intended to see the thing through to the
finish. He offered me every consideration, even to
tolerating my young friend here, whom he happens to dislike."

Caleb looked a little uncomfortable, but no
smiles answered Major Heath's.

"I propose to stick to the main track in this business," he went on, after a moment's hesitation,
"and I shall therefore leave out Whipple's part
in it. No one, of course, thought the colored boy
Jem had anything to do with Justice Frazier's
murder. Of course Whipple hadn't the knowledge
I had to build on; and in not giving it to him I
was merely following Justice Frazier's first gen-

eral warning to me. About Whipple's motives I have nothing to say.

"It was too dark to do much that night, but I did what I could with a flashlight. Whipple's men had searched the house and grounds, as best they could, for the weapon. They found none. Well, it's almost unheard of that when a crime is committed in a crowded house there isn't some attempt to implicate an innocent person. I waited, therefore, for the revolver to turn up. You all know how it did. There is also the possibility that the shrewd criminal would plant the revolver on himself—and it has often been done. Mrs. Mellish made a grave mistake, of course; if she'd left the gun in her husband's pocket he could have disposed of it the next morning, when he waited on the river bank for Vaughan and Xanthopoulos. However, I would probably have seen him, for I was there myself, a little earlier."

I thought Pericles moved a little uneasily in his chair. He went through a fruitless search of his pockets for a cigarette. Major Heath pushed a lacquer box across the table towards him and went on.

"There is, of course, the little drama of the duck shooting. I suppose the story has become known that in reality Mr. Vaughan was knocked overboard. So he was. Senator Mellish saw it, and so did I. But my eyes are a little better than the Senator's, I fancy. I could plainly see Vaughan's hand slowly moving back towards the trigger of his shotgun, which was pointing at his friend in front of him; and I saw Mr. Xanthopoulos drop down quickly against the side of the boat so that Vaughan lost his balance and went over. I suppose there's no harm now, since this whole matter is finally settled, to introduce Mr. Xanthopoulos to you as an able and respected agent of the United States Treasury Department—the agent, in fact, whom Justice Frazier had intended me to meet."

We stared at Pericles! I thought Senator Mellish's eyes would pop out of his head. The faintest flush appeared on Pericles's handsome olive features. I don't think we'd have been more surprised if Caleb had suddenly been announced as president of the Lord's Day Alliance.

"Xanthopoulos," Major Heath continued imperturbably, "had known that Vaughan was implicated in the liquor business; how seriously he had not known until Vaughan made an unquestionable attempt on his life. And Vaughan, of course, had discovered Xanthopoulos's real status. Well, when Senator Mellish came to me with his story of the attack, which I had no reason to doubt was made in bad faith, I very naturally assumed collusion between Vaughan and himself. Which, I may remind you, fitted in pretty well with the alibis all you people had given me.

"Mr. Radstock was called to the telephone at 4:15. Sebastian was listening to his son over the radio. Xanthopoulos had dashed off to the river. Mellish had followed him—the fact that Xanthopoulos was Greek discredited him, I'm afraid, in Senator Mellish's eye—but remained on the terrace to meet Justice Frazier. Had Xanthopoulos followed his instructions, I must say, Justice Frazier would in all probability have been alive to-day. Instead of waiting with Senator Mellish on the lower terrace as Frazier had directed, he went down to the river to watch the fishermen.

"When he got back Justice Frazier was dead. Early next morning I saw the prints of a medium-sized shoe on the turf just outside that window. When I took Whipple there at ten o'clock they were gone. Miss Xanthopoulos had had the lawn mowed—thinking she was destroying her brother's footprints. You see, even she was unaware of her brother's connection with the government's intelligence service. A European reticence that must be almost unknown in America.

"Miss Xanthopoulos had seen more, however, than footprints—as Senator Mellish observed. She did know that her brother was to meet Justice Frazier at 4:15. She left Miss Frazier in the kitchen at about 4:23 and ran out to speak to him —and all but fell over the dead body of Frazier. Hence her sudden determination when she saw the prints next morning. She told me all this last evening when I told her I knew she had seen the body before the gardener discovered it.

"In the meantime Senator Mellish waited for ten minutes on the lower terrace. He came up towards the house, saw the body, and saw, lying on the ground near it, his own revolver. He assumed at once, he says, that it was a 'plant'; that if his gun were found there his political career was over. He picked up the revolver, came in through the garden door, and settled himself in the library. No one saw him as he passed the drawing-room door, and he was first discovered to be there when Mr. Radstock spoke to him at 4:30.

"Now when I found that the footprints had been eradicated, I was much more interested in them than I had been. I naturally inspected everybody's feet. The prints—roughly, of course, for their outline was not very sharp—fitted all of you, except—and this was Miss Xanthopoulos's great mistake—Mr. Xanthopoulos, whose feet are narrower and longer. I was able to rule out, besides him, Mr. Radstock, of course, and Sebastian, who has the large and I'm told typically gnarled feet of the old Negro. That left me Vaughan, John Radstock, and Senator Mellish. Senator Mellish has very small feet for his size. We are about the same height and weight; I wear a ten, he wears seven and a half."

Major Heath paused to fill and light his pipe. There was no sound in the room. I remembered the day I sat in that very room and looked at everybody's feet, because someone I'd read said people's feet always gave them away. It was true, then, in this case, though in a very different sense.

Major Heath at last got his pipe going satisfactorily and continued:

"Later I saw those same footprints, or something very like them, on the black velvet rug in the inner room at Madame Rosa's, where Priscilla Stone was strangled. I learned that Vaughan, young Radstock, and Mellish were all away from Monckton Hall that afternoon. I knew I had only to follow the right one of them to get to my goal. That night, when, after I'd put Mrs. Volney's car in the garage, I was shot at from the woods, I felt I was getting on. It was no amateur hand that fired that shot. Fortunately I've hunted a good deal myself, and I have ears that were trained in the jungle. I heard the stealthy, quick steps of my assailant, and I heard them suddenly stop; and I know that when that happens it's time for you to stop too and move back. If I hadn't—well, no telling what might have happened. Then I lay there in the road, naturally, as I had no weapon, though I wasn't badly hurt, until Mrs. Volney and eventually the rest of you came down from the house. Norman Vaughan was not there; John Radstock and Senator Mellish were in pajamas; it was Miss Xanthopoulos who first noticed—besides myself—that the pajamas had not been slept in.

"We now come to the part played in this tragic business by Priscilla Stone.

"I think I may as well explain her as best I can. I haven't much sympathy for her, but I think she must have in a sense been getting back some of her own. You know her early life better than I do. When her father was alive, her mother's position

in society was an important one. When Priscilla
was left with no money she became, socially,
pretty much an object of charity. Kind relatives
and friends provided for her and used her un-
deniable charm and tact for their own ends. They
probably in many instances made her feel her
obligation to them—people usually do. And of
course underneath her vivacious naïveté Priscilla
Stone had a spirit that was as proud and vindictive
as it was determined.

"She decided, I fancy, during the war to do
something about it, and in the general burst of
freedom she took to journalism. She was a feature
writer in 1919, and in 1920 she took over the gossip column of the *Chronicle*. It was in 1920 also
that she created Madame Rosa. Where she got the
idea I don't know. That she had it, and was aware
of some of its possibilities, is clear from Madame
Rosa's bank account, which began in a small way
that year.

"For ten years, to the day of her death, she carried on a restrained but consistent blackmail; as
Madame Rosa when threats would suffice, and
openly as Priscilla Stone when pressure had to
be applied and it was perfectly safe. In many instances her victims, unless they were pretty stupid,
would know there was collusion between the two
—when Rosa learned things that appeared later
in the *Chronicle*—but there was of course no
reason to suspect the identity of the two. Sometimes she was perfectly open. In her last column,

for instance, she tells us that Vaughan is leaving the country, and adds the malignant opinion that he has had enough shooting. Just what she was planning to get out of that, I don't know. Nothing, probably. Maybe it was just a parting shot at an old friend.

"I've read her collected works of the last two years, and I think I know pretty well how she levied her toll. It was quite simple. She stated, in such a way that only her victim recognized it, what she knew. Further down in the same column she mentioned, in a totally different connection, the sum of money that would satisfy her. And as far as I can make out, from the time of that payment on she played her game fairly. She never demanded more; and so in a certain perverted sense may be said to have built up her clients' confidence.

"And now we come closer home. She left this house Sunday night at nine o'clock. She telephoned Mr. John Radstock from the little store in the woods, and she came back here at half-past eleven, to lead up to an important move in what, had it been successful, would undoubtedly have been her greatest *coup*. She met Mr. John Radstock in the garden at the end of the wing, and told him—I imagine with only a sort of insolently shallow pretense of disinterestedness—that she had just been told by the fortune teller, Madame Rosa, some information that had shocked her profoundly. Madame Rosa knew something that very closely affected him, but which, because it is false, and chiefly concerns a perfectly innocent person, I'll not repeat."

In spite of myself I stole a glance at John. Beads of perspiration glistened on his forehead; he kept moistening his dry lips with the tip of his tongue, and his knuckles showed like ivory balls on his clenched fists.

"Which, of course, shows how very shrewd Priscilla Stone was. She happened to dislike John Radstock, for some reason I can't make out—just as she happened to like Williams here for a reason that's equally obscure. And she knew that in a few days she would have Mr. John Radstock so completely in her power that he couldn't move. She worked on his fears and his chivalry, and, although I doubt if she knew it, on the fears he had for Jocelyn Frazier. Had Miss Stone been a man, I fancy she would have been knocked down. As it was, John Radstock became her dupe, and attempted to get ten thousand dollars to pay to Madame Rosa. As a lawyer he acted very unwisely; as a man I'm not sure most of us wouldn't have done the same thing."

When he paused this time I managed not to look at John. I knew he'd had a rotten time, but I'd only suspected how rotten it was.

"His father, of course, refused flatly to lend him the money. That he finally relented enough to give Mrs. Volney a check for that amount, to pay the woman and silence her until legal action could be taken, is not strange. He could have felt, of course, and I think wisely, that Mrs. Volney would be able to cope with the woman far better than his son. John Radstock tried to keep the appointment Miss Stone had made for him with the woman. He saw Mrs. Volney enter her house, and he saw me in the street outside. He went away and telephoned from the Union Station, to try to get a later appointment. He heard my voice at the telephone and rang off, thinking, I fancy, that something had gone wrong. He returned to Monckton Hall very much worried. He knows best what he did from dinner time until he joined the others in the road when I was shot at.

"Most of which, you see, goes to prove not that John Radstock was a foolish man, but that Priscilla Stone was a very shrewd woman. Some day I'm going to find out if possible where she got the idea of combining the jobs of society columnist on the one hand, and society fortune teller and psychic adviser on the other. Her great merit was that she perfectly understood the limitations imposed on her by that combination. She could never marry and continue it, for instance; and though she liked men she didn't allow them to interfere with her dual career. She liked Williams here, and it's entirely due to her affection for him that Thalia Xanthopoulos escaped a very subtle persecution."

I thought Pericles looked rather surprised at that.

"That brings me to Miss Xanthopoulos herself, through whom I found out, at last, how Priscilla Stone discovered the secret of another, and what it was she discovered. Miss Xanthopoulos, as I've pointed out, is a very shrewd young woman herself; and she had, for a long time, had a passionate hatred of Miss Stone. And she had felt, in a vague way, that Miss Stone was not as naïve as she appeared. The treatment her mother had received was always in her mind, and it was only because it was preposterously absurd that she came only subconsciously to her conclusions. Priscilla was a member of her own class, some people liked her, and so on. But having come to her conclusions subconsciously, she set out to harass Miss Stone at every point. I think that she was frightened sometimes, even, by her appalling rudeness; and I have no doubt that even to the last she actually accused Priscilla in her own mind of being no more than a hypocritical busybody who printed everything she heard.

"I've no doubt that this didn't pass unnoticed. Miss Stone was as wise as a serpent in the ways of women. And at the best Miss Xanthopoulos must have been a little transparent. She let her go because she had a genuine regard for Mr. Williams, and she thought he was fond of Miss Xanthopoulos. As indeed I assume he is."

Caleb got rather red, but no one paid any attention to him.

"Well," Major Heath continued, "Priscilla

Stone is the key to the problem here. As I say, she was a clever and shrewd woman, and her combination of jobs trained her in the exercise of an almost unnatural ingenuity. She had eyes like a cat and ears like an owl. And she was used, I have no doubt, to collecting information by their means. She was alive to every move that was made, of any unusual nature, and she guessed and measured the significance of it. She first betrayed herself by underestimating another woman. Miss Xanthopoulos was nearly as quick as she to see things, but she was not trained in making deductions from them. So when you were sitting in the room over there that night when Justice Frazier's body was brought in, you all heard what Priscilla heard, but you didn't make from it the brilliant—and fatal—deduction that she made. You didn't at that moment know who had killed Justice Frazier. Priscilla Stone did know, and it was that knowledge that killed her."

We were leaning forward, every nerve strained to hear the terrible case that this man was building up so inevitably against someone.

He went on quietly: "Thalia said, if you'll remember, 'I hear footsteps approaching on horseback'; and in a flash Priscilla had whipped around from the door, like a fury for an instant. Thalia caught her look and was surprised; she didn't know what the matter was. None of you, not even Mrs. Volney, noticed that sudden change. For an instant she thought Thalia had come to the same conclusion that she had. Then, acute and quick-witted, she saw in just that brief instant that Thalia meant only a rude flippancy; and at once she was innocent and ingenuous again. Well, there you have the germ of it.

"Then Priscilla relaxed a little, scheming what to do, how best to utilize her knowledge, savoring her triumph in anticipation. She sat around, not vivacious as usual, but, as Thalia put it, like a boa constrictor who'd had two rabbits and was licking his chops for a fourth. She was waiting, and I doubt if anyone ever knew better how to wait. It's one of the hardest things in the world to do, for the criminal—or for the detective, for that matter. While she waited, she watched; alert as a cobra, ready to strike in a split second. And as she watched she began to see that there was a purpose to what she'd found out. There was something else in the picture. She redoubled her attentions to Mrs. Mellish. When she found out that Mrs. Mellish was afraid of her, she withdrew at once; but not, I suspect, before she had found out that Mrs. Mellish did not know what was going on. And in the course of these attentions she betrayed herself a second time: Mrs. Mellish recognized her as Madame Rosa. And Mrs. Mellish told that to her husband.

"It was then that she left Monckton Hall and returned after pretending to have seen Madame Rosa to bait John Radstock.

"I said he was a part of her grandest *coup*. He was important, but he was not nearly as important as other matters. Priscilla Stone took with her when she left that night something far graver and far more dangerous to herself than the knowledge that she had trapped John Radstock. She took with her the two secrets of Monckton Hall. She knew why Senator Mellish roamed the river bank. She gathered those cat berries in the copper pot there on the river bank herself, in the only real walk she took while she was here. And she also knew who had murdered Blanchard Frazier.

"That Saturday evening, when they took Frazier's body upstairs—that second when she turned on Thalia Xanthopoulos—she knew the secret which she could not know and live. She made her last mistake by underestimating the shrewdness, the subtlety, and the cruelty of her opponent. When she heard the dull tread of the bearers' footsteps on the stairs she heard two lighter steps, unburdened by the dead weight of Justice Frazier. She heard them go up evenly and steadily, and with no sign, except to a very shrewd and ingenious mind, that one pair of those feet was carrying a burden greater than Justice Frazier's mortal remains. A burden on his soul, the burden that Cain bore: the burden of murder."

We waited, scarcely daring to breathe, for him to go on. His cool steady gaze rested appraisingly on each one of us in that little circle for an instant, before he said, "It was all in Priscilla's

column on Tuesday morning; and Tuesday afternoon Priscilla was dead. Here you have it."

He took the next to the last clipping out of the
portfolio and read us a part of it.

Monckton Hall down the Potomac carries on, now
that Death has closed those two.

Mr. Radstock's lameness has kept him out of the
swirl that made his two friends more publicly known.
But it needn't have. His ability has made him a power
in the legal world. And now that his old friends have
passed one likes to think of him as an Emerson or
Thoreau, the Sage of Monckton Hall.

REQUIESCAT IN PACE

★   ★   ★

When I came back to town I found the town had
left me a little behind, so I went at once to Madame
Rosa. I'd forgot about her. Of course I know a great
lot of people who go to her for advice because she
knows the ropes in Washington. Especially political
ladies who are newcomers. Mrs. Mellish, the wife of
the Senator, was telling me about her the other day,
so I went around.

But she's too discreet. She wouldn't tell me a thing.
I did learn something while I was there, though, but
not from her.

Adèle d'Acosta is going back to Madrid or Paris.
Diplomatic changes are responsible, I understand.

I also heard that a certain somebody is out just
exactly $20,000.

I'm sure I'd be glad to go to Paris, or Timbuctoo
for that matter, for $20,000 cash.

Major Heath looked at us gravely for an instant when he had finished reading that, and went on:

"The footsteps on the stairs never faltered under that burden, or under the burden of a secret that they'd concealed for years. With a flash of brilliant intuition Priscilla Stone leaped from observation to knowledge; she knew, but for once in her life she was not subtle enough to see the danger of her course—or avoid it. Those same feet stepped behind her and stopped her from ever telling what she knew—except that in her way she had already done it; they'd told their own story. In the excitement of that moment, Jacob Radstock had forgot to limp. The master of Monckton Hall was not lame; and it was he who murdered his oldest friend, when that friend had at last discovered that it was Jacob Radstock who had organized and controlled the great ring that trafficked in liquor and spread corruption on all sides in the federal government."

CHAPTER TWENTY

JOHN RADSTOCK got unsteadily to his feet, his face white and distorted with pain, and started blindly towards the library door. Major Heath laid his hand on his arm.

"Sit down, Mr. Radstock," he said quietly, but with a definite note of authority in his voice. "Your father asked me to tell you that he wishes not to be disturbed until he has finished his notes on your brief. It was his wish that I should tell you all his story; that's why I'm choosing this way."

I must have stared stupidly at John, sitting there hunched down in his chair, looking fixedly at the floor, bewildered, ashamed and hurt, terribly hurt. I was too stunned myself to think very clearly, but I saw that Mr. Radstock's message was for me, not for John. Major Heath knew it too. When I looked up our eyes met for a moment. He knew of course that I adored Mr. Radstock. I still do. And just then I had so much to remember; so much that I couldn't ever forget.

So when Major Heath went on with his painful recital of the events that led up to our double tragedy, I felt in some way that he was talking to me, although he didn't look at me once. I suppose I'm fairly callous, but it seemed to me, as I heard the story he had to tell, that the tragedy of it wasn't Justice Frazier's death and Priscilla's—it was Mr. Radstock's life.

"As I see it, the life of Jacob Radstock was governed by two overwhelming traits. One, his complete and absolute contempt for the human species. Only second to that, his passion for Monckton Hall. I think he's the coldest man I've known, under an exterior of suave urbanity, the result of good breeding and a cultivated mind. He told me quite frankly that he had known but one person in his life for whom he had any genuinely deep affection. He had combined with these things a coolly twisted sardonic sense of humor.

"And this is the story of that strange development of his. As a child he was always frail and unskillful. Sebastian, with whom he played—they were the only boys of the same age on the plantation—was cleverer than he in all physical accomplishments. When Sebastian accidentally pushed him into the well, the superior, terrified at what he had done, became suddenly a willingly devoted slave. That day was born the hoax that Mr. Radstock carried on for years. It gave him a simple weapon; when he was lame everyone deferred to him. He had brains, ability of a very high order. The lameness put him apart, saved him from pastimes and people he despised. His friendship with Mrs. Volney's father and Justice Blanchard Frazier was a sort of personal triumph. His success as a consulting attorney was another. But behind this was a longing to throw it all in their faces and live here, alone practically, with the old Negro, whose bondage, pleasanter than the freedom of most of his race, was the price that he continued to exact—an exaction the right of which was never questioned."

John raised his head. "Does Sebastian know that?" he said in a low voice.

"No," said Major Heath calmly. "Nor do I see any reason why he ever should. To go on: Mr. Radstock's passion for Monckton Hall was at the bottom of all of his efforts. The need of money to keep it drove him on; to provide an heir for it, he married; and when he retired to come here it was all he wanted in the world. When he learned the possibility of restoring it to its ancient beauty he realized that his moderate wealth was not enough. He was afraid, if he turned it over to his son without handsome endowment, that his son would naturally dispose of it. The idea was a nightmare. One day his son suggested that he leave the country and come to New York to live. That was enough for Mr. Radstock.

"He decided to make money for his house, and he decided to do it as the original Radstocks had made their money, with which they had built Monckton Hall. As a child the secret passage to the river—which I discovered in the cellar and wasted a good deal of time on before learning that it had nothing to do with this case—had fascinated him. I doubt if the idea of smuggling had ever been far out of his head as he dreamed of his house. The river leading to the sea was an open highway.

"But I'm not interested in his liquor traffic, except in so far as it applies to what happened later. He built up an organization that now has ramifications in all branches of the government. He had two assistants—let me call them: one for this country, one who superintended the ordering of foreign cargoes. Norman Vaughan was the local assistant. Only those two knew that the shrewd and ruthless intelligence directing the organization was Jacob Radstock. And they were completely in his power; and I think, very little in his confidence. His organization controlled, and controls, the illicit liquor business in the Capital; so-called diplomatic immunity was skillfully extended to the entire District.

"As I say, that doesn't in itself interest me, and Xanthopoulos's job is to stop it, not to prosecute it. When Justice Frazier began to suspect his oldest friend I don't know. Senator Mellish also, as we know, had been independently after the same object, and he had got an inkling that a woman was connected in some way with the ring—hence his interest in Miss Xanthopoulos. Xanthopoulos meanwhile had been set to work, and Senator Mellish, by a stroke of genius, had cultivated the acquaintance of Priscilla Stone, who he suspected might be able to help him along. Caleb Williams was also trying to help.

"Williams began his helpful work by making a frightful blunder." Major Heath cast a sardonic but not unkindly grin in Caleb's direction. "One night at the Cosmos Club he told Mr. Radstock more or less of what was going on. In so doing he sealed Justice Frazier's fate, and very nearly that of his friend Xanthopoulos—and may I add that of his friend and admirer J. P. V. Heath. For Frazier had discussed the situation with Radstock in the beginning without the faintest suspicion that he was the man; and reading without great trouble between the lines, Radstock knew from that night why Frazier had not lately confided in him. Justice Frazier was thereupon offered inducement to give up his search. He declined. He was then offered, through sources they best know, the fulfillment of his greatest ambition. He declined that. Mr. Radstock, a man who hesitated at nothing, then began the scheme to do away with his two leading enemies at a blow."

Quite sharply at that moment something brought back to my mind that night on Dupont Circle when Jerry Blaine and I were late getting to the Fraziers'. Of course; subconsciously I had recognized Mr. Radstock when he came briskly down the stairs. Only consciously I knew it wasn't he, because he didn't limp. I heard Major Heath only dimly as he went on. I was wondering if Mr. Radstock knew when he came out of the Fraziers' house then that Justice Frazier was to die the next day.

"When Senator Mellish arrived, and Sebastian found in his bag the revolver with silencer attached, the whole affair was providentially simple. Mr. Radstock knew—as Senator Mellish knew—that however unfounded the evidence that connected him with Justice Frazier's murder, he would be politically ruined. And when the emergency came, Senator Mellish's conduct was undoubtedly opportunist, but it was not dishonest."

Senator Mellish bowed. Still no one spoke.

"Justice Frazier had made a mistake in not telling his right hand about his left. Had Mellish known, and Xanthopoulos, who each other was, it would have saved a great deal of trouble. Well, we come to Saturday afternoon at 4:15 o'clock. Frazier and Radstock had talked frankly, there in the retiring room; they had come to an impasse. When Radstock was called to the telephone Justice Frazier formally warned him that he was then going to meet, on the lower terrace, Senator Mellish and a federal agent; and that they would there put him under arrest unless he would agree irrevocably to disband his organization and give up his traffic. A chance phrase betrayed to Radstock that neither Mellish nor the agent had been taken into Justice Frazier's confidence; he asked Frazier to meet him by the box hedge in a few minutes before consulting the others. He went directly to his study in the wing, answered the telephone, walked calmly out of the hyphen door into the back garden with Senator Mellish's revolver in his pocket.

"He shot Justice Frazier with no more compunction than you or I would feel in shooting an animal that was trying to bite us. He put Senator Mellish's gun on the ground by him, and ran swiftly back into the wing. On the grass he left the telltale prints that Miss Xanthopoulos next morning had erased, thinking they were her brother's. Mr. Radstock was taking just one chance—that of being seen. If he was not seen—as it turned out—it was impossible, barring the impossible-to-be-foreseen, that he could have done the crime. And the only people, as it turned out, who could have seen him were Norman Vaughan, his right-hand man, and Mrs. Volney. Mrs. Volney was writing letters. Well, that was the only chance he took. The deed was done with the coolness, and particularly the simplicity, that makes the really intelligent, and in this case almost undetectable, crime."

I shuddered at the thought that I might have just glanced casually out of my window at that terrible moment; then the thought came to me— what would I have done? I caught an amused flicker in Major Heath's eye. He seemed always to know what was in one's mind.

"Given only slightly different circumstances, it would have been the perfect crime. No one in the world knew, or dreamed, that Jacob Radstock could move with normal rapidity. That Priscilla

Stone was here; that she, so used to deception in herself, constantly looked for it in others; that, by a bit of most unusual observation and intuition, she should have detected that one instant, probably, of all the time he'd played at being lame, in which he relaxed; that by attempting to blackmail him she had warned him of her knowledge; and that she left her warning in a form in which others could read it: those are the factors that were entirely accidents of circumstance, unprecedented and unpredictable.

"For that, of course, as you've seen, is the point of Priscilla's column. She made references to footprints in the sands of Time, and to his lameness— and observed that it needn't have hindered him; and that she'd go anywhere for twenty thousand dollars. Mr. Radstock's deduction and decision were as swift as Priscilla's.

"Mrs. Volney had told him the story of Madame Rosa's blackmail of Mrs. Mellish; John's story fitted in; and Priscilla had already signed her death warrant.

"We left that afternoon at two o'clock. Mr. Radstock, as I learned at the stables, by the simple process of asking as soon as I'd got sense enough to do so, left just after us. He went directly to Madame Rosa's, and his work there was short. He walked calmly out and came straight home. He answered the telephone when Mrs. Volney called him at about seven-thirty. Again the perfect simplicity. Everyone, even I who am supposed never to assume, assumed that Mr. Radstock would not leave the place. No one ever wondered if he might have been out of his study that afternoon.

"And that, I think, is about all. It was he, of course, who fired the shot at me when I was coming into the garden from the garage. He ran swiftly, after firing it, back into the house from the *front;* knowing, of course, that anyone who happened to be out quickly, as Mrs. Volney was, would dash directly out the garden door. It was a good shot."

There was a short silence. Not even Senator Mellish seemed to want to say anything. After a moment Pericles said quietly, "What about the letters that were taken from Justice Frazier's table?"

Major Heath shook his head.

"That we will probably never know," he said with a smile. "I'm afraid they'll have to stay in the limbo of forgotten things. After all, they aren't important now."

I never saw Mr. Radstock alive again. He shot himself while we were listening to Major Heath. I suppose we all knew he would do so, because I think none of us were so terribly shocked as we would normally have been. I went into his room and saw him, with Sebastian weeping, on his knees, by the side of the table at which he'd been sitting. His face was as peaceful, as dignified, as urbane, as I had ever seen it. On the table were his notes on John's brief. John told me some months later that the head of his firm had called them one of the most acute, closely reasoned, and powerful statements of the law he had ever seen.

Jocelyn and Thalia came back from Kenworthy. Jocelyn, it seemed, had had some curious notion that Norman Vaughan was the man who had come to see her father at midnight, but she'd not known how to go about proving it. She is going abroad for a few months with Thalia, and then she and John are to be married. There's no doubt they're perfectly matched.

John went back to New York after his father had been buried in the Radstock plot overlooking the Potomac. I stayed at the house. I couldn't leave it somehow. Thalia and I were sitting in the drawing room in front of the fire the night before she left with Jocelyn and Pericles to go to Caleb's mother's country house near Richmond.

"Rotten, isn't it, Diane?" she said. "I liked Mr. Radstock."

I smiled quietly at her.

"I suppose you know I'm going to marry Caleb when he's older," she went on, after a silence measured by the slow even beat of the old clock.

"Isn't he old enough now?" I asked. "He's twenty-eight."

"I know, but I'm only twenty. I don't believe in girls marrying until they're twenty-two anyway. So he'll have to wait until he's thirty. And if he

gets as dull as John I'm damned if I'll marry him
at all. Do you know, Diane, if it had been John
that had done in Priscilla I'd have married him
then myself. That's one thing I can't forgive Caleb.
That and Camels."

They'd left, and the house was curiously quiet.
Major Heath came back to have lunch with me
the next day. It had rained all night, and the
misty gloom made Monckton Hall different, in
some way. We sat in front of the fire. Neither of
us said anything for some time.

"Well, I suppose it's my ego that really brings
me back, Mrs. Volney," he said, with a twinkle
in his eye.

"Is that all?"

"Oh, by no means—but I'd fancied you rather
hoped you'd seen the last of me."

"Not at all," I protested.

"Then you're kinder than I'd thought."

"Why does your ego bring you back?"

"Well, I'm sailing to-morrow," he answered.
"And I couldn't go, somehow, without letting you
know that you didn't fool me."

"Meaning?" I asked.

"That you were the woman Senator Mellish
was hunting for."

I smiled.

"As a matter of fact, when I reflected that you
were upstairs, and Vaughan was upstairs, I thought
for some time that you'd both been eye-witnesses.
Well, I concluded later that you hadn't. I wasn't

sure about you until Mr. Radstock took a shot at me the night we came home. Somehow I knew perfectly that you hadn't known about that. I think you'd like to have got rid of me, but I'm sure you didn't want me killed."

He grinned so that his face was curiously young. I smiled back at him.

"No, I didn't want you killed. And I didn't have the faintest suspicion who killed Justice Frazier— or that he was going to be killed. I thought all along that it was Sebastian."

He shook his head.

"Radstock never left his dirty work for subordinates. He was undoubtedly anxious that you shouldn't know; he didn't want you to have guilty knowledge. I suppose you know you're the only person he was really fond of."

I nodded.

"You know he left Monckton Hall to you? And quite properly, I think. Be a shame to have John as owner. He was afraid, by the way, when I talked to him that time, that you wouldn't want to live here after what had happened. He said he hoped you would regard it as a trust, for him."

I nodded again, not quite daring to speak.

"And by the way, Mrs. Volney," he said, still with the quiet smile, "I'm not in the least interested in the Volstead Act. It's quite none of my business. I don't care how much it's violated, or who does it. But no one except myself—and of course I'm the soul of discretion—knows you're

the person who attended to the foreign end of
Radstock's business. That it was something quite
apart from Louis Quinze damask that took you
abroad four or five times a year. Well, you know,
I wish you'd give it up."

He lighted his pipe. I noticed that he'd got a
new bit for the same old pipe he was smoking
just after we'd read Priscilla's columns together.

"I've stopped," I said.

"O. K., as you people say. Oh, just one other
point. I'm anxious, you see, not to leave you
a poor impression of myself professionally.
Wouldn't you like to know, just as a point of interest, who took the letters from Justice Frazier's
table?"

"I might as well," I said.

"It was you, Mrs. Volney. That was the first
clue I had. I saw them in the pocket of your
ermine evening coat the night we were at Joe's.
Seems a long time ago, doesn't it? Of course you
were the only person who could have done it. You
just pocketed them as you went out. And how
clever of you to burn them in the fireplace of
Marl Castle, and then let me sit and look at their
ashes!"

I lighted a cigarette. He wasn't looking at me,
and I didn't look at him.

"It shows how prejudiced we are in spite of
ourselves," he added after a little. "I should have
supposed I came to this business with a completely open mind. I realized I didn't when I

found it so hard to convince myself that you had really taken those letters, that you had a reason for taking them, and that reason—you were concerned in this . . . rum-running. I'm not sure I really believe it now—or understand it. Perhaps some day you'll explain it to me."

We were interrupted by a quiet shuffling footfall. Sebastian's kinky head was whiter, his steps slower.

"Ah jus' thought Ah might tell you-all, Miss Diane; theah's one mo' bottle of Mistuh Jacob's ol' port, Miss."

I managed a smile.

"Will you stay for dinner, Major Heath?"

"With pleasure. Mrs. Volney," he replied with a grin.

THE END

9 781434 459909